Readers love the Sucker for Love Mysteries by K.L. Hiers

Acsquidentally In Love

"This book has a bit of everything I love, a good mystery, magic, romance, humor, and Action. K.L. Hiers has me hooked and I can't wait for more!"

—Bayou Book Junkie

"Hiers rolls worldbuilding mythology, delicious flirting, erotic scenes, and detective work into a breezy and sensual LGBTQ paranormal romance."

—Library Journal

Kraken My Heart

"I am so in love with this series… This is a really good series. It is one that is worth reading over again, just for the fun of it."

—Love Bytes Reviews

Nautilus Than Perfect

"If you're new to the series – WHAT the hell are you waiting for, go and read the first book! Especially if you love *tentacles*."

—Reading under the Rainbow

By K.L. Hiers

SUCKER FOR LOVE MYSTERIES
Acsquidentally In Love
Kraken My Heart
Head Over Tentacles
Nautilus Than Perfect
Just Calamarried

Published by DREAMSPINNER PRESS
www.dreamspinnerpress.com

JUST
CALAMARRIED

K.L. HIERS

Published by
DREAMSPINNER PRESS

5032 Capital Circle SW, Suite 2, PMB# 279, Tallahassee, FL 32305-7886 USA
www.dreamspinnerpress.com

Just Calamarried
© 2022 K.L. Hiers

Cover Art
© 2022 Tiferet Design
http://www.tiferetdesign.com

Trade Paperback ISBN: 978-1-64108-362-1
Digital ISBN: 978-1-64108-361-4
Trade Paperback published March 2022
v. 1.0

Printed in the United States of America
⊗
This paper meets the requirements of
ANSI/NISO Z39.48-1992 (Permanence of Paper).

CHAPTER 1.

SLOANE BEAUMONT had known and persevered through many hardships: the death of his parents, losing his job as a detective, and the struggle of establishing his own private investigation business.

Oh, and saving the world from ancient murderous eldritch gods who wanted to awaken their even more murderous father and destroy all of humanity, of course.

He was a fighter, a warrior, a Starkiller amongst mortals.

It was hard to believe he was being beaten by morning sickness.

Then again, it was crazy enough dealing with the fact he even had it to begin with, since men usually couldn't get pregnant. Most men, however, weren't married to a very well-meaning but ultimately irresponsible god.

"You are the most beautiful creature in all of the universe," Loch was soothing. "Even when you are depositing your stomach contents into the porcelain bowl, you are stunning, my sweet mate."

"Oh, by the gods." Sloane groaned and rested his head against the toilet seat. "That's very nice. And very gross. Thank you."

"Here, my love." Loch presented him with a slitted tentacle, the tip ghosting over Sloane's lips.

"Thanks." Sloane lightly sucked on the tentacle, closing his eyes as a rush of sweet liquid flooded his mouth. It was the divine nectar of a god, easing his nausea and the cramps in his stomach immediately.

It was also technically Loch's come.

Though it was sort of weird to drink it so casually, it had incredible healing properties, and Sloane could use all the help he could get right now.

Carrying the child of an ancient god was turning out to be a real pain in the ass.

"I don't understand," Sloane grumbled as he got up to wash his face. "The first three months were great. Solved some cases, went apartment hunting, got the one with the extra bedroom I liked, got everything packed and moved, no problems. Not a one! Awesome. I didn't get sick, I felt wonderful, I was happy. And now…." He threw up his hands. "This!"

"I'm sorry, my sweet Starkiller." Loch frowned. "Gods don't usually spawn with mortals. I'm not sure exactly what we should expect with this pregnancy."

"What happens with the gods?" Sloane dried off with a towel. "There's not much written about the actual spawning. Just that, you know, some of you choose to do it by yourselves whenever you want."

"It can vary. Many gods mate and one will carry a spawn for nine months exactly as mortals do. The triplets, Eb, Ebb, and Ebbeth, on the other hand, were spawned directly from Baub's breast with a mere thought. My half sister, Chandraleth? Salgumel carried her for a hundred years before giving birth."

Sloane paled. "I might be pregnant for a hundred years?"

"No!" Loch paused. "Probably not. It's unlikely. You could always lay an egg instead of giving live birth. I think one of my uncles did that."

Groaning, Sloane dragged himself into their bedroom. "By all the gods, I'll be in a nursing home by the time I'm having our egg baby!"

Loch was right behind him and gently swept him up in a tentacle-filled embrace.

The touch of Loch's true flesh was always wonderful and flooded Sloane's entire body with a rush of sweet warmth. It was the touch of a divine being, and it was without comparison. Even so, Sloane's thoughts were determined to make him miserable.

"Two words," Sloane grumbled. "Egg baby."

"My sweet Starkiller, all will be well," Loch promised, kissing Sloane's hands. "My family will be visiting soon for your Neun Monde celebration. My mother is the goddess of fertility! If anyone can help us with your pregnancy, it is she."

"Yeah, but my 'Neun Monde' might not be nine months! It might be a century! When are we supposed to have it?"

"I am not qualified to answer that."

"Is there any way you could maybe call your mom now? Maybe she can hook me up with one of her blessings?"

"I can call my sister. She always hears me. I'll let her know to bring Mother as soon as possible so we can take care of you."

"Thank you." Sloane sighed in relief. "There, now I feel better."

"Really?" Loch beamed.

"Yes." Sloane kissed him. "I love you."

"I love you, my beautiful mate." Loch nuzzled against Sloane's neck. "I worry you are still angry with me."

"For what? The baby?" Sloane closed his eyes, leaning into Loch's soft kisses. "No, I'm not mad. I'm just… well, I'm scared. I'm worried about our child, how all of this is gonna work."

"I swear by all the stars in the sky that no harm will befall you or our child." Loch hugged Sloane, and more of his tentacles unfurled from his arms to hold him closer. "I will take care of you. Always."

"What if I get fat?"

"Growing with child is a beautiful miracle, and there is nothing to be ashamed of."

"Even if my hormones get all crazy?"

"And you require more attention of a sexual nature? I'm always up for more mating, and I believe it would honestly improve our marriage."

"What if I start craving weird foods?" Sloane challenged. "Like pickles and pineapple on pizza?"

"Then I shall learn to make the pickles and pineapples on pizza for you."

Sloane chuckled. "I seem to remember someone having trouble with cookies. Think you can handle pizza?"

"Ah!" Loch turned up his nose. "The cookies were not my fault! Their wretchedly burned bottoms were the fault of your inferior cookie sheet!"

"Oh, clearly."

Loch picked Sloane up and carried him to their bed, cuddling with him and petting his stomach. "Once I added parchment paper as Chef Ramsey suggested, the issue was resolved."

"You could use your godly powers and poof some perfect cookies into existence, you know." Sloane laid his hand over Loch's. "Be a lot easier. And probably safer."

Beneath his very attractive redheaded vessel, Loch was a giant tentacled dragon deity named Azaethoth the Lesser. He was the god of thieves and divine retribution. He was also a huge fan of cooking shows and had become a bit obsessed. However, his godly powers hadn't exactly translated into a natural culinary gift, and Sloane now kept two fire extinguishers in the kitchen.

"That would be cheating," Loch protested. "I will master the culinary arts without the aid of magic, as Chef Ramsey does, and I will use these skills to woo you."

"Still mad about our wedding cake, aren't you?"

"You moaned."

"It was really good!" Sloane tried not to laugh.

"*Moaned.*"

"I won't ask your mother to make it ever again." He kissed Loch's pouting lips. "Promise."

"You're a very considerate husband. Thank you." Loch's tentacles wound around Sloane's legs and hips. "Mm, how are you feeling now?"

"Better. Not as sick." Sloane placed his hand over Loch's on his stomach. "Can I…?"

"Of course, my love."

With a thought, Sloane could now feel their baby's heartbeat fluttering beneath his palm through Loch's hand. It was fast and strong, and it made Sloane smile. No matter how many times he had to throw up or whatever else he might have to face, it was going to be worth it.

"Our child," Loch whispered reverently.

"It's amazing. Scary and weird, but still amazing." Sloane grinned. "Can you tell if it's a boy or a girl yet?"

"Not yet. Soon, if you'd really like to know."

"Maybe we should let it be a surprise. Decorate the nursery in purples and greens, something neutral."

"I still do not understand how colors have genders. This makes no sense."

"It's how people do things." Sloane shrugged. "It's what's expected."

Loch huffed. "Well, I am a god, and I will do whatever I want. I do not care for doing what is 'expected' of me."

"What about when I told you to quit threatening the mailman and expected you to stop?" Sloane cracked a smile.

"After I stole the keys to his mail transportation vehicle and saw him cry, peeling his skin off seemed pointless. He is not a worthy opponent."

"You're awful." Sloane kissed his cheek and sat up with a groan.

"I'm wonderful." Loch rubbed Sloane's back, his tentacles still curled around him. "Why are you moving? It's difficult to properly snuggle you in this position."

"Because I have to go to work," Sloane reminded him. "I have a ton of paperwork to catch up on, and we have a new case. That thing I do to make money to pay for things, like the rent of our new apartment."

Expecting a child had dictated a home with an extra bedroom for a nursery, and they'd moved a few weeks ago with little incident.

Well, other than Loch threatening the moving staff with his godly wrath for dropping a few boxes.

"How about—" Loch leaned in close and smooched Sloane's neck. "—you allow me to go on a caper with Lochlain and steal something to make money?"

"No. Because that's illegal." Sloane shivered. "And... and... mmm, that feels good."

"Just one teeny, tiny little theft," Loch pleaded as his mouth continued to move along Sloane's jaw. "It will be most profitable."

"It's not about the money. It's about the crime."

"Then I will return the item once we've stolen it," Loch promised. "Is that acceptable, my love?"

"Mmm, maybe."

Expecting the god of thieves not to steal ever again was like hoping water wouldn't be wet.

"If you swear you'll take it back," Sloane began, "whatever it is, and you won't let Lochlain get in any trouble...."

"As if I would let any misfortune befall my most devoted disciple!" Loch actually looked offended by the thought.

"Well, he did technically get murdered that one time."

"Oh, that is *down*."

"I think you mean 'that's low'?" Sloane teased.

"Your father is very mean," Loch whispered loudly to Sloane's stomach. "Bringing up my failings like this is cruel."

"Hey, if he hadn't been murdered, you would have never come down here and taken over his body to get revenge, remember? We wouldn't have ever met." Sloane fluffed Loch's curly hair. "So I, for one, am thankful for your failings."

"Hmmph."

"Not that you ever really fail, because you're a perfect and absolutely infallible immortal who I'm madly in love with and enjoy mating with for hours and hours." Sloane smirked. "Better?"

"May I assist Lochlain in a caper?"

"As long as you promise to return what you steal and behave yourself, yes."

"There. Now *I* feel better."

"Good." Sloane wasn't sure if giving his husband leave to commit a potential felony was wise, but Loch did look so happy right now. Sloane didn't want to take that away from him.

And besides, Loch was the literal god of thieves. He should be able to handle any theft with ease.

"Is it time for the work now?" Loch asked.

"Yes. Missing persons case."

"Ah, I'm very good at those!"

"Oh?" Sloane stood and stretched, rubbing his belly as he headed into the kitchen. "Since when?"

"I solved the last one," Loch said proudly.

"No, you didn't!"

"Yes, I did," Loch argued. "The cat did it."

"The cat who was actually a shapeshifting Asra from Xenon." Sloane poured himself some juice from the fridge and took a thoughtful sip. "Okay, I'll give you that one. But only because you figured out he wasn't actually a cat."

"Tell me the details of our new case." Loch took out some eggs and milk, bustling around to make breakfast. "I shall solve it as effortlessly as I provide you and our child with morning sustenance."

"Missing person is Nathaniel Ware," Sloane replied. "He's twenty-four, last seen two weeks ago at work. Never came home after his last shift. Lives with his sister, Daphne Ware, and she's the one who called us. She says the police aren't doing enough to find him."

"Ah, the sister did it, then!" Loch declared as he whipped the eggs around in a bowl, using his tentacles to add salt and pepper while his hands stirred. "Calling us was merely a ruse to avoid suspicion. I've done it again."

Sloane ignored him and continued, "He'd just gotten a new job working at a bar, really seemed to like it. He was trying to save for college, wanted to study art. Oh, and get this. She said he was getting involved with a local Sagittarian coven."

"Sages?" Loch perked up. "There's a coven here now?"

"Apparently. Better than another cult, I guess."

"Oh! Unless the coven is actually a new cult hiding in plain sight, and they're harboring fugitive Salgumel cultists like the ones who escaped when we helped Uncle Gordoth and Chase save Ollie."

"Okay, first of all, you've been watching way too many movies again, but... strong maybe."

Loch and his ancient immortal family were once worshipped by witches called Sages. After the gods fell into a deep sleep called the dreaming, their worship declined over many centuries until the religion faded into near extinction.

Sloane was raised Sagittarian by his devout parents, but he had never even met another Sage until Lochlain at that fateful party last year. The Sagittarian faith was considered a joke by most, and having enough followers to justify the need for a coven was surprising.

It was also troubling.

"Do you think it's because of my brothers?" Loch asked, frowning.

"Yeah. I mean, what else could it be?" Sloane fidgeted with his glass. "Between Tollmathan and Gronoch and all their crazy schemes, more and more people are finding out the gods are real. Look at how many people know just from me finding out."

"It's not *that* many."

"Milo, Lynette, Lochlain, Robert, Fred, Ell, Jay, Alexander, Rota—"

"Rota doesn't count because he's already a god."

"Ollie, Chase. I won't say Merrick because yes, okay, he's also a god."

"Fine, so there are... more than a few." Loch snorted.

"And think of all those people who were working for Gronoch at Hazel and all the Salgumel cultists with that Jeff Martin guy. They all saw you and Merrick in all your godly glory when we saved Ollie from the whole human sacrifice thing. That's even more people. It's bound to keep spreading."

"And potentially cause worldwide mass panic?" Loch carefully poured the eggs into a frying pan on the stove.

"I sure fuckin' hope not," Sloane mumbled. "But yeah." His cell phone rang. "Huh."

"Who is it?"

"It's Chase." Sloane answered the call on speaker. "Hey, Chase! How's it going?"

Elwood Q. Chase was a detective with the Archersville Police Department. He and Sloane had worked together years ago, before

Sloane was fired for abusing police resources trying to solve the murder of his parents. Chase was loud, a bit crass, but a fine detective.

"Hey," Chase greeted him. "Good, good! How's, ahem, the little godly bun in the oven?"

"Good. Great." Sloane grinned. "How are you and Merrick? Everything all good on your side of godly love land?"

Detective Benjamin Merrick was actually Gordoth the Untouched, Loch's uncle, and the Sagittarian god of justice. The real Merrick had died and, like Loch had done with Lochlain, Gordoth had taken over Merrick's body.

He had also recently started dating Chase.

"Oh, fuckin' awesome!" Chase cleared his throat. "I mean, you know, it's good. Anyway."

"How's the mating going?" Loch asked loudly. "Uncle! Is he there? Can you hear me? Did you get the artificially strawberry flavored lubricant I recommended?"

"We're looking into it, Loch." Chase chuckled.

"What's up?" Sloane asked. "Is Ollie okay?"

Ollie was Chase's nephew, who had narrowly survived being a human sacrifice recently.

"Oh, he's okay. You know, uh, he's staying close to the house." Chase sighed. "I'm keeping an eye on him."

"Good."

"I want to know about their lubricant usage!" Loch demanded impatiently.

"I'm sure they didn't call to talk about lube," Sloane drawled.

"They might have!" Loch argued. "I've also been thinking that Uncle Gordoth should change his name. Seeing as how he's been touched many times now by Chase, the 'Untouched' makes no sense."

"Loch, we can talk about that later—"

"I would like to suggest Gordoth the Slut."

"Yeah, no. I don't think he's gonna go for that." Chase cleared his throat to stifle a laugh. "Do you remember the whole thing with the Salgumel cultists maybe increasing their bullshit 'cause they got an eyeful of Merrick and Loch doin' their godly thing when we saved Ollie?"

"Kinda hard to forget," Sloane replied. "We were actually just talking about it."

"Well, we think it's going down."

Sloane exchanged a worried glance with Loch. "What do you mean?"

"There's two registered Sagittarian covens in Archersville now. Both formed in the last month. One is led by some fuckhead named Ronald Tip, the other by a guy named Gerard Ziol."

"Ziol? Why do I know that name?"

"He's a big-time fancy Sage scholar from the West Coast, and he specifically traveled here to start up a coven. Was on TV fightin' last week with the Lucian church about that damn tree."

"The Tree of Light."

"What's that?" Loch whispered loudly.

"It's this big tree that they say magically popped up in the city park," Sloane explained. "Just came out of nowhere, bam, full-grown tree where there wasn't one."

"Ah! A Xenish Sprig!" Loch exclaimed.

"Huh?"

"They appear when the veil between worlds has been torn. They glow like white fire and have immense magical power."

"This is just... a tree. I've seen it. It doesn't glow."

"Oh. Perhaps it's broken."

"Well," Chase said, "Ziol seemed to think it was one of those magical Xena tree things, and the Lucian church said it was a gift from the Lord of Light."

"Pffft." Loch sneered. "The Lord of Light is a mortal fabrication. Therefore, the tree must be a Xenish Sprig."

"Whatever the fuck it is, it's about to get fuckin' bulldozed. They're expanding the playground, and that tree is gonna get real friendly with a wood chipper."

"I saw people protesting it on the news." Sloane frowned. "I didn't realize they were Sages."

"Not all of them are. That's the problem. I got two groups of idiots who want the same damn thing, but one is Lucian and the other is Sagittarian. Fun fact, they don't get along very well. One of the guys from the coven threatened to kill this Lucian priest, and then some of the Lucian guys threatened to kill the Sages right back."

"Well, that's not good."

"It is exceptionally not good because Deacon Thomas Hills, the Lucian priest in question, was murdered yesterday," Merrick's grumpy voice interjected. "We are looking for the member of the coven who made the threat, but we have not been able to locate him."

"And it gets worse," Chase said. "While we're trying to find our suspect, turns out he was real close with Ziol, so we go over there to see what's up. Guess who else is dead."

"Ziol." Sloane's heart sunk. "So, a Lucian and a Sagittarian priest have both been murdered?"

"Yup. Within hours of each other. Looks like Ziol was killed first, then the Lucian guy."

"Someone retaliating? You think the Lucian was payback for Ziol being killed?

"Lookin' like a very strong maybe, but that's not why I called you."

"What is it?"

"Me and Merry are here at Ziol's house, and, well, we got some goo."

"Goo?" Sloane's stomach sloshed. "As in, the godly kind of goo only the gods leave behind?"

"That's the one. As if that wasn't freaky enough, Ziol has got research notes all over the fuckin' place about Salgumel. Looks like he was trying real hard to find a way to wake him up. So, yay that he's dead, I guess, but uh, he has a whole coven of followers who might all be on the same 'let's wake up Sally boy and end the world' train."

"Shit." Sloane's stomach kept churning. "It could be the cult all over again."

"Yup."

"Uh, any leads yet?"

"We ain't got shit for who killed Ziol other than the mystery goo, but our suspect for the deacon is primo. It's this kid named Nathaniel Ware—"

"Hey!" Sloane's eyes widened. "That's our new case! His sister says he hasn't been home in almost a week!"

"We believe the sister is responsible," Loch chimed in.

"He probably ain't been home because his crazy little ass has been at these stupid tree protests," Chase drawled. "He's the one who screamed he was gonna kill the damn deacon, and we got him on a security camera outside fleeing the crime scene."

"Did his sister mention anything unusual about his behavior?" Merrick was now on the line. "Anything at all that might be useful?"

"Nothing that would lead me to think he decided to go murder a priest," Sloane replied. "Missing for two weeks, didn't come home after work one day and, no offense, but she didn't seem to think the police were looking that hard for him."

There was a pause on the other end of the phone.

"We will confirm it, but I do not believe any missing persons case was filed for Mr. Ware," Merrick said carefully. "The sister may not be being honest with you."

Loch waved his spatula triumphantly.

"Huh. Weird." Sloane tried not to smile at Loch's ensuing victory dance. "Well, we just got the case yesterday. I haven't even met with her yet. We just talked on the phone."

"You got time to swing by here?" Chase asked.

"Yeah. Not meeting her until noon. Text me the address and we'll come right over. I'm guessing Milo is there with you?"

"Yeah. He's here. He's gettin' samples and all that, ahem, off the record. See you guys when you get here."

"Be there soon. Later, guys." Sloane hung up and groaned. "Great. Our missing person who wasn't actually missing is now missing, and he's also a murder suspect."

"And his sister is a big, fat liar," Loch said smugly, plating the contents of the pan with the utmost precision and care.

Sloane sipped his juice thoughtfully. "It's such a weird thing to lie about. Why tell us the police weren't doing anything when she hadn't even filed a report?"

"She is clearly a criminal mastermind."

"I still can't believe there's a real coven here in Archersville. Do you know how much I got made fun of for being a Sage when I was little? It was horrible."

"Why would anyone do that?"

"Because no one thinks you're real, and kids are dicks." Sloane sighed. "I guess I should be happy that people are coming back to the old ways, but... I don't know if it's for the right reasons."

"Ah, yes. Are they actually hearing the call of the gods, or do they want to awaken my father and be a part of ending the world?"

"Yeah, that."

Loch took a dish towel and wiped the edge of the plate. "I do not know, my sweet mate. It is troubling."

"Like this kid, Nathaniel. Was he a serious convert, or did he get sucked into Ziol's bullshit?"

"We can ask him when we find him if you'd like."

"Maybe. I don't know if knowing would make me feel any better."

"Well, do you know what will?" Loch wagged his eyebrows.

"I swear, if you say mating...." Sloane grinned.

"That's obvious. No, I was going to say breakfast!" Loch proudly set the plate of eggs in front of Sloane. "Behold!"

"Wow!" Sloane was impressed. The eggs were fluffy and bright, the plating was flawless, but there was something off about the smell. "What, uh, what did you season these with?"

"Salt, pepper, and garlic."

Sloane's stomach sloshed again. He knew Loch had worked hard on preparing this meal for him, and he took a big bite despite his gut's warning.

That was a mistake.

"What's wrong, my sweet mate? You do not look well. Are these jostled bits of unborn birds not palatable?"

"Loch, it's just, *erp*... oh gods." Sloane slapped his hands over his mouth and prayed to every deity he could think of that he made it to the bathroom in time.

He did, but barely.

Loch hovered near the door, frowning as Sloane shoved his head down into the toilet. He patiently waited for him to finish before asking, "I take it that means no?"

"Definitely no," Sloane wheezed. "A really big no."

CHAPTER 2.

AFTER CLEANING up and opting to nibble on some crackers with another splash of divine nectar, Sloane felt confident enough to leave without puking again.

"I am sorry the eggs were so offensive," Loch was saying as they drove over to the crime scene. "I measured the garlic with my heart, and I thought it would please you."

"It's okay," Sloane promised. "Really. You know I love your cooking."

"I must be able to give you proper sustenance."

"Microwave me some chicken soup."

"Processed food?" Loch sneered. "Never again."

"Not even frozen breadsticks?" Sloane grinned, pausing at a light to eye Loch.

Loch thought it over before conceding, "There may be some exceptions."

Sloane chuckled. "I think it's very sweet you want the absolute best for me and the baby. Maybe we should do the nursery in purple, then, since that's Great Azaethoth's color, huh?"

"Although my great-great-great-grandfather is the most powerful of all the gods, he is not the best. That would be me."

"Do you have a color?"

"Yes."

"Well, what is it?"

"Purple, obviously."

"We still need to think of names," Sloane said, hiding a fond smirk. "And before you ask me, I'm still not sold on 'Azaethoth the Lesser Junior'."

"Fine. What pitiful mortal names did you have in mind?"

"I'd honestly like to name them after my parents. Daniel for a boy or Pandora for a girl. Maybe just for middle names, I don't know. I want them included somehow."

Loch's expression softened, and he reached over to take Sloane's hand. "If that's truly what you desire, I would be happy to honor your wishes."

"Really?" Sloane beamed.

"I think Daniel Azaethoth the Lesser Junior sounds lovely."

"Perfect."

Ziol's house was a modest two-story home with a very tidy front yard currently full of police officers when they arrived. Sloane parked where he could, in between two cruisers off to the side, and took a deep breath.

"Okay," he said. "Are you ready?"

"Of course I am." Loch cocked his head. "Why wouldn't I be?"

"I wanna make sure you know it's time to behave and be a normal boring mortal."

"Yes," Loch groaned. "Sometimes I wonder if you actually trust me."

"I do trust you. You just have this bad habit of doing things that make me not want to."

"Hmmph. That is almost certainly not true."

Sloane smiled at Loch expectantly.

"Okay, so there have been a few times my judgment may not have been perfect." Loch leaned over to kiss Sloane's cheek. "I promise, husband, that I will behave."

"Thank you." Sloane got out of the car to head into the house with Loch, but an officer stopped them at the front door.

"Can I help you, gentlemen?" he asked, glancing between Sloane and Loch warily.

"We're here to see the murdered corpse and render our expert opinions," Loch replied.

"Could you please let Detectives Merrick and Chase know that Sloane Beaumont is here?" Sloane asked, smiling politely.

"Sure." The officer frowned but stepped inside the house.

When Sloane was fairly sure no one was looking, he elbowed Loch.

"That's assault!" Loch declared.

"Stop it!" Sloane hissed. "You can't say that with a bunch of cops!"

"They will arrest you, and you'll have our egg baby in prison. It will be very sad."

"Loch, you promised you'd behave!"

"Fine, I will drop the charges."

"Hey!" Chase popped up at the door with a big grin. He was a big pasty redhead, and he had tidied up his once slovenly ways quite a bit since he'd started dating Merrick.

It wouldn't have been unusual for Chase to show up for work with two different shoes on before. Today his suit was sharp and pressed, and his long hair was brushed neatly back beneath his ever-present fedora.

"Come on in," Chase said. "Merrick is waiting upstairs. You guys doin' okay?"

"Sloane assaulted me," Loch whispered defiantly.

"You probably deserved it."

Sloane snickered while Loch complained the entire way upstairs about rude mortals. What Sloane saw of the house seemed normal: clean, tidy, and lots of books.

Merrick was waiting for them in a large and cluttered master bedroom. It was full of more books and papers, some of them in fancy glass cases locked with magical seals or thick locked frames up on the wall. There was a connecting bathroom and no immediate signs of foul play.

"Here we are," Chase announced. "Scene of the crime."

"Hello, Uncle," Loch greeted Merrick. "You're looking well."

Merrick was a handsome black man with bright blue eyes, and he was impeccably dressed in a black suit. He allowed himself a small smile as he said, "You as well, Azzath."

"Hey, Merrick." Sloane waved.

Merrick awkwardly waved back.

"They've already taken the body away, but we found him in here." Chase gestured to the bathroom.

The bathroom was spacious, with a large tub and a walk-in shower. A long, thin window ran along the top of the adjacent wall, and neatly arranged toiletries lined the sink. There was blood splatter on the tile inside the shower and a large puddle right outside it on the floor.

Sloane cautiously pulled the shower curtain out of the way to peek inside with a perception spell, but he didn't see anything of interest.

"The drain is filthy," Loch observed.

"Noted." Sloane smirked and kept looking around.

There were wards of protection over the window, but they appeared to be intact.

"How was he killed?" Sloane asked.

"Shot," Chase replied. "Good ol' thirty-eight caliber."

"But you guys are magical enforcement, not homicide. Are you keeping the case?"

"Yup. Check this shit out." Chase grinned. "Doors were all locked from the inside. Same protection wards on the windows and all the doors were also on him. None of them were broken except the one we busted to get inside.

"We found Ziol buck naked, facedown right there. Bullet entered his nose and came out the top of his head. Weird angle, right? But not so weird if he was in the shower with his head back, rinsing his hair out. It lines up with someone possibly shooting him from that tiny-ass window."

"But the window isn't broken."

"And the shower was bone-dry when we got here."

"So, why would he have been holding his head back like...." Sloane smirked. "Okay, fine, now I know why it's magical. Because it doesn't make any damn sense?"

"You remember what it's like. Crazy weird shit going down with no physical evidence that defies explanation and might be a tough case? Give it to the magic guys."

"And no weapon found, I take it."

"Nothing. So, gonna say a big no on suicide 'cause there's no gun."

"Where was the, uh, goo?"

"Most of it was on Ziol's body. His shoulder and his head." Chase leaned against the doorway. "Small bit here on the bathroom door and the front door."

"Shooting someone is kind of an odd way for a god to kill someone, though. I mean, I get a mortal opting for a gun since protection wards won't stop a bullet, but a god?" Sloane glanced to Loch and Merrick. "You guys could just break them, right?"

"Absolutely," Loch replied.

"There are a few very old wards that can guard from our power," Merrick said. "These are not it. These do not even prevent teleportation."

"So a god may not even be responsible," Sloane pointed out. "They're not the only ones who can teleport."

"Yeah." Chase shrugged. "Ziol could have been fuckin' murdered by one of his coven members or maybe one of those very passionate Lucian dudes, but—" He held up his hand. "—we already checked them out. Nobody's licensed for teleportation magic. Plus, nobody mortal leaves goo."

Anyone who used magic had to be registered and licensed for it. After testing, they would be assigned a designation based on the Lucian system of elements—air, water, earth, fire, or the divine. Divine was the most powerful and encompassed the power of all the other elements. The Sages called it starlight, and it was very rare. Sloane was registered as a starlit witch, and it allowed him to cast spells with only his hands and without actually having to speak the words.

There were special skills that could be learned by talented witches, like teleportation, but such spells required an exclusive type of licensure. Because these magics had the potential to be dangerous and harmful to others, anyone licensed to practice them was always very closely monitored by magic enforcement authorities.

Granted, there were rogue witches, usually Sages who didn't like the modern Lucian system and refused to be registered, who might possibly have these spells in secret, but Chase was right—no one mortal would have left that strange magical goo behind.

"Right. And the goo was on Ziol. So our mystery god comes over, pokes at him, and doesn't take over his body." Sloane smirked at Loch. "How weird."

"Maybe they weren't that close," Loch suggested. "I only possess people I'm very fond of."

"Excluding present company, gods don't usually make a habit of possessing the dead," Merrick said dryly.

Sloane wandered out of the bathroom into the master bedroom. He was drawn to one of the crowded bookshelves. The books here were older and thicker than the ones he'd glimpsed downstairs, and Sloane recognized them as Sagittarian grimoires.

These would have been a family's collection of spells and rituals, and it made Sloane's heart ache to see so many abandoned. After all, if they were here in this guy's bedroom, he could only assume the families who had once kept them had died or lost their faith.

Before he even knew it was happening, Sloane was crying.

"My sweet mate?" Loch was alarmed and beside him in an instant, hugging him close. "What is wrong?"

"All these books… the families that owned them… they're all dead." Sloane sniffled. "Like my parents. My grandparents. My whole family. They are all gone."

Loch cradled Sloane against his chest. "I'm so sorry, my love. I didn't know this would upset you."

"I didn't know either!" Sloane rubbed at his face and tried to will the tears to stop. The sudden surge of emotions was overwhelming, and he was nauseated again. "Ugh. What is wrong with me?"

"Baby blues?" Chase asked kindly. "When my sister-in-law was pregnant, anything and fuckin' everything made her cry. Hormones are a bitch."

"I assume you've called for your mother?" Merrick frowned at Loch.

"I spoke to Galgareth." Loch rubbed Sloane's back. "She should be waking Mother soon."

"Sorry, guys." Sloane hurriedly wiped away his tears. The wave of sadness subsided, and he was embarrassed now. "I didn't mean for all of that to spill out."

"It's all right, my sweet Starkiller," Loch soothed.

"Thank you." Sloane gently pushed Loch away and took a deep breath. "Okay. Lemme think. Protection wards weren't broken, which means no one forced their way in here. Doors were locked from the inside and there was no one else here, which means no one got out, so Ziol was alone."

"Quite a feat to get murdered by yourself," Loch mused.

"Portals are still a possibility," Sloane suggested. "Jeff the crazy Salgumel cultist can teleport, and that wouldn't have broken these wards."

"It's been hours," Chase said. "If anybody ported in or out of here, there wouldn't be any fuckin' trace left by now. No way to tell."

"Was there any sign of godly goo at the deacon's house?" Sloane asked.

"Nope. His back door was busted, wards broken, and he was strangled with some kind of magical piece of rope. Couldn't find it."

"Damn. Two killers."

"Two?" Loch frowned.

"There's two completely different murder weapons, one magical and one not, and two different methods of entry, one that broke wards and one that didn't," Sloane explained. "What's really weird is whoever used a magical murder weapon didn't use magic to sneak in, but the magic-type entry used a gun. This means there could be two killers."

"Ah. I knew that. I was merely testing you."

"Now you see why we called you." Chase held up his hands. "Even without the godly goo, it's real fuckin' weird."

"Very." Sloane looked over the books, and he felt his eyes well up again. "Ah, so, what are you thinking? Nathaniel Ware came here, found Ziol dead, and he killed the deacon?"

"It's thin, but we do got him on camera leaving the deacon's place. Definitely interested in asking some very murder-themed questions."

"We'll let you know what the sister says. Maybe she has some ideas where he might be."

"Keep your eyeballs out for more goo," Chase cautioned. "I mean, Loch kinda has a point. It is weird she waited this long to call you if she really thought her brother was missing."

Loch beamed.

"Yeah. Let me check it out real quick." Sloane headed back toward the bathroom. "You said there was some over here, right?"

"Yes," Merrick replied. "On the knob."

Sloane walked over to the bathroom door and held up his hands for a perception spell.

There on the knob was the prismatic glimmer of something immortal. It shimmered like no other substance Sloane had ever seen, but it seemed... broken.

"Huh."

"The fractures," Merrick said knowingly. "Unusual, are they not?"

"Yeah. It's like looking at a crystal. There's all these different facets to it." Sloane scratched the back of his neck. "It's not as bright as the others I've seen either. It's sort of muted."

"What are you thinking?"

"I don't know. Something about it is just off. I can't figure it out." Sloane grinned sheepishly. "Maybe it's pregnancy brain."

"It looks like that dreaded little Asra's aura," Loch sneered. "Ugh."

"That's what it is!" Sloane gasped. "It looks like Asta!"

"Asta the Asra, the prince of Xenon?" Merrick frowned.

"Well, not exactly him, but the way it's sort of faded reminds me of him. Godly auras like what you and Loch have are super bright, and this one is like Asta's. Like the color got turned down a bit."

"Like a bad filter?" Chase suggested.

"Yeah," Sloane confirmed. "I don't know what the weird little fractures are, though. Maybe it's not a god at all, but some other member of the everlasting races, like a Vulgora or something."

"Explain for the class, please." Chase raised his hand. "Are those the fish guys or the kitty-cat monsters?"

"The Vulgora are an aquatic race of serpentine fish-worms," Merrick replied. "The Asra were the first of the everlasting races, and yes, they are large feline beasts."

"So, our mystery goo might be a giant kitty cat?"

"Possible, but doubtful. All of the everlasting people either perished or fled to Xenon, where the Asra have ruled for thousands of years. They have no reason to travel here, and there should not be any left here in Aeon."

"Knock-knock!" Milo Evans called out cheerfully from the bedroom door. "Everyone put their tentacles and godly bits away! Innocent mortal eyes coming in!"

"Hey, Milo!" Sloane grinned.

Milo was round and bearded, and he and Sloane had been best friends since college. He was a forensic tech and a new Sage, having converted after Loch revealed his true godly nature to him last year.

"You cannot say things like that," Merrick scolded. "Someone could hear you, and they may actually believe you."

"Sorry, your godliness." Milo bowed his head respectfully and pulled Sloane into a hug. "How's my favorite daddy-to-be, huh?"

"Emotional and puking." Sloane sighed. "Not a great combo."

"Aw yeah, Lynnette watched one of those commercials about saving little baby animals and sobbed for, like, twenty minutes last night." Milo patted Sloane's shoulder. "Sorry, dude. You should try ginger for the spewing. Helped Lynn a bunch when we figured out Urilith's blessing doesn't cover all sickness vanishing away."

"Thanks, man."

"No greeting for me?" Loch crossed his arms. "Your *favorite* and most important god?"

"Right, sorry, Your Most Holy Tentacle-ness!" Milo made sure to bow extra low. "It's really good to see you too!" He grinned. "Merrick and Chase get you guys up to speed?"

"Yeah." Sloane nodded. "We know as much as you guys do, and I'm just as confused."

"I'm not." Loch snorted. "It's obviously the perp's sister. She committed these crimes and framed her brother!"

"Huh?" Milo blinked.

"Nathaniel Ware," Sloane explained. "The guy seen on the security footage leaving the deacon's house? His sister called me yesterday to ask for help finding him, claimed he's been missing for two weeks."

"Which is real funny, 'cause we know he's been at the tree protests, and no missing person's report has been filed," Chase chimed in.

"Weird." Milo frowned. "Maybe the sister didn't know what he was up to? Did she try calling the cops?"

"She said she had, and she told me the cops weren't really doing anything. Which, of course, after talking to Chase and Merrick, is a lie."

"Did you find anything useful downstairs, Mr. Evans?" Merrick asked sternly.

"Nothing except this guy's book collection is worth a fortune." Milo gestured to the cases. "Some of these are the only known copies in existence. Super rare Sagittarian texts, antique grimoires, the works."

"And none are missing?" Chase whistled. "This has gotta be personal. For someone to figure out how to sneak on in here and not snatch even one book?"

"It is strange," Merrick agreed.

"Well, shit." Milo shrugged helplessly. "What now?"

"We're gonna start tracking down members of Ziol's coven," Chase said. "Find out if they're really Salgumel crazy or not, see if anybody knows somethin' about Ware."

"The protests at the Tree of Light are still ongoing." Merrick cringed. "Once the deaths of Mr. Ziol and the deacon make the news, we must expect the situation there to escalate between the two groups."

"We'll go talk to Ware's sister." Sloane rubbed his stomach. He was absolutely starving. "Ugh. After I get something to eat."

"Check back in tonight? Compare notes?" Chase clapped. "Yeah, I think that's a pretty solid plan."

"Excellent." Loch held his head high. "I will feed my husband a nutritious meal, provide him additional relief by mating with him thoroughly, and then I will confront this treacherous sibling."

"Take care." Merrick cracked a smile as Sloane blushed. "I wish you both well."

"Thanks, guys." Sloane hugged Milo farewell while his face burned. "We'll see you guys later, okay? Tell Lynette we said hey."

"Have fun mating!" Chase teased.

"Goodbye, Chase!" Loch waved. "Goodbye, my beloved uncle, Gordoth the Slut!"

Merrick gaped. "Gordoth the *what*?"

"Bye, guys!" Sloane scrambled to leave the house, not stopping until he and Loch were back in the car. He let out a big sigh of relief, groaning, "Wow."

"Double homicide, two killers, mysterious goo." Loch was positively giddy. "A religious feud over a tree? This is very exciting."

"This is stressful," Sloane corrected. "I was hoping for a simple missing persons case, but nooo."

"My sweet husband, we are not obligated to help them." Loch frowned, and he reached for Sloane's hand. "If this is going to be too much for you, we need not continue. It can't be good for you and the baby."

"That's very sweet of you, and I want what's best for our baby too." Sloane started the car and headed to his office. There were a few fast-food places on the way, and he wanted something disgusting and greasy. "But…."

"But?"

"But when I think about it, I have to help them. This is all my fault."

"That is ridiculous."

"When I found my parents dead and called to my gods, it was my prayer that woke up Tollmathan. He woke up Gronoch and who knows who else." Sloane squeezed Loch's hand. "All of this shit is because of me, what I did."

"My sweet mate," Loch soothed, "you can't think that way. If it had not been you, my brothers would have woken up by some other means, and their plans to awaken our father and end the world would be the same. You are not the one who put hate in their hearts."

"Yeah, I'm just the one who pulled them out of the dreaming," Sloane grumbled. "Even that damn tree. If it really is a Xenish Sprig, I might have brought it here. I could have torn the veil."

"You cannot hold yourself responsible for others' actions," Loch insisted. "You're no more at fault for me pilfering Chase's badge—"

"You took it *again*?"

"—than you are for anything my brothers do. And yes, I took it. It's shiny, and I like it."

Sloane laughed. He couldn't help it. Loch was smiling so earnestly, and the heaviness in his chest eased.

"He's gonna know it was you," Sloane warned.

"I'm not giving it back." Loch kissed Sloane's hand.

"I love you. Thank you for making me feel better."

"Do you?"

"What?"

"Feel better?" Loch frowned. "I'm serious about not taking the case if you believe it would put you and our child at risk in any way."

"I feel like… I feel like this is what I need to do." Sloane struggled for the right words. "I want to help fix this. I can handle it."

"If at any moment I feel you or our child are in immediate danger, I will use all of my godly powers to stop you."

"I wouldn't expect anything less."

They went through the drive-through of a burger joint despite Loch's protests, and Sloane got three double-cheeseburgers and a large vanilla milkshake. He only had part of a burger left by the time they arrived at the office, and he really was feeling better.

He would do what he could to assist with the case, and if it became too overwhelming, he would take a step back. He had a responsibility now as a father to see to his child first.

Mystery goo be damned.

Sloane's office was a bit cluttered with files from previous cases he needed to tidy, and he lit some incense to help him focus. Loch had stolen this incense bowl from a museum because it had reminded Sloane of one his mother once used.

Sometimes his thieving ways were downright thoughtful.

Once Sloane finished eating, he clapped his hands to sort the paperwork into neat stacks. "Okay, we've got some time before Daphne gets here, and I need to put this stuff in the right folders."

"May I be of assistance?" Loch asked, peering over the papers.

"It's okay. It's my notes from the cultists and the paintings Ollie helped us translate."

"Mmm." Loch stood behind Sloane, and one of his tentacles crept down the front of Sloane's shirt.

Sloane saw it was one of the slitted ones, and his breath caught.

Loch had three tentacles for copulation; two slitted ones that gave the most amazing blowjobs and felt great inside of him, and the *tentacock*, a massive knotted phallus that had no right fitting inside a mere mortal body.

Oh, but when it did, *wow*.

"What are you doing?"

"Well, I was not able to provide you with a nutritious meal because you elected to eat garbage," Loch replied. "The least I can do is provide the relief I promised."

Sloane's pants magically unzipped, and the slitted tentacle wiggled its way inside.

"B-but I'm working!" Sloane protested. He groaned when the tentacle mouthed around his soft cock, and he quickly hardened.

"Come along, my sweet Starkiller." Loch kissed Sloane's neck. "Let me take care of you."

"Mmm…." Sloane closed his eyes, and he groaned as the tentacle began to suck on the head of his cock.

It had been a very stressful morning, after all.

Maybe just a quick—

The office door suddenly opened, and a young woman with a hooded cloak walked inside. "Hello? Mr. Beaumont? I know I'm early—*oh*!" She gasped and turned around. "I'm so sorry!"

"Shit!" Sloane jerked and quickly smacked Loch's tentacle away.

Loch grumbled in annoyance.

Sloane clapped to right his clothes, praying Daphne hadn't seen what had just slipped out of his pants. "Hi! Miss Ware! I'm so sorry!"

"I, I should have knocked!" Daphne was still turned, and she pulled her hood around her face tighter. "I'm sorry!"

"Mating is perfectly natural," Loch said. "There is no shame in exploring the body of a loved one—"

"We're decent now. Please." Sloane sat at his desk and waved at the chair in front of him. "Have a seat. Tell me how I can help you. Trying to find your brother, right?"

"Right. Yes, I'm Daphne Ware." She hovered by the chair, hesitating to take it. "You are a Sage, right? You follow the old ways?"

"Yes. My family has been Sagittarian for many generations." Sloane subtly raised his hand.

Her aura: glowing, prismatic, air, *fractured*.

As Daphne sat, she swept a large thick tail up into her lap. She dropped her hood, revealing a very normal face—save for the greenish-yellow skin and tusks peeking out between her lips from her lower jaw.

"As you can see, I'm not exactly… human."

CHAPTER 3.

"AN ABSOLA," Loch whispered, "but... not?"

Sloane had seen drawings of the Absola people. They were big troll creatures with large snouts, sharp tusks, and long pointed tails. This young woman still looked very human in most aspects, but the tusks and tail definitely indicated she was something more.

"Yes," Daphne replied nervously. "I'm part Absola and, well, we think Faedra too. It's kinda complicated." She fidgeted. "This is why I wanted to make sure you were actually a Sage and wouldn't freak out."

"Uh...." Sloane was tempted to freak out. "Is it okay if I ask you... some questions?"

"Of course."

"When you say 'part' Absola, what do you mean? Are you not from Xenon?"

"Xenon?" Daphne laughed. "No! I'm from Ohio originally. Me and my whole family."

"Do they...."

"Do they look like me?" She smiled, her big tusks gleaming. "No. Not for a long time, from what I understand. You know the story about the gods all going into the dreaming and what happened to the everlasting people who were left behind?"

"Some went to Xenon, where the Asra rule, and the others—" Sloane glanced sympathetically to a mournful Loch. "—perished on Aeon."

"But not all of them." Daphne smiled brightly.

Loch perked up.

"They learned how to change their shape," she said, excitement rising in her voice. "Not just the Asra, but all of the everlasting people. And they got spells to glamour themselves, found places to hide! And later they actually married mortals and had children. The children would look perfectly normal, but then every few generations—" She gestured to herself. "—you might get a really big surprise."

"Yeah, I can imagine." Sloane nodded, and he touched his stomach. For the first time, he wondered what his and Loch's child would look like. "So there's people running around now who are descendants of mortals mingling with the everlasting races?"

"There's probably thousands." Daphne shrugged. "A lot of them may not even know. That is, unless they're born with obvious, ahem, signs."

"Is your brother, uh, like you?"

"Yes. We both use glamour charms to hide what we really look like. You know, the little pieces of jewelry that cover zits or whatever, but a very powerful one. Mine broke a few weeks ago, and I've been having trouble getting a new one. We were sharing his so I could still go to work, and well... I had to take some time off. I can't go to work like this."

Sloane couldn't explain why, but he got the feeling Daphne was embarrassed.

"It's okay." Sloane smiled. "You didn't come here to tell me all about your personal business, although I certainly appreciate you sharing about your family. It's really amazing."

"Thank you." Daphne smiled, clearly relieved.

"You need help finding your brother, yes?"

"Right." Daphne seemed to relax, but she then noticed Loch staring at her. She blinked a few times. "Uh, yes?"

"Yes, you kidnapped your brother," Loch challenged, "or yes, you can hear me?"

"The second one! Wait! What?"

"Loch," Sloane said between clenched teeth.

"The Absola's tusks are quite beautiful, but they often interfere with verbal communication." Loch leaned over Sloane's desk, still staring Daphne down. "They developed a language of hand signals, very similar to human's sign language, and oh, also, they're telepathic."

"Wow." Daphne was impressed. "Are you some kind of scholar? Most Sages don't even know that."

"Not quite."

"Yeah, uh, I can hear thoughts when they're really loud or emotional." She narrowed her eyes at Loch. "Do you really think I kidnapped Nate?"

"No," Sloane said.

"Possibly," Loch mused. "We must entertain all the possibilities."

"Please." Sloane grabbed at Loch's waist and pulled him back. "Uh, so. Right. Let's try to get back on track here. Your brother went to work two weeks ago, everything totally normal, but he never came home?"

"Right."

"Any friends he might have gone to stay with? Boyfriend, girlfriend, anyone like that?"

"Well." Daphne cringed. "He might maybe have gotten involved with a coven. There's... well. It's just...."

"What is it, Miss Ware?"

"Guilty conscience?" Loch accused.

"Okay, maybe a little?" She sighed, and her tail dropped by her feet. "Since I haven't been able to get a new glamour charm yet, I haven't really been able to leave the house. I maybe sort of teeny tiny bit lied about talking to the police. I was afraid they'd want to see me in person."

"And your appearance would cause mass panic?" Loch said knowingly.

"That and I'd be hauled off to some government lab for experimentation." Daphne grimaced. "No one can know we exist. Our hidden world has to stay hidden! No one can find out. We'd be hunted again, we'd be—"

"Trust me," Sloane interrupted gently, smiling. "Your secret is safe with us. I always give my clients one hundred percent confidentiality."

"Thank you."

"So, tell me what happened with your brother. From the beginning."

"Right. We've never been that religious, but we tried to keep the sabbaths and be good Sages. A few weeks ago, we started hearing stories about the gods returning. There are people, right here in Archersville, who swear they saw two gods battling it out in Babbeth's Orchard. Nate got really excited, did some research, and started talking to this coven he found online. He seemed to like it, but he was suddenly going all the time."

"Did anyone at the coven know what Nate really was?"

"He said no, but I think he told the coven leader, this man named Ziol. They talked on the phone a lot. Like way a lot. He went over to his house all the time too."

"Ah."

"Nate was getting obsessed, and he was convinced the gods were really walking here amongst us. I got mad at him, told him he was taking all of this too far. We had a big fight… and well, the next day, that's when he didn't come home.

"I saw him at the protests on the news, so I knew he was still with the coven, but then he wouldn't answer any of my calls. I kept thinking he'd come back home, so I waited. But then yesterday afternoon, he sent a really weird text, and that's, well, that's when I called you."

"May I see the text?"

"Here." Daphne handed her phone over.

"Thank you." Sloane read it and tilted it so Loch could read it as well.

Don't trust anyone. I'm in trouble. Please don't believe what they're going to say about me. It's not true. Ziol is gonna help me. I love you.

"I don't know what it means," Daphne said softly, "but I have to find my brother as soon as possible. I'm really worried about him."

Sloane grimaced and looked to Loch. They needed to tell her the truth.

"Wait, tell me what?" Daphne flinched.

Right. Psychic.

"Your brother is wanted for a heartless, bloody murder—"

"Loch!" Sloane snapped.

"What?" Daphne gasped in horror. "No, no, that can't be true!"

"Miss Ware, I'm very sorry to be the one to tell you this, but it's true." Sloane grimaced. "You've seen the protests on TV, so I'm sure you know there's been some fighting between the Sages and Lucians. Well, the deacon was murdered yesterday. Someone broke into his home and killed him. And, uh…." Sloane grimaced. "Mr. Ziol was also killed yesterday."

"By all the gods!" Daphne's eyes widened, and her tail curled around her feet.

"The police believe your brother found Ziol murdered and killed the deacon for revenge," Loch said, pausing to add, "which would have been justified a few thousand years ago, but everyone frowns on that now." He rolled his eyes. "Prudish mortals."

"No." Daphne hugged her tail to her chest, and her eyes were glistening with tears. "No… that… that can't be. My brother is a dumbass, okay, but he's not a killer! There's no way he killed anyone!"

"I'm really sorry, Miss Ware, truly, and I want to help you," Sloane said earnestly. "I want to help your brother too."

"Ha, do you mean find him and turn him over to the cops? Turn us both in for being monsters?"

"No. Nothing like that. I have no intentions of turning him in to the police unless I am convinced he is guilty."

"I can prove he's innocent!" Daphne insisted. "You said this deacon guy's house was broken into, right?"

"Yes?"

Daphne vanished from the chair and was now standing on top of Sloane's desk.

"Oh!" Sloane jerked back in surprise. "You can, uh, teleport. Without saying a spell. Or using your hands. Or a glyph. Or... wow, okay."

In another blink, Daphne was back in the chair. "We have Faedra in our family. We can teleport at will, always could, me and my brother both. He would never break into someone's home."

"Because he wouldn't need to," Loch observed, looking thoughtful now. "You know, if he's cleared of the murder charges, he would make an excellent thief."

"But to be clear, he hasn't actually been charged with anything yet," Sloane said quickly. "There's no warrant or anything. The police only want to talk to him."

"Hmmph." Daphne didn't seem convinced.

"You know I can't tell them he's part Faedra, and I can't say he teleports because then they'll hit him for using unregistered magic."

"Why do they think it's him?"

"Apparently he made some threats against the deacon, and they have him on camera fleeing the crime scene."

"Shit." She squeezed her tail. "I get how that can look bad, but you believe me, don't you? My brother would never hurt anyone."

"We are reserving judgment at this time," Loch declared.

"Ignore him," Sloane said. "We believe you, and we're going to help you."

"Thank you!" she gushed. She sank back in the chair, clearly relieved. "Thank you so much!"

"So, uh, any ideas where your brother might be?"

"There are a few places, secret places, where people like us go. I should warn you, they can be... well...."

"What's wrong?"

"They're a little rough." She grimaced. "One is a bar that's run by hidden people. It's called Dead to Rites."

"Ah, I'm familiar with it."

"They have a very dismal shrine for Azaethoth the Lesser," Loch said sourly. "It's insulting."

Sloane and Loch had visited the bar before when they were trying to help Merrick and Chase track down the Salgumel cultists. Rough hardly began to describe it.

"There's also a strip club, the Velvet Plank," Daphne went on. "Not quite as scary, but it's definitely packed full of hidden people. Just be careful. They don't like when strangers come around asking a bunch of questions."

"That's okay," Sloane reassured her. "We can be very discreet."

"Yeah, well, be super discreet." Daphne laughed. "They say the man who runs it is a gangster. I mean, they also say he's an old god in disguise, but pffft, that's just crazy."

"Says the troll girl," Loch griped under his breath.

"What was that?"

"We'll check out the bar and the club," Sloane said smoothly. "Do you have anything of your brother's I could have for a tracking spell?"

"We're both warded against it." Daphne made a face. "Most hidden people are. We make it a habit not to be able to be found if our identity is ever compromised."

"Right." Sloane glanced over her tail and tusks. "If you'd like, I could create a glamour charm for you? It wouldn't last very long, but hopefully until you can get a proper replacement."

Daphne brightened. "You'd do that for me?"

"Of course." Sloane smiled. "You've gotta get back to work, right? And it's one less thing you have to worry about. Do you have something I can enchant?"

"Please! Yes!" She patted her wrist. "Huh, I swore I had my watch on."

Sloane stared expectantly at Loch.

Loch batted his eyes.

Sloane cleared his throat.

Loch shrugged.

Sloane pointed emphatically at his crotch and shook his head.

Loch's eyes widened, and he conceded, "Fine. Yes. Oh! Here it is!" The watch appeared in his hand. "You must have dropped it."

"Ah, great! Thank you!" Daphne smiled. "I really appreciate this. Thank you, Mr. Beaumont. And thank you, too… uh…. Wow. I'm so sorry. With all of this going on, I never got your name!"

"I am Azaethoth the Lesser—" Loch began, puffing out his chest and smiling wide.

"Lochithoth Leslie," Sloane blurted out. "Loch for short. Lochithoth Leslie Beaumont. My husband."

"I never agreed to take your last name," Loch huffed.

"Oh! Well, it's nice to meet you." Daphne smiled, and her tail wagged. "I'm so glad I found you. As soon as I saw the Sage's Cross on your logo, I knew you were the right one."

Sloane laid the watch over his desk, and he focused his magic. A simple glamour charm wasn't too complex for his starlight's power, and he finished the spell with a clap. "There we go."

"Thank you." Daphne took the watch back and buckled it on her wrist. Her tusks and tail vanished, and her skin took on a normal hue. She ran her hands through her hair and pushed her hood back. "Wow! Seriously! This is amazing."

"My husband is a talented witch of starlight," Loch said proudly. "There is nothing he cannot do. Including but not limited to finding your brother."

"Thank you." Sloane was honestly touched by the sweet compliment, and he half expected Loch to say something crass to ruin it. When nothing came, he was even more pleased.

"Is there anything else you need from me?" Daphne asked. "Anything else that might help find my brother?"

"Normally I would ask for some sort of personal item for tracking or hope for a watchman's spell, but you guys are all warded against that." Sloane cracked a little grin. "It's okay. We'll have to do this the old-fashioned way. Don't worry. I'll find him."

Standing, Daphne said, "Okay. And you'll call me if you guys find anything?"

"Of course." Sloane stood to shake her hand. "Thank you for trusting us with so much, Miss Ware. We won't let you down."

"Thank you, Mr. Beaumont. Mr. Leslie."

They waved farewell, and Sloane sunk back into his chair as soon as the door shut. "Well, holy crap. That was… something."

"What's wrong, my love?" Loch petted Sloane's hair. "Are you angry that your pleasure was denied?"

"Loch!" Sloane gestured helplessly around them. "Did you not fully process what she told us? That there are everlasting people here on Earth? It's incredible!"

"Yes, I have processed. I am quite pleased, even if these hidden ones are but mere shadows of their ancestors."

"Did you see how she teleported? That was so cool!"

"I fail to see how that's so fascinating when you are wed to true godliness and I can whisk you away to your very own private world with a thought."

Sloane reached over to pat Loch's arm. "Mm, I'm sorry. You are the most amazing god ever." He sucked in a breath. "But...."

"But what?"

"It's still *cool*, isn't it? Just think! All of these hundreds of years, and these hidden people were here with us!" Sloane grinned. "I wonder if Asta and the other Asra know?"

Loch turned up his nose.

"I owe you a very sincere thank-you, by the way."

"Of course you do." Loch paused. "But what for specifically this time?"

"For mostly behaving and not revealing your true godly nature. Our little secret club is at capacity, you know."

"We should be much more discerning moving forward."

"Agreed. Okay, so." Sloane struggled to get his thoughts together. He was having some trouble focusing, and he tried not to let it frustrate him. "If Nate can teleport, that would explain how he got in and out of Ziol's house without setting off the wards."

"He wouldn't have been able to get through mine."

"Well, you're a god."

"I'm just making sure you have your facts gay."

"Don't you mean *straight*?"

"No." Loch grinned at his own joke.

Sloane laughed. "By all the gods, I really do love you."

"Mmm, and I love you, my beautiful Starkiller. Now! Let's continue making sure our facts are very gay. That only explains how he was able to get into the house. It does not absolve him of guilt."

"I know. And we still have him on camera fleeing the deacon's house." Sloane frowned. "I wonder, though… do they have him *entering* the house?"

"A good question to ask my uncle and Chase." Loch's tentacles slithered out and rubbed Sloane's shoulders.

"Maybe Nate went to talk to the deacon about the tree, or maybe Ziol even sent him there for something. I don't know. He pops in, but then some crap goes down, and he can't teleport so he runs."

"And fleeing the home breaks the wards." Loch zeroed in on a particularly sore muscle. "How's that, my love?"

"Mmm, very good." Sloane closed his eyes as his aches melted away beneath Loch's magical touch. "He could have even witnessed the murder… damn, Loch. That's amazing."

"Of course it is." Loch preened. "I'm a god."

"Mmm…."

"There is a problem with your theory, though."

"What?"

"By assuming Nate's innocence, you eliminated our only suspect, and there are two treacherous murderers afoot." One of Loch's tentacles massaged Sloane's chest. "We should fetch some more suspects."

"More suspects, mmm…." Sloane's pulse climbed as the tentacle slipped inside his shirt, rubbing over his nipple. Another tentacle crept down his stomach and teased along the zipper of his pants. "We… should…."

"Yes, my sweet Starkiller?"

"We should talk to the deacon's followers too," Sloane said firmly as he tried to resist Loch's advances. It felt good to struggle, especially when he knew he was going to give in. "We should go look at his house too. Look, uh, look for clues."

"Oh, I love clues." Loch leaned over Sloane's shoulder, sliding his hand over Sloane's chest as his tentacles opened up Sloane's pants.

"Clues! Hmmm. The, the killer… maybe left more clues…."

"We shall find all the clues," Loch promised. "Now, I believe I had some relief to bestow upon you."

"Just… mm… lock the door." Sloane panted, and he groaned excitedly when Loch's tentacle enveloped his cock. It was hot, tight, and he bucked up instinctively. "Ah, fuck!"

"I will take care of you." Loch kissed along Sloane's neck, and his other tentacles curled around Sloane's arms and waist.

The tentacle sucking his cock was intense, and Sloane knew he wouldn't last long. He was shivering, his hips twitching, and he loved how Loch's other tentacles were wrapped all around him.

He weakly thrust into the divine heat, letting his head fall back as he moaned. Loch's mouth was working up by his ear now, and he turned into the sensation.

"I cannot wait to taste you," Loch whispered.

"Yeah," Sloane breathed. "I wanna, mmm, I wanna taste you too."

"Yes?" Loch offered his other slitted tentacle, gently stroking Sloane's lips.

"Mmph!" Sloane sucked the tentacle into his mouth, relishing the smooth sensation against his tongue. The tentacle thrusted slowly, giving Sloane time to swallow and suck, and he rubbed his tongue along the firm shaft.

The tentacle on his cock had taken him all the way down, its undulating pressure coaxing Sloane toward orgasm. It was too hot, too perfect, and all of his muscles were tensing up like little springs.

He opened his mouth wide, inviting Loch to push deeper, and moaned when the tentacle teased at the back of his throat. He whimpered, spit pooling around his lips, and he gave himself over to Loch's intense affections.

"Come along, love," Loch purred. "I want you to come for me… over… and over again…."

That sultry rumble sent Sloane over the edge just as surely as the magnificent tentacle sucking his dick, and he came with a muffled cry. His body melted into the chair as his cock pulsed, every drop swallowed by the eager tentacle. The pleasure came in heady waves, making his eyes water and his thighs twitch, and it wasn't over.

Far from it.

The tentacle kept sucking away, but Sloane never felt the agony of overstimulation. His orgasm simply didn't end. He kept coming, his hips thrusting of their own accord, and his skin buzzed with bliss. His heartbeat thundered in his ears, and he barely had a moment to breathe in through his nose before another wave of pleasure came over him.

It was impossible to tell where the first orgasm ended and the next one began, the intense sensations rolling together seamlessly. His mouth was suddenly filled with Loch's hot seed, and he fought to swallow it all, new warmth surging through him.

This was the divine touch of a god, an ecstasy that no mortal could ever provide, and it wasn't just any god; it was Azaethoth the Lesser, his husband, who loved him more than anything in the entire universe.

"You're so beautiful," Loch whispered, nuzzling Sloane's flushed cheeks. His eyes had turned from green into endless black pools full of stars, and he smiled. "My beautiful Starkiller."

The spent tentacle withdrew, and Sloane wheezed in a deep breath, exhaling a deep groan. "Ohhh, f-fuck!"

"Good, my love?" Loch smiled, kissing Sloane's cheek.

"So good," Sloane panted. He gasped as Loch's tentacle pulled off his cock, and he lurched forward. His head was still spinning, and he braced himself against the desk. "Wow."

"Do you now feel more relaxed?"

"Very." Sloane grinned. "Thank you."

"Anytime." Loch beamed.

"Mmmm, wow." Sloane ran his fingers through his hair, and there was a sudden tug in his stomach.

No, wait, that was a *kick*.

"Oh!"

"Are you all right, love?" Loch frowned.

Sloane pushed his shirt up to cradle his stomach, and he laughed. Some of it felt like little flutters, soft bubbles, but then there were very definite kicks. It was as bizarre as it was wonderful. "It's our baby!"

"What's wrong?"

"Nothing! They're kicking! Here!" Sloane took Loch's hand and pulled it over to feel. The moment Loch touched him, it stopped. "Oh damn. Well, hang on, wait."

Loch petted Sloane's stomach, allowing a few beats of silence to pass before conceding, "It's all right, my love. I will feel the kicking at a later time."

"Stubborn little booger." Sloane poked his tummy. "Not even born yet and they're making trouble." He frowned. "Wait, should I even be able to feel kicking yet? At three months? Is that normal?"

"I'm not sure if the particulars of normal mortal gestation would apply to our situation." Loch patted Sloane's shoulder. "We can ask Mother when she and Galgareth arrive."

"Okay." Sloane rubbed his stomach. "Hope they're okay in there."

"I am sure they are fine." Loch kissed the top of Sloane's head. "Do you require more relaxing, my love?"

"I'm good for now, thank you." Sloane cracked his knuckles. "Now we get to work."

"Ah! Beating the curb for more suspects, pounding the truth out of them?"

"No." Sloane smirked. "Not quite."

Loch sighed. "Research?"

"Riveting, insightful, exciting, very important research."

"I don't agree with any of those words."

CHAPTER 4.

SLOANE FINALLY finished his paperwork and got to work on his laptop. Loch entertained himself first by listing all the many words he would use to describe research, such as boring, pointless, and insufferable agony. He then found amusement rearranging things in Sloane's office and chatting about preparing for their new child.

"I will not allow them to eat any of the processed garbage that you sully your body with," Loch was saying. "Although I am hurt they did not allow me to feel them kicking, I have decided to be a forgiving father and not hold that against them. I will gather fresh fruits and vegetables, and I will make baby food from scratch."

"Huh." Sloane paused. "Will they need to eat? I guess that's a weird question, but you don't ever need food."

"I am a god. Our child is only half. They will be everlasting, but not immortal. They will still feel the pangs of hunger and thirst. Keeping them well-nourished is essential to their growth."

"Ah." Sloane went back to reading.

"I heard that Abigail the Starkiller fed her child morning dew mixed with stardust and honey to nourish them." Loch scratched his chin. "I'm thinking... bananas."

"Uh-huh."

Loch plopped in the chair in front of the desk. He scooted forward so he could peer over the top of Sloane's laptop. "You must be focusing very hard. You haven't even noticed that I turned all of the picture frames on the wall around."

"Sorry, was looking at this article. In typical prudish Lucian fashion, our pal the deacon was trying to get a bunch of places shut down for rampant immoral behavior. Some bars, a topless restaurant, adult-type stores."

"The adult-type store is where they sell pornography and the sexual toys, yes?"

"Yes."

"We should visit one. I am curious. We still have many gift cards for the custom sex toy fabricator to spend."

Sloane ignored that reminder with a sly grin and went on, "It looks like a lot of people were getting really annoyed with him. He was arrested for trespassing and had numerous complaints for disrupting businesses." He turned the laptop around so Loch could see. "Including the strip club, the Velvet Plank!"

"Fascinating. Relevance?"

"Relevance being that Daphne told us to look for her brother there, and the deacon had the owner arrested for assault after they had some words. I think we should go check it out. We can look for Nate and ask the staff there about the deacon."

"Can we stop by the adult store on the way?"

"No."

Loch pouted.

"Okay, strong maybe, but on the way back." Sloane grabbed his cell phone. "I'm gonna call Chase and update them before we head out."

"I am ready for adventure."

Sloane smiled as he dialed, waiting for Chase to pick up.

"Hey, Sloane," Chase said. He sounded annoyed. "Tell Loch to give me my badge back. I know it was him."

"Yeah, sorry about that." Sloane grinned. "We'll get it back to you soon, I promise."

"Damn him." Chase snorted in laughter. "So, what's up? How did it go with the sister?"

"Good," Sloane replied. "Her name is Daphne, very sweet, and she confirms Nate was really getting into the coven scene with Ziol. Gave me some places to go look for him. Dead to Rites and the Velvet Plank."

"Rough spots." Chase whistled. "We got three open homicide cases just at Dead to Rites, including this real fun one where one of our old cultists buddies drowned in the alley out back."

"He *drowned*?"

"Yup. On seawater. You sure that you and Loch good to go?"

"No offense, but better us than two cops strolling in."

"Fair."

"Also, I checked into the deacon. He was not a friendly guy."

"Yeah." Chase sighed. "I know. I swear his dick only got hard when he was pissing people off."

"Like Sullivan Stoker?" Sloane read the name off the newspaper article on his screen.

"Somebody's been doing their homework."

"Yup." Sloane clicked back through the searches on his laptop, and he remembered what Daphne said. "I heard he's some kinda gangster?"

"He's *the* gangster. Moved to town a few years ago and set himself up real pretty running drugs, curses, and all kinds of illegal magic. Stay the fuck away from him."

"Why have I never heard of this guy before?"

"He's real quiet. Keeps his shit locked down tight. We've never been able to pin anything on him. He likes to make people who bother him fuckin' disappear."

"You're shaping him up to be a nice suspect. Looks like the deacon bothered him a lot. Had him arrested for assault, went after him in civil court when all the charges got dropped, and then...." Sloane clicked. "He *stole* Stoker's cat?"

"Let us handle Stoker. If there's any connection between him and the deacon's death, we'll take care of it. Right now, I'm still in favor of Nathaniel Ware."

"I don't think he did it."

"Why?"

"Okay, so." Sloane took a deep breath. "First of all, you cannot freak out. Secondly, I'm telling you as a friend and a Sage, and you can't tell anyone else."

"What is wrong, Sloane?" Merrick's voice asked.

"Hey, this goes for you too," Sloane said firmly. "No freaking out or reporting them or trying to arrest them."

"I will agree to nothing until you tell us what you are hiding."

"He agrees," Chase drawled. "Go on, Sloane."

"Daphne and her brother aren't human," Sloane said. "They're descendants of Absola and Faedra that survived here on Aeon. It's incredible. She and her brother can both teleport—"

"Truly?" Merrick sounded amazed.

"Ah!" Chase grunted. "Which is how the little bastard got in without breaking the fucking wards!" He paused briefly. "Okay, and which ones are the Abfola and Faery things?"

"The Absola are long-tailed trolls with telepathic powers, and the Faedra are behemoths with the ability to manipulate time and space," Merrick explained.

"Got it. Still doesn't tell us why we got the kid on camera fleeing the fuckin' crime scene."

"It does, however, explain why we have no footage of him entering the home."

"I'll be sure to ask Nathaniel all about it when I find him," Sloane said. "Worth mentioning, uh, Daphne said that Dead to Rites and the Velvet Plank were places these hidden people like to go. All the descendants of the everlasting people, I mean."

"There's more of them?" Chase asked incredulously. "How many are we talkin'?"

"I'm not sure exactly. But I'm guessing more than a few."

"Tread carefully," Merrick warned. "If that is true, there is much more than mortal magic to fear."

"I will be with him," Loch said confidently. "There is nothing to worry about."

"I disagree."

"You guys make any headway yet?" Sloane asked.

"Nobody at the fuckin' coven wants to talk," Chase griped. "Everybody is all, 'Oh, Ziol was just so fuckin' amazing, the best ever,' and, 'No, Nate would never hurt anyone,' and blah blah blah."

"That is not accurate," Merrick grumbled. "That is not what they said."

"Close enough. They get the idea. Nobody is talking. They were real fast to point fingers at the deacon for stirring shit up, though."

"Which doesn't help us." Sloane sighed. "Makes all the members of the coven look like suspects."

"On a brighter note," Merrick said, "none of them seemed particularly obsessed with Salgumel. Despite what we found in Ziol's home, he taught the high pantheon of gods and venerated Great Azaethoth above all else."

"Well, that's good at least."

"It's the little things, right?" Chase laughed. "I've never been so happy we have a double murder and magical creatures runnin' around 'cause it's better than some crazy-ass cult."

"Or fighting a god," Sloane mumbled.

"If we actually find anything fuckin' useful, we'll call," Chase promised. "Check in after you head down to the Plank, okay? Be fuckin' careful."

"Will do. Talk to you later."

"Farewell, Uncle!" Loch said, waving at the phone.

"Farewell, Azzath. Sloane." Perhaps Merrick waved back.

"Later, guys. And don't forget my badge, Loch!" Chase hung up.

"How rude." Loch had the badge out, spinning it around his finger by the chain. "As if I could forget this wonderful little prize."

"He meant don't forget to give it back." Sloane put his phone away and stood, stretching his arms over his head. "Mm, okay. Let's get going."

"I noticed you didn't mention what Daphne said about the owner potentially being a god." Loch made the badge vanish and batted his eyes. "I like this sneaky side of you."

"It's not sneaky!" Sloane protested. "It's just a rumor, and they're already worried about us. Besides, me and you are more than enough to handle a god."

"Obviously."

"See, so there's nothing to worry about." Sloane kissed Loch's cheek. "As long as we're together, we can do anything."

"I believe the proper word for this situation is 'duh.'"

Spirits high, Sloane drove them to Dead to Rites. It was an old funeral home that had been converted into a bar, and they'd been here before when Chase's nephew, Ollie, was missing.

Their visit was as unhelpful as it had been the last time they were here. No one seemed to know anything about Nathaniel. Most of them claimed to not even know who he was. Even with a truth spell, it was difficult to tell if anyone was lying. Knowing now that these people might not be human made Sloane wonder if they could all manipulate the spell, and Loch spent his time complaining about the lackluster shrine to Azaethoth the Lesser.

Having gained nothing, they decided to head over to the Velvet Plank and hoped it would be more productive. After a short drive, they arrived, and Sloane parked around back. The lot was mostly empty, to be expected at such an early hour. The large building must have once been quite magnificent, and it was obviously a theater long ago.

The marquis had lots of Xs and names of people Sloane assumed were featured exotic dancers. Instead of advertising films, there were posters boasting male revues three nights a week and prime rib lunch specials. The scrolling woodwork featured waves and seashells around the doors, and the ticket booth was damaged but still breathtaking.

The plywood nailed over one of the doors, however, was an eyesore.

There was no one at the ticket booth, but the door that wasn't boarded up was unlocked.

Loch insisted on going first, and Sloane allowed it, following him inside.

It was a massive space, and the stage had been extended with the addition of a long catwalk. There were two smaller stages built on either side, with multiple tables scattered between them all. What may have been concessions was now a bar, and the private boxes up in the balcony were hidden by thick curtains.

Sloane noticed an added design of tentacles weaving in and out of the oceanic reliefs above the stage and bar, and he wondered what it must have been like to see this place when it first opened. It was miles away now from whatever that had been.

The longer Sloane looked around, the worse it all was: there were tears in the faded carpet, cobwebs hanging in every nook and cranny, the tablecloths were frayed and stained, and the faint odor of vomit and cigarettes permeated the air.

Despite it not even being quite lunchtime, there was a lithe woman up on the main stage, busy entrancing a handful of men to fork over their cash while she danced on the pole at the end of the catwalk. There was a man working at the bar, stocking the shelves with liquor bottles.

To the bar Sloane went, and he offered the man behind the counter a friendly smile. "Hi."

"What can I get for you gentlemen?" the man asked, gesturing for Sloane to take a seat.

The man looked like the club, beautiful but damaged by the passage of time. His buzzed hair was more silver than gray, and his fierce blue eyes were plagued with dark circles. He was wearing a black T-shirt with the Velvet Plank logo imprinted across the front in neon pink.

Sloane couldn't quite place how old he was, but perhaps in his forties or late thirties. The gray made it difficult to be sure, and there was something off about the way he moved: too smooth, too *liquid*, like a snake.

"Information," Sloane replied, waving his hand casually to cast a truth spell.

"Cops?" The man was instantly wary.

"No, private investigator. Name is Sloane Beaumont. Trying to find a young man by the name of Nathaniel Ware."

"Is that so?"

"Yes," Loch said as he leaned over the bar. "You would be wise to cooperate. We could make things very difficult for you. Send you straight up to the big house."

The man laughed. "Oh really?"

"I was hired by his sister, Daphne, to find him," Sloane said earnestly. "She told me I might be able to find him here."

"Mmm, did she?"

"You ask a lot of questions when you should be answering them," Loch noted. "Not very helpful, are you?"

"I'm helping myself quite well," the man retorted. He poured a glass of an amber-colored liquid and took a sip. "Even if I had seen Nathaniel, I don't get why I would tell you."

"His sister is desperate to find him," Sloane said. "She's worried about him."

"That sounds an awful lot like her problem and not mine. I didn't lose him."

"Do you know where he is?"

"Maybe."

The man's dodgy answers weren't setting off the truth spell, so Sloane tried, "Can you help me find him?"

"It depends on what you have to offer." The man snapped his fingers, and two sigils appeared on the bar, one in front of Sloane and the other in front of Loch.

Sloane steeled himself not to react.

Only witches of starlight and gods could cast magic without speaking a spell. Some mortals could learn to cast one or two things without saying the words, but it was not common. Either way, this mere bartender was powerful. The sigil he cast was one designed to read auras.

But there was something weird about it, something that had been changed....

"Go on." The man waved. "Let's see what you can do. Aura first, and then we'll talk terms."

Sloane went first, placing his hand on the sigil. It lit up and turned bright white, the light prismatic and brilliant before fading away.

"Starlight," the man observed. His eyes cut to Loch. "You."

"Yes?" Loch blinked.

"Go on. Touch it."

"Ah, never on the first date."

"Loch," Sloane urged. He knew Loch could hide his godly aura and mimic any number of things.

"Fine!" Loch fussed but placed his hand on the sigil. It glowed brightly, and it suddenly sparked, erupting in a flurry of rainbow-hued flashes.

A god's aura.

"Well, that's not good," Loch said, his eyes wide as he tried to pull his hand away.

"Loch!" Sloane hissed. "What the fuck are you doing?"

"I can't move my hand—!"

"You had one job, one simple job!"

"I really don't see how this is my fault—"

"Ahem." The man cleared his throat. He was calm for someone who had just revealed a stranger to be a god.

Sloane glared. "Release him at once."

"If you don't let me go immediately, I'm afraid I'm going to do something very mass-panic-causing," Loch warned.

"Not yet," the man replied. "I'm curious how a witch of starlight and a god happened to come walking into my establishment and think they can try to trick me with a truth spell and start asking all sorts of questions about a friend of mine."

"You're Sullivan Stoker," Sloane realized.

Gangster, entrepreneur, possible god.

"And you're the new Starkiller everyone is talking about," Stoker mused. "Which makes this one Azaethoth the Lesser."

"A pleasure." Loch beamed. "We really are the Jay-Z and Beyoncé—"

"No! No pleasure! No Beyoncé! Don't get excited because he knew our names." Sloane placed both of his hands on top of the counter. He felt resistance when he tried to cast, and then it clicked.

That's what was different about the sigil. Not only could it apparently trap gods, it identified auras and silenced whoever touched it.

No problem.

Sloane focused and effortlessly broke through the sigil's hold. He summoned his magic, a surge of starlight, and the bar rattled.

"Huh." Stoker seemed intrigued. "The sigil didn't silence you."

"I once had a man with the soul of a god burn a silencing ward right into my skin," Sloane declared. "I ripped it out with my bare hands. This was nothing." The bar shook harder. "I didn't come here to deal with any stupid bullshit. I'm going through a lot of crazy stuff right now, I'm getting really hungry, and all I wanna do is find Nathaniel. So you can either help us or not, but no more bullshit games!"

Loch had never looked so proud, and he clapped.

"If you keep fucking with me, I will send you right to…." Sloane stared at Loch's free hands. "Wait! How did you…?"

"Oh right!" Loch grinned. "A trap is sort of like a lock, isn't it? And I am the god of thieves. I merely needed a moment to pick it open."

Sloane groaned.

"You're both very impressive," Stoker praised as he took another drink from his glass. "Your reputations are well deserved."

"How do you know who we are?" Sloane asked.

"Part of my business involves the acquisition of valuable information." Stoker smiled. "A Starkiller and gods in Archersville? Very valuable to know. Fear not. Your secret is safe with me."

"Yeah, and how do we know that?"

"I've kept it this long, haven't I?"

"Are you going to help us now?" Sloane didn't know how long Stoker meant, and he was not going to address the fact that Stoker had said 'gods' and not 'god.' Sloane removed his hands from the bar, but he kept a flicker of starlight in his palm just in case.

"I won't tell you where Nathaniel is, but I can tell him you're looking for him." Stoker glanced at his nails. "Though his sister means well, I'm sure you can understand why he wouldn't want to make an appearance right now."

"I need to talk to him," Sloane insisted. "I believe he's innocent, but I can't catch the real killers without him."

"I may be able to provide a private channel of communication." Stoker leaned forward, smooth and graceful, eyeing Sloane. "But I will want something in return."

"What?"

"You probably already know I was no fan of the deacon. He took something very precious to me, and I want it back."

"Your cat."

"You've been doing your homework. Bring my cat back and I'll let you talk to Nathaniel." Stoker smirked slyly. "Do we have a deal?"

"Do we have to steal the cat?" Loch asked with wide eyes.

"Probably."

Loch grinned.

"I actually have a few questions for you first," Sloane chimed in.

Stoker drummed his long fingers on the edge of the bar and hummed. "That's not part of the deal, Mr. Beaumont."

"How about we make it part of the deal?"

"Mmm, and what? You'll owe me a favor?" Stoker's smile was positively wicked. "Were you an unwed man, I might ask you for something unseemly. Say, to lay in a bed with no clothes on for a few days while I explore every inch of your skin?"

Sloane hated how he blushed, and he couldn't even think of a reply. No one had flirted with him so aggressively since he'd first met Loch.

The chances of Stoker being a god had just jumped up.

Either that or he was a creep.

Maybe both.

"Do you know what one of my favorite pastimes is?" Loch asked Stoker with a sweet smile, his eyes turning black. "I love braiding. In particular, making internal organs into external ones and braiding those is very exciting."

"My apologies." Stoker bowed his head. "I meant no offense, but I simply cannot think of anything else he could possibly offer me."

"Ah, the next words out of your mouth had best be a much more sincere apology," Loch warned, "or I am going to leave my mortal vessel, assume my godly form, and pull out your lower intestinal tract with my teeth to practice my fishtail."

Stoker flinched.

Sloane's loins were assaulted by a wave of lust, and he had a new appreciation for Loch being a totally badass and terrifying deity. He made a mental note to show his appreciation later.

"Sloane Beaumont, please accept my most humble apologies," Stoker said solemnly. "As a token of my sincerity, how about I answer some of those questions you wanted, hm?" He winked. "Starting with, yes, I am single."

"Flirt with my husband again and I am going to eat you." Loch wagged his finger.

"What are you?" Sloane demanded.

"A business owner." Stoker rolled his eyes. "I know you're still using a truth spell. You're going to have to be more clever than that."

"Are you human?"

"No."

"Are you a god?"

"No." Stoker snorted dryly. "We're going to be here a very long time if you want to go through every single magical creature ever known trying to figure out what I am. Trust that I am old, I am powerful, and I have little desire to fight a god or a Starkiller."

"Because you'd succumb to failure?" Loch taunted.

"Because I'm tired."

Sloane lifted his hand for a perception spell and found Stoker was changing his aura's hue like a twirling kaleidoscope. Scowling, he griped, "You know, that's not helpful."

"I don't see how it's any of your business," Stoker replied shortly. "You want to find Nathaniel and prove his innocence, and I want my cat. It is a fair deal, and this interrogation is annoying me."

"Did you kill the deacon?"

"No. Murder is bad for business. Would you like to ask me if Fishboy is real? Do unicorns really poop rainbows?"

"Wow. Hilarious. I think we're done here." Sloane hopped off the barstool. "Where's your damn cat?"

"The deacon took him and placed a spell on him so he could not be removed from his residence by mortal hands." Stoker waved at Loch. "You should have no problem freeing him."

"And if we do this, you'll tell us where Nathaniel is?"

"No, but I will let you speak to him." Stoker smiled. "It's been an absolute pleasure meeting you both."

"Yup. A real blast."

"Remember." Loch narrowed his eyes, walking backward to keep glaring at Stoker as he followed Sloane to the door. "Me, you, intestinal braiding."

"Noted." Stoker saluted with his glass. "Farewell, Azaethoth and Starkiller."

"Let's get the fuck out of here," Sloane mumbled under his breath. The lustful simmer from earlier was still there, and he was hungry for more than food.

Loch turned around to walk forward, patting Sloane's shoulder. "Worry not, my love. When this is all over and he is no longer useful to us, I can still eat him."

"That's sweet of you." Sloane leaned in close. "You know, speaking of eating, I am absolutely *starving*." He lingered on the last word, hoping Loch would catch his meaning.

"Oh? Oh!" Loch grinned. "For food, mating, or both?"

"Both. Definitely both. How about we go home, get naked, and—"

As Loch opened the door for Sloane to exit the club, there was an old black woman with long braids and a blue-haired teenage boy trying to come in. They nearly collided, and Sloane scrambled to get out of the way.

"Sorry! Excuse us!" he said. "We were trying to…." He grinned at the boy. "Wait. Toby?"

"Oh! Look! Breasts!" the old woman exclaimed as she peered in through the open door.

"Sloane! Brother!" The boy immediately hugged them both. "It's so good to see you!"

The teenaged boy was Toby, the vessel of Galgareth, goddess of night and serendipity. He served as her host whenever she came to Aeon now.

"You both look wonderful!" the old woman gushed, also pulling them into big hugs.

"Mother." Loch smiled happily. "Ah, our family. All together again!"

The old woman was Urilith, Loch's mother and the goddess of fertility. She was in a different vessel than the one she'd used before, but it was definitely her: same rib-crushing hugs.

Sloane could feel Stoker staring at them, and he urged, "Let's go outside. Too many eyeballs in here."

"Oh, of course!" Urilith led the charge back out to the sidewalk. "We came as soon as we could. I fear the delay is my fault. The dreaming is so hard to wake from, and then I had some trouble finding a vessel! My old one died, bless them, but this is Joanna, and she's very lovely and quite alive!"

"It's all right." Loch went in for another hug. "Mm, you're both here. That's all that matters now."

"Is everything all right, my sweet child?"

"Oh yes! We're on a quest to solve two heinous murders, track down a vile suspect hiding from justice, and I threatened a gangster with internal organ braiding for insulting my husband."

"Wow." Galgareth laughed. "You guys have been busy, huh?"

"That's not even the best part!"

"What is it?"

"We're going to steal a cat!"

CHAPTER 5.

"A CAT?" Galgareth wrinkled her nose. "What in the world have you guys gotten yourselves into this time?"

"A whole steaming pile of crazy," Sloane drawled. "Come on. We'll tell you about it on the way home."

"But we have a cat to pilfer!" Loch protested. "And you said we could visit the adult store!"

"Not with your mother and your sister here!"

"The sooner we get the cat, the sooner we can talk to our vile suspect and peruse adult wares."

"He is not a vile suspect, and I really need to eat." Sloane rubbed his stomach. He would attend to his baser needs later, but food was an absolute priority.

Urilith reached for Sloane's belly. "May I?"

"Oh yes! Please." Sloane stepped a little closer, hoping this wouldn't look too weird if anyone glanced their way.

Urilith rested her hand on Sloane's stomach and snuck a yellow tentacle from her sleeve to slip up his shirt to meet bare skin. "Ah, yes. Healthy, happy… and, oh!"

The baby suddenly kicked.

"Hungry," she chuckled.

Sloane was relieved, but he still had to ask, "They're okay? Everything is normal? Well, you know, as normal as can be."

"Yes," Urilith promised.

The baby wiggled again and gave another kick.

"They are very strong."

"How can I feel them kicking like this right now?" Sloane frowned. "I'm not even showing."

"Your body will adjust as it needs to. Your pregnancy may mimic a mortal's in some ways, but this child is still half god. It feels like they are getting impatient…." She grinned as she withdrew her hand. "I believe we need to plan for the birth soon."

Sloane squeaked. "Like how soon?"

"Before the next full moon," Urilith said. "We have much to do to prepare."

"Wait, was our child kicking again?" Loch put his hand on Sloane's stomach and sighed grumpily when there was nothing to feel now. "Our child is doing this to spite me."

Sloane was a little dizzy as they headed around the club to get to his car. The full moon was less than two weeks away. "Wow. Uh, is that why I've started getting sick all of a sudden?"

"Yes," Urilith confirmed. "Your little one has decided they're ready to be born. The increase in growth is a strain on your mortal body. I have given you one of my blessings, but I am not sure if it will help. A pregnancy such as yours is most unusual."

"Don't worry," Galgareth was quick to reassure. "We will be here to help take care of you and the baby when the time comes."

Flopping behind the wheel, Sloane tried taking a few deep breaths. "We don't have a nursery. We don't even have diapers or anything. I thought we had more time." He was getting weepy again. "I didn't think it was gonna happen like this."

"It's all right, my love," Loch promised as he took the passenger seat. "We will all be right here for you. This is what family does."

"Thank you," Sloane sniffed.

"Families also do fun things together. Bowling, baseball games, bikini waxes—"

"Loch."

"—petty theft. Lots of possibilities."

"We have a new child to get ready for!" Urilith scolded, getting settled in the back seat next to Galgareth. "The theft can wait!"

"Yes, Mother." Loch fidgeted. "What about visiting an adult store?"

"No!" Sloane griped. "We can go some other time when your family isn't here! I'm not looking at giant weird dildos with your freakin' mother!" He glanced back at Urilith. "No offense."

"Oh!" Urilith smiled. "None taken, sweet child."

Loch pouted.

As they drove back to Sloane's apartment, they caught Galgareth and Urilith up on what was going on with their latest case. Although Loch complained about the disgusting horrors of processed food, Sloane stopped at another fast-food place to grab something to eat.

They also made sure to tell them all about their recent familial discovery.

"Uncle Gordoth is Detective Merrick?" Galgareth gasped. "I can't believe it! This is awesome!"

"See! This is exactly why we couldn't find him in Zebulon for the wedding!" Urilith exclaimed. "He was right here with us and we had no idea!"

"And your love readings turned out to be most accurate," Loch said proudly. "I am very happy to announce our dear Gordoth is no longer 'untouched,' thanks to Detective Chase."

"Aww, how sweet!" Galgareth gushed.

"I'm voting for Gordoth the Slut, but he hasn't really warmed up to it yet."

"They're really happy together." Sloane smiled as he drove up to his apartment building and parked. "Who knows, might have to help plan another wedding soon."

"One celebration at a time." Urilith chuckled. "We must get the preparations for the Neun Monde underway at once."

"More like Three Monde," Galgareth teased.

"Three really short Mondes," Sloane grumbled. "I don't even know where to begin."

"You begin by letting us take care of everything," Loch said confidently. He was already out of the car, and he swept Sloane into his arms the moment he shut his door. "Starting with I have decided you no longer need to walk on your own."

"Oh, by the gods, you're ridiculous!" Sloane laughed, but he let himself get carried inside the apartment. He had to admit it was nice to be spoiled. Plus, his feet kinda hurt.

Urilith and Galgareth made themselves at home and went through the fridge and cabinets. Loch deposited Sloane on the couch and propped him up with pillows and blankets.

"Have you thought about where you want to set up the nursery?" Urilith asked. "The second bedroom, yes?"

"Yeah." Sloane stretched out in the cushioned nest Loch had made for him. "There's just boxes in there right now."

"You guys really haven't done squat, huh?" Galgareth smiled sympathetically.

"I thought we still had months! At least five more, you know. We haven't even settled on names."

"Yes, we did." Loch frowned. "Daniel Azaethoth the Lesser Junior."

"Oh?" Sloane laughed. "What if it's a girl?"

"Pandora Azaethoth the Lesser Junior. Obviously."

"There is not enough food here for a proper feast." Urilith put her hands on her hips. "You don't even have any fresh lavender."

Sloane cringed. "I am the worst witch who's ever witched?"

"Mother and I are going to take Toby's parent's credit card and go baby shopping," Galgareth soothed. "Don't worry. We got this. Now let's see. We need lots of lavender and ginger, oh, some fruit. Mm, some kind of fish. And gifts! Oh!"

"We have to get the birthing gifts!" Urilith gushed. "Yes!"

"I need to find my bell," Sloane suddenly realized. "From my birth. I still have mine that my mother gave me."

"I will help you, my love," Loch promised. "We will find it."

"Do I get a crown too?"

"Of course you do." Loch snorted. "You're giving birth."

"When we did this for Lynette, I never thought we'd ever be doing it for me." Sloane took Loch's hand. "Funny, isn't it?"

"If by funny you mean incredible and wonderful, then yes."

"We should probably go ahead and send out invitations for the Neun Monde," Galgareth mused. "Milo, Lynette, Uncle Gordoth, his new mate. Mm, who else?"

"Should we invite the entire super-secret Sages' club?" Loch asked Sloane.

"Lochlain and Robert maybe?" Sloane smiled wearily. "I think that's plenty."

"What about Fred?" Loch frowned. "What if he's having problems with his penis again?"

Fred was a ghoul, a person who had died and whose soul was bound to a copy of their original body. Unlike Merrick and Loch, whose godly essence kept their mortal bodies intact, ghouls always ended up rotting away.

"He hates when you ask him about that, but fine, yes, Fred can come too." Sloane smirked. "Which means Ell is coming."

"I like Ell. I respect his choice in personal lubricant."

"Shall we say tomorrow night?" Galgareth asked. "That should give Mother and I enough time to cook up a truly magnificent feast."

"Perfect," Sloane confirmed. "Thank you both so much for this."

"Of course, little one." Urilith flitted over to pet Sloane's cheek with a tentacle and kissed his hair. "My blessing should ease some of your sickness, so you can rest now."

"All right. We're going." Galgareth used a tentacle to poke Loch. "You, stay here and pamper your mate."

"Will do." Loch smiled.

"See you guys later!" Sloane waved as the goddesses left, and he sank into the pillows with a huff.

Even with all of this immortal help at his disposal, it was overwhelming to think of everything they had to do to get ready for their child. That wasn't even taking into consideration their new case and the cat theft looming over them.

"What's wrong, my love?" Loch kneeled beside the couch and offered his tentacles for Sloane to snuggle with.

"Feeling crazy." Sloane smiled wearily. "I know your family is gonna do everything they can to help, but wow, it's… it's a lot. And I'm a little scared."

"Of what?" Loch's tentacles curled closer around him.

"Birth. Our baby. Making sure they're safe and happy and…." Sloane groaned when his eyes teared up again. "I wish my parents were still here so I could ask them for advice. You know, all the normal parent stuff I don't get to have."

"My mother loves you like her own."

"Which is great, and I love her too, but she's not… she's not *my* mother." Sloane wiped at his face. "My mother isn't here to see her grandbaby. She's not here to tell me that everything is gonna be okay and what crazy little things I did when I was a baby." He shook his head, pressing the heels of his hands against his eyes as if he could stem the flow of tears. "Ugh. I'm sorry."

"My love," Loch purred, "don't ever apologize for your feelings. I am not frightened or put off by emotions." He kissed Sloane's forehead. "If you'd like, we can visit her and your father once the baby is born. I'm afraid the trip might be too stressful right now while you're with child—"

"Really?" Sloane sat up and hugged Loch's neck. "We can go back to Zebulon?"

"Of course." Loch rubbed Sloane's back, and his tentacles clung to him. "I told you we can visit them whenever you'd like. Your mortal body limits your experiences with them to only that of their light, but—"

"I can still talk to them! Even if it's just for a few seconds!" Sloane cried against Loch's shoulder. "A few seconds… please…."

Whatever dam had been holding back his feelings was broken, and he openly sobbed, clinging to his husband.

He missed his parents so much, and starting his own family had sharpened the pain of their loss in a way he hadn't expected. He couldn't call his mother to ask about diaper rash or picky eating, and he couldn't ask his father about what kind of fabric softener to use or what good remedies for teething he knew.

He was so alone.

No… not alone.

Not now.

Though he could not fix the hole his parents' death had left in his heart, he did not have to shoulder the pain on his own. He had an eclectic godly family who would do anything for him and dear friends who absolutely adored him.

He could never replace what he'd lost, but he didn't want to spoil what he had now with the sorrows of what could have been.

After all, he knew with total certainty that one day they would all be together again.

That wasn't a gift many people had.

Not to mention he had the love of an immortal being who was right this very moment drying all his tears with a thought and summoning a flurry of starlight to gently rain down upon him.

"I love you," Loch whispered, holding him close and rocking him gently as the starlight sparkled around them. "I love you so much."

"I love you too," Sloane whispered back. He sniffed loudly and let the warmth of the magic seep into his skin. Finally spent from his tears, he leaned back to wipe off his face again. "Fuck, I'm such a mess."

"It's all right." Loch bumped their noses together. "You're a beautiful mess."

"Mm, thank you." Sloane rolled his eyes, but he cracked a smile. "I wish I had some of your godly confidence right about now."

"Think me so confident, do you?" Loch bit his lip. "Would you like to know a secret?"

"A secret?"

"I'm scared too."

"Of what?" Sloane scoffed. "Your shrines being too small? Us not mating enough? Burning your cookies?"

"Of being a father."

"Really?" Sloane was honestly stunned, and he cringed for being so shallow. "But I've seen you around kids before. You freakin' love them, and you're great with them. Bee summoning spells aside, ahem. You have been nothing but excited and super happy about our baby."

"Ah yes, and I am excited, and yes, super happy." Loch turned his head away. "And also scared. I've not exactly had the most impressive father figure in my life, as I'm sure you're aware."

"Salgumel."

"To you, he's the mad god of dreams and sleep who abandoned mortals the very moment we had competition for worship. He took the gods into the dreaming and that was that, yes? But for me... as his youngest child, he's been gone much longer."

Sloane touched Loch's cheek, and he settled his other hand on one of the many tentacles coiled around him. "You don't ever talk about him. I didn't want to ask you... I guess, I thought, well... that it might be rude."

"He promised all of Aeon to Tollmathan and my brothers. A kingdom for them to rule, the same one they long to regain by remaking the world, waking him up. I never wanted any of that. I didn't care about ruling." Loch closed his eyes. "I just wanted my father."

"You wanted your family."

"I think perhaps that's why I was always so drawn to Great Azaethoth." Loch smiled sadly. "My own father didn't want to spend time with me, but Azaethoth was there for me no matter what. And what more of a father figure could I ask for than the creator of all?"

"Well, you are his favorite." Sloane grinned, hoping to cheer Loch up.

Loch's smile did brighten a bit, and he teased, "Ah, but do you know why?"

"I assume because you're so wonderful and charming?"

"You forgot humble."

"That too."

"Tell me."

"At the very first Dhankes, the one my mother first made her cake for that caused you to moan so erotically, Great Azaethoth lit a magnificent bonfire for the feast. This is the same fire mortals emulate by lighting candles to welcome back the spirits of the dead."

"Right."

"Well, I was a very young god, I was a bit bored...." Loch grinned. "And I stole it."

"The fire?" Sloane laughed. "You stole the damn bonfire? The whole thing?"

"Oh, I most certainly did. Everyone was quite furious with me, but not Great Azaethoth. Not him. He thought it was hilarious. He laughed so hard that some of the stars fell from the sky that night. Ah, he was always so very kind to me. Encouraged me, guided me, helped me find my place as a god...."

Sloane could see Loch's eyes getting damp as they turned into deep black pools, and he reached for Loch's hand to comfort him.

"The creator of the entire universe, the greatest of all the gods, *made time for me*...." A glittering tear slid down Loch's cheek. "Even when my own father didn't."

"Well, it sounds like you didn't need Salgumel around anyway." Sloane squeezed his hand. "You had Great Azaethoth to show you what it means to be a great father. And you are going to be a great father too. I can't think of anyone else I would want to raise a baby with."

"You mean that, don't you?"

"Yes. You love our child so much already. I mean, that's why you're scared. It's because you care enough to worry about being a good dad. You're gonna be awesome. I already know that you'd do anything to keep our family safe."

"Like braid the intestines of our enemies?" Loch beamed.

Sloane laughed, and then groaned loudly. "Ugh, yes. I'm very aware."

"Thank you for listening, my love."

"Hey, thank you for listening to me." Sloane hugged him. "We're gonna kick ass as parents. We got this. We can handle this crap. We saved the damn world!"

"Twice."

"Exactly!" Sloane stroked Loch's tentacles. "You know, somebody once told me we can do anything together."

"That was me, yes?"

"Yes."

"Good." Loch smoothed his hands through Sloane's hair and kissed his forehead. "Now tell me, my earthly husband, my deliciously insatiable mate, my beloved Starkiller amongst mortals, how may I serve you?"

"Serve me?" Sloane chuckled. "Ah, because your sister told you to pamper me?"

"Pampering you would have been my intention even without her direction."

"Well, I'm still kinda hungry," Sloane confessed.

"Would you like me to cook for you, my love?"

Sloane's stomach dropped. "Uh, I don't want to trouble you."

"Oh, it is no trouble!"

"Then that would be wonderful."

Loch sprang up, all of his tentacles vanishing back into his body in a whirl. "What would you like, hmm? I can make anything that your dear heart desires."

Sloane didn't want his concerns about Loch cooking to be too obvious, and he decided to pick something simple. "Spaghetti with those frozen breadsticks sounds good."

"Consider it done." Loch marched into the kitchen with his head held high and proceeded to raid the fridge and pantry for ingredients.

"Hey, I was thinking about something," Sloane called after him.

"Is this a something that will make you cry again and require physical comfort?"

"No." Sloane chuckled quietly. "I think I'm okay on crying for a little bit. No, I was thinking about that Stoker guy. Do you think he's really a god in disguise?"

"It is possible." Loch filled a pot of water to put on the stove for the pasta and another for the sauce. "He could also be one of the hidden people like Daphne and her brother."

"Who can cast without speaking and make a sigil that traps a god?"

"I was not trapped." Loch held up a tomato, waving it at Sloane to emphasize his words. "I was lightly *restrained*."

"Whatever." Sloane grinned. "It was still pretty impressive."

Loch snorted. He cut up tomatoes while his tentacles opened a can of tomato paste to dump into the sauce pot.

"Whatever he is, he's doing a good job of hiding it. And he knows who we are."

"Why are you so interested?" Loch hesitated. "Do you find him... attractive?"

"What? No! He's a jerk. Not to mention a criminal and probably a murderer." Sloane sighed. "I'd feel better knowing what was sneaking around in our backyard."

"We don't have a backyard." Loch frowned. "We still live in an apartment. Did the move confuse you?"

"I mean I'd like to know if there's another potentially crazy god out there close by."

"Ah." Loch added the diced tomatoes to the sauce and sprinkled in some herbs.

"It's bad enough we're waiting around for the Salgumel cultists to pop back up and whichever one of your siblings decides they want to end the world next. I thought... maybe instead of waiting around for once, we could be proactive."

"Like going after the criminal with the shoulders you could hang a bedspread on and the moldy eyes?"

"Smoldering eyes."

"Yes, those."

Sloane raised his brow. "Hey, are you sure you're not the one attracted to him?"

"No." Loch turned up his nose and dumped the pasta into the water that was now boiling. "I am only making observations."

"Uh-huh."

"I am also observing that you have made a good point. He knows who and what we are. It would be nice to be on equal webbing."

"Footing."

"That too."

"But how to draw him out? Make him reveal himself?"

"Oh." Loch smirked. "I'm sure I can think of something."

Loch finished cooking and proudly presented Sloane with a savory plate of spaghetti and a chunky red sauce. It actually looked and smelled incredible. Sloane was very impressed, except....

"You forgot the breadsticks."

Loch cleared his throat, and a breadstick magically appeared on Sloane's plate.

"What happened to not using magic for cooking?" Sloane chuckled as he grabbed the breadstick to take a big bite.

"I have a hungry husband who wanted to enjoy the incomparable taste of reheated frozen garlic bread. I am obligated to provide it at any cost, even if it means compromising my culinary ethics."

"I love you."

"And I love you."

Sloane finished eating and flopped back in his pillowy nest with a full stomach. Loch cleared his plate away and came back to snuggle with him, easing his head into his lap and petting his hair.

"That was delicious," Sloane praised. "Your cooking is really getting better. Nothing even caught on fire."

"Mmm... you didn't moan."

Sloane rolled his eyes and gave him a lusty, loud moan. "Ohhh, it was so good, Loch."

"You don't mean that." Loch narrowed his eyes.

"It was really good. Seriously." Sloane snagged one of Loch's tentacles and kissed it. He was full and sleepy, and it would be so easy to drift off.

"What else can I do for you? Would you like a sensual massage? Do you hunger for my flesh, my sweet Starkiller?"

"I hunger for a nap." Sloane grimaced. "I'm sorry. I'm so exhausted all of a sudden. I think Urilith's blessing helped because I don't feel sick, but ugh. So very full."

"You're growing a tiny god or goddess inside of you. It is no easy task." Loch picked Sloane up, holding him against his chest with his arms and tentacles.

"Mmm, where am I going?"

"Bed." Loch took Sloane to their bedroom, reverently tucked him into bed, and then kissed his cheek. "You are going to rest here for as long as you want while my family and I are making our home ready for our child."

"We still need to work on the case," Sloane argued. "And, I hate to say it—" He yawned. "—mm, but we really need to go steal that damn cat for Stoker. We've gotta talk to Nathaniel."

"All in good time, my sweet husband."

"You're lucky I'm really sleepy. Mm, and I haven't forgotten how hot you were when you threatened to braid Stoker's intestines for me."

"We can be detectives and vigorously mate as much as you want later. Sleep well, my love."

Sloane grumbled, but he closed his eyes. He was exhausted, and his hips were aching. He had no idea what he'd done to aggravate them, but he decided a quick nap would help him recharge to jump back on the case.

And on Loch, of course.

The angle of the bullet that had killed Ziol was bothering him. If the shot hadn't come from the window, the only other possibility was the shot originating from the floor as Ziol stepped into the shower. That didn't make any sense, but....

Damn, he was tired.

Sloane dozed for a while, deep and dreamless, only waking up when there was a firm kick in his belly.

It was still such a marvel to feel the life growing inside of him, and he slid his hands down to rub his belly. He groggily thought about calling Loch in so he could feel it. It was so magical and sweet, and he really liked—wait, by all the gods, what the hell was wrong with his stomach?

Jolting up in bed, Sloane stared to find his abdomen was hugely distended. He looked pregnant now, the full nine months in the space of a nap, and he had to quickly unbutton his pants to relieve his new belly.

"What in the *fucking* fuck?"

"My love?" Loch had to have heard him as he came charging into their bedroom, tentacles whipping wildly. "What's wrong? Is it...?" His eyes widened. "Oh."

Sloane gestured helplessly to his giant belly.

"Huh. Well, that's new."

"No shit!"

CHAPTER 6.

"ARE YOU in pain?" Loch sat next to Sloane on the bed.

"Kinda? Sore. My hips and my back and my fuckin' everything! By the great fuckin' horns of Great Azaethoth!" Sloane's mind was spinning. "Look at me!"

"You look very beautiful—"

"I look like I swallowed a beach ball!"

"That beach ball is our child!"

"What's the matter?" Urilith was at the doorway, and she gasped when she saw Sloane. "Oh!"

"Yeah, oh shit." Sloane groaned miserably. He was hesitant to touch his belly, and his skin was shockingly tight when he finally did. "What's happening to me?"

"Here, let me take a look at you." Urilith came over, her thick yellow tentacles spiraling out to stroke Sloane's stomach. Her brow was furrowed in concentration.

"Is everything okay?" Galgareth was now at the door, and she looked equally shocked when she saw Sloane's belly. "Wow! Sloane! Uhh…."

"I know," he grumbled.

"I'm sorry," Galgareth said quickly. "We don't see mortal men, uh, in this condition usually. Little bit of a surprise."

"Guarantee it's a much bigger surprise to me!"

"My sweet husband, we talked about this," Loch soothed. "Growing with child is natural."

"How long was I asleep?" Sloane demanded.

"Mmm, a few hours."

"That's not fuckin' natural!"

"Because it's *magical*." Urilith withdrew her tentacles and smiled warmly. "Your little one is nearly ready. I know the sudden change must be upsetting, but even gods experience periods of instant growth like this."

Taking a deep breath, Sloane tried to calm down. "So we're both okay? Everyone is healthy?"

"Yes." Urilith patted his knee. "I think they may emerge as an egg first, and then they'll hatch."

"Huh?"

"Because you are mortal, the gestation may be safer if it takes place outside of your body."

Sloane felt faint.

"Is that what Abigail did?" Galgareth asked. "I don't remember her having an egg."

Abigail was the first Starkiller, a mortal who summoned a sword of starlight to kill the god Halandrach to claim Halandrach's mate, Zunnerath, as her own. It was always told as a romantic tale, but Sloane had to wonder if Abigail would have done it knowing there were egg babies in her future.

"She did with her son." Urilith nodded. "I helped her build the nest. He's your cousin, Beltara and Abeth's little brother. I believe they named him… hmm… Jake."

"How exactly am I going to have an egg?" Sloane asked weakly.

"It will leave your body."

"Yes, but *how*?"

"Magic." Urilith smiled again. "Trust in the ways of the gods, my dear child. The laying process may be uncomfortable, but it will not harm you."

"I might be sick."

"May I help you?" Loch tried to offer one of his slitted tentacles to him.

"Ugh, no, not in front of your mother!" Sloane breathed through the nausea and leaned into Loch's arms. "Okay, this is fine. Totally fine. Gonna have an egg baby. Yup."

"What can I do, my love?" Loch frowned.

"I don't know." Sloane grimaced. "I definitely did not expect to wake up like this. I feel gross and bloated and… what is that smell? Is something burning?" He stared suspiciously at Loch.

"Oh! No! That's me!" Galgareth sprang out of the room, presumably to the kitchen.

"We're still working on the Neun Monde feast." Urilith stood. "The nursery is ready, if you'd like to go see." She glanced between them with a knowing smile. "I'll let you have a few moments, hmm?"

"Thank you." Sloane tried to cheer up, but his gut was still sloshing. "I'm sure it's great. I'll go look in a sec."

Loch waved farewell as his mother left the room, and then he turned his full attention to Sloane. "I hate to see you in such distress, my sweet mate. I want to make you happy."

"I am happy. I'm also really freaked out." Sloane gestured to his belly. "I can't even wear pants!"

Loch grinned slyly.

Sloane tried not to laugh. He really did, but Loch looked so lecherous that he couldn't help it. "I already know what you're going to say, and don't you dare."

Loch petted Sloane's stomach gently. "I will not, but it is very true. Not wearing pants is hardly a problem."

"I just told you… ugh. You're impossible."

"And you're gorgeous." Loch bowed his head to kiss Sloane's belly. His tentacles were out and on the move, curling possessively around Sloane's hips and thighs.

"You're insane. I look horrible." Sloane's breath caught when Loch's tentacle squeezed his leg. The touch made his face hot and his cock twitch, and he gulped. "You can't be serious right now."

"About what?" Loch asked innocently.

"You're coming on to me." Sloane hated his new belly, and Loch's insistent affections stirred up a confusing surge of shame. He didn't understand how Loch could still be attracted to him like this.

Even weirder was how much it was turning him on.

"I usually do." Loch nuzzled Sloane's throat. "As often as I can. You look incredible like this, my love. I enjoy knowing that planting my hot seed deep inside your tight bodily chasm—"

"My *what*?"

"—is what has made you so full with child. The very sight of you is making me ache. I want to give you my knot and fill you until you are dripping."

"Maybe, uh, maybe not right now?" Sloane sputtered and pushed Loch's tentacles away. As worked up as Loch's dirty talk was getting him, this was still too weird right now.

Hell, he wouldn't even be able to look down and see his own dick.

Loch pouted a little, but he withdrew obediently. "Perhaps later?"

"Later. Yeah."

"Would you like to cuddle?"

"No. Thank you." Sloane carefully got out of bed, a little wobbly with the new weight he was now carrying. "I want to go see our nursery, get some snacks, and then we have a cat to swipe."

"Are you sure you're up to cat swiping adventures in your... condition?"

"I can make some kind of glamour charm to hide my stomach, and I'll wear... uh." Sloane tried to think of anything in his closet that would fit him. The glamour magic would give the illusion that he wasn't ridiculously pregnant, but he still didn't have anything to fit his real body.

"Ah! I have just the thing for you." In Loch's hands appeared a pair of jeans with a wide stretchy band at the top. "These are mortal maternity pants."

"You're a genius."

"Oh, I know."

Sloane had to admit the pants were pretty darn comfortable. The elastic stretchy bit over his stomach was a little odd, but more so because it made his new shape inescapable. He found an oversized T-shirt, enchanted a watch with a quick flash of glamour, and decided he looked non-pregnant and presentable once he put his coat on.

The waddling, however, was still going to be obvious.

The weight of the baby was throwing off his entire center of balance, and he couldn't walk without setting his legs far apart and *waddling* forward.

Great.

"Are you all right, my love?" Loch was watching him walk, and he looked concerned.

"I'm good. I got this." Sloane feigned confidence as he trudged into the kitchen, greeting Urilith and Galgareth. "Hey! It smells great in here!"

The kitchen was an explosion of flowers, meat, and produce, and the stove was packed with bubbling pots. Sloane could pick out the scent of lavender, and the rest was a lush mix of savory and sweet, and it made his mouth water.

"We should have everything ready by tomorrow," Urilith said. "I'm trying to create an Asran dessert that usually takes weeks to ferment, but I think I can, hmm, what do they say? Ah! Swing it! I should be able to swing it."

"It's gonna be fabulous, Mother," Galgareth reassured her.

"Thank you both so much," Sloane said. "For everything."

"I helped too," Loch whispered loudly.

"Thank you too."

"Would you like to go see the nursery now?" Loch asked. He was excited, and some of his tentacles kept peeking out.

"Yes." Sloane smiled and took Loch's hand. He knew Loch and his family had worked hard on this, and he couldn't wait to see. He'd deal with the waddling later. "Show me."

Loch practically dragged Sloane to the second bedroom, and he threw open the door with a flourish. "Behold!"

Sloane stepped inside and gasped.

It was gorgeous.

A crib was in the center of the room, framed by gossamer fabric hanging from the ceiling. The crib was made of wicker and overflowing with soft blankets that glittered with shining thread, and there were lights suspended in the air above.

Sloane couldn't resist and tapped one of the lights. Soft music began to play, the soothing twinkle kind from a music box, and the lights floated around and through the fabric in a lazy circle.

It was absolutely mesmerizing.

The rest of the room was equally awesome: a wicker changing table, a shapely dresser, and a tree—that suspiciously looked like the palm tree Loch had once stolen from their local grocery store—decked out in festive lights in the corner that faded out in long painted branches along the walls.

There was a rocking chair by the window, and a fuzzy stuffed eldritch monster was perched in the seat. It looked like it could have been Galgareth or Salgumel because it had big bat wings and a beard of tentacles. It didn't escape Sloane's attention that it was purple and green, as was the rest of the room.

"You did purple and green." Sloane turned to hug Loch, and he had to fight back a fresh burst of tears. His heart was simply too full. "Oh, Azaethoth."

"My proper name!" Loch beamed. "I did well, yes?"

"Very well. It's amazing. I love it." Sloane kissed him deeply, but he soon found it was hard to get close with his belly between them. It made the kiss a bit awkward, and he pulled away. "Mm, sorry."

"It's all right, my love." Loch rubbed Sloane's back. "Do you really like everything? Is there anything missing?"

"Just a baby." Sloane touched his stomach. "Or an egg, heh, I guess."

"Are you feeling well enough to investigate?"

"Yes, I'm okay. I just need a snack or five and I'll be good to go."

"Whatever you desire, my beautiful mate."

SLOANE'S DESIRE turned out to be a ham sandwich, leftover spaghetti, a breadstick, and two pickles. As they drove over to the deacon's house, he was already hungry again. He didn't think normal pregnancies involved eating this much food and chalked it up to growing a tiny half-god.

He called Chase on the way to give them a heads-up on what they were up to but specifically made no mention of his recent physical development.

It was already too weird without sharing it with anyone else.

He kept catching Loch staring at his stomach, prompting him to ask, "What?"

Loch jerked his eyes up. "Hmm?"

"Can you see through the glamour?"

"Mmm, in a sense. Looking at a glamour is sort of like looking at someone who's shaved off their eyebrows. Something is amiss, but you can't immediately deduce what."

"You're saying if I shaved off my eyebrows, you wouldn't notice?"

"I would definitely notice if yours were missing because they are luscious and beautiful, and they're one of my favorite things on your face."

Sloane chuckled. "Mm. So, like with Daphne? Could you see through the glamour I made her?"

"Not exactly. It always looks like something is missing, but I cannot tell what. Mortals use a lot of glamour. It's become quite common now. Lynnette uses it to cover her hideous pimples."

Sloane laughed. "Oh, come on. Don't be mean."

"I only assume they're hideous since she's using magic to hide them." Loch shrugged. "Ell uses it as well."

"To cover his hideous pimples?"

"Probably." Loch's gaze drifted back to Sloane's belly.

"You're doing it again."

"Hmm?"

"Why do you keep staring at me?"

"Because you're beautiful and stoke the fires of my primal lust?"

"Why my stomach?"

Loch wagged his brow.

"Wait. You... you like my belly?" Sloane realized. "Like, you *like* like it?"

"I find it very attractive, yes."

Sloane squeezed the steering wheel—the steering wheel he had to move his seat back for so his stomach wouldn't hit it—and tried to process Loch's newfound obsession. He usually didn't mind Loch's insatiable passions, but he was having trouble with this one.

"That bothers you?" Loch pressed gently.

"Not that you like it so much, but the fact that I have it." Sloane frowned, trying to gather his thoughts. "Maybe I would feel differently if it had happened gradually? Like, a little at a time? But literally waking up, I can't see my own dick, and wow, I have to suddenly pee again—"

"Did you not relieve yourself before we left?"

"I did! And I have to go again!" Sloane sighed. "It's way too much at once. You can tell me how much you love me and wanna invade my bodily chasms, but right now, I'm...."

"Are you having an 'ugly day'?"

"A what?"

"That is what Lynnette says when she is feeling unattractive. Or gassy. Or bloated. They are all somehow connected."

"Well, I'm having one of those times a million."

"I will simply wait until you feel better to make any attempt to initiate mating." Loch patted Sloane's knee.

"Really?" Sloane quirked his brows.

"Why do you sound so surprised?"

"That's very sweet of you. Thank you."

"I am always sweet."

"You also have the libido of a tweaked-out bunny rabbit on prom night."

"I don't know what prom is, but I will take that as a compliment."

Sloane reached over to take Loch's hand. "I love you."

"I love you too."

The deacon's home was a sprawling ranch-style house made out of white stone with a three-car garage. Sloane even spotted a pool around back as they drove up. He whistled low, parking the car in front of the garage and taking a moment to look over the fancy house.

"Are you flirting with the house?" Loch asked.

"Huh? No."

"You whistled at it."

"It's also a way mortals express awe or surprise." Sloane opened the car door, struggling to pull himself out. "Ugh, it's just, ah, kind of a big house for some humble priest."

"Maybe you should try being a priest instead of a private investigator," Loch mused. He got out of the car and stepped around to offer Sloane a hand. "It appears to be far more lucrative."

"Apparently." Sloane groaned as he finally escaped the car, holding his aching hips. "Damn."

"Are you all right, my sweet mate?"

"I'm okay." Sloane eyed the house. "Let's go steal ourselves a cat."

"Are we expecting a great battle?" Loch peered in through the windows of the garage. "Foes to defeat?"

"No. There shouldn't be anyone else here."

"There are other cars here."

"I guess the deacon owned a lot of cars?" Sloane shrugged and headed to the front door. "We'll be in and out—"

The door opened.

A tall man in a white suit was on the other side, staring at Sloane and Loch with a snotty scowl. "Excuse me? Can I help you?"

Shit.

"Hello!" Loch said cheerfully. "We're here to steal a cat. Have you seen one?"

"My name is Sloane Beaumont," Sloane said quickly. "I'm a private investigator."

"Hugh Barman." The man's frown deepened. "I saw you pull up on the cameras. You're here for Madame Sprinkles?"

"If that's the cat the deacon stole, then yes." Loch hummed. "I was actually really looking forward to stealing it back. Can you shut the door so we may break in, please?"

"Huh?"

"We'd like to take the cat and to maybe look around." Sloane smiled politely.

And use the damn bathroom.

"I'm not sure if I can do that." Hugh fidgeted.

"Do you live here?" Loch asked. "Hmm? Were you the deacon's illicit secret lover?"

"Wh-what?" Hugh stammered. His scowl had been replaced by a startled worry. "No! I was… I was just stopping by to, to check in on a few things! That's all!"

"I'd be more than happy to contact the police," Sloane suggested casually.

"You, you go ahead and do that!"

Hugh was bluffing.

"Fine." Sloane shrugged. It was hard as hell to play cool when he was about to pee his pants. "I'm starting to get the feeling one of us is not supposed to be here, and it's you."

"Two of us," Loch mumbled. "There's actually two of us, my love. Three if we're being technical—"

"Okay, okay, okay!" Hugh threw up his hands. "I have a key. I let myself in. I work for the deacon. I'm the one that found him…. We were close."

"Ah! Lovers?" Loch asked.

"No!" Hugh scoffed. "Look, the cops said it's still a crime scene, and I know I'm not supposed to be here. I… well…."

"How about we talk about this inside?" Sloane urged. "After I use your bathroom, huh?"

Hugh reluctantly moved out of the way and waved them in. "Bathroom is at the end of the hall. First door on the right."

"Thank you." Sloane stepped inside, taking a quick look around.

The first thought he had was the ding of a cash register because this place was loaded with rich goodies. There were multiple fine paintings, gilded objects, big cabinets full of antique books and religious artifacts. Even the carpet beneath his feet felt extra plush.

He could *hear* Loch squealing under his breath and saw how wide his eyes got.

"No!" Sloane hissed. "Don't touch anything!" He quickly waddled to the bathroom to relieve himself, and he groaned. Going to the bathroom had never been so oddly satisfying.

After washing his hands, he attempted to fix his posture and find where Loch and Hugh were. He followed their voices to a lavishly decorated den.

"And you're sure you and the deacon were not sexually involved?" Loch was asking.

"Yes! Very sure!" Hugh shook his head. "What is wrong with you?"

Sloane sat on a cushy sofa next to Loch, offering Hugh a friendly smile. "So, uh, care to tell me why you came by here?"

Hugh hadn't taken a seat, but remained on his feet with his arms crossed and back to his sour expression. "I had left some personal items here, and I wanted to get them back. The deacon was letting me stay with him for a while until I got back on my feet. I lost my job recently."

"But you said you worked for him?"

"I worked for the church. They made the decision to terminate my position, and the deacon was nice enough to let me stay here while I looked for another job."

"Were you home the day of the murder?" Sloane leaned back, casually casting a truth spell.

"I already went over all of this with the cops."

"Humor me. Unless you want me to call them up and ask them."

Hugh scowled. "Yes, I was here. I'd gone out to check the mail, and when I came back, the deacon was lying facedown on the kitchen floor. I heard someone run out the front door, but I never saw who it was."

"Ah! There is no mail on Sundays!" Loch suddenly declared. "You're lying! You did it!"

"It was Tuesday!" Hugh blinked.

"Oh." Loch pouted. "Carry on, then."

"That's it." Hugh uncrossed and crossed his arms again. "The police said it's pretty obvious that heathen from the protests did it. He was on the cameras leaving the house, and I was there when he threatened to kill the deacon."

"You can't think of anyone else who might have wanted to harm the deacon?" Sloane asked. "Any other death threats?"

"No." Hugh paused. "Well, other than Mr. Stoker. He and the deacon have not exactly had the best relationship. He threatened to kill him over the cat."

"Speaking of, where is it?"

"What?"

"The cat."

"Oh. It's around here somewhere." Hugh rolled his eyes. "The police told me they have some expert coming in to try and remove the ward that's been placed on it so they can get it out of here."

"I'm such an expert." Loch stood with an eager smile. "Give me a moment to locate this cat."

"And only the cat," Sloane warned, all too aware of his husband's penchant for taking things that didn't belong to him.

Loch kept smiling and strolled out of the room, lightly humming to himself.

Sloane was a little worried, but he wanted to keep questioning Hugh. So far Hugh hadn't said anything to set off the truth spell, but it was possible to work around it by telling half-truths or giving vague answers.

Hugh wasn't being overtly suspicious, but Sloane remained on guard.

"Had you worked for the deacon long?" he asked.

"Eight years," Hugh replied. "I was baptized in the Lord of Light's radiance as a child, and I was drawn to service in the church. It was my calling. The deacon later took me on to work for him directly, and, well, the church made the financial decision to let me go."

"Financial, hmm?" Sloane found it hard to believe that the same church that paid for this fancy house had to fire someone to save money.

"You know, losing our beloved deacon has devastated our congregation," Hugh went on, seeming to ignore Sloane's prompting. "He truly was a vessel of the Lord of Light's love. My only comfort is that he died with his crest in his hand."

The Lucian crest was an angular starburst said to represent the Lord of Light's luminance. They were worn as pendants or bracelets, often held during prayer and meditation.

Sloane understood how passing away with one in hand would be comforting, but it was clear Hugh was using that little anecdote to avoid answering his question.

Hugh probably suspected Sloane was using a truth spell.

"That's nice?" Sloane forced a smile. "So, what are you going to do now that the deacon has passed, hmm?"

"You don't really care about me." Hugh snorted. "You're only here to pick up a cat for that criminal. Which makes you as crooked as him."

Sloane ignored the insult, and he was even more sure Hugh was deflecting now.

But to hide what?

Before he could ask another question, there was a loud crash, glass shattering, and the yowl of a cat.

"What the…?" Sloane grunted, struggling to get up from the couch. He probably looked ridiculous with the way he was fighting to stand, but he couldn't help it.

"What was that?" Hugh demanded.

"Stay here." Sloane gasped as he finally got to his feet, wobbling forward. "I'll go check it out—"

"Hello!" Loch came strolling back in, and he smiled brightly. "Wow! That was exciting!"

"Loch!" Sloane frowned. "Are you okay? What happened?"

"Good news!" Loch announced. "I removed the ward, the cat is free, and it is definitely not one of those vile fiends from Xenon."

"Okay. Where is it?"

"Ah, you see, that's the bad news."

CHAPTER 7.

"EXPLAIN THIS to me one more time." Sloane massaged his throbbing temples. "How did the window get broken?"

"Ah, when I threw the bed," Loch replied.

"And why did you throw the bed?"

"It was in my way of searching for the cat."

"But you did find the cat, right?"

"Yes! It was hiding underneath the bed. But after I removed the ward, it jumped out the broken window."

Sloane sighed.

"It was very distressed for some reason."

"I know how it feels."

With no cat left to steal inside the house, Sloane and Loch bid farewell to Hugh. Sloane assumed Hugh was going to keep squatting at the deacon's place, but that really wasn't any of his business.

Figuring out if Hugh had something to do with the murder, on the other hand, was definitely his business. As long as Hugh was staying there, at least they'd know where to find him.

Their immediate priority, however, was to find that damn cat.

A clap of Sloane's hands repaired the broken window as they walked by, and he waddled around the yard in search of the lost pet. "What does the cat look like?"

"Fuzzy. White. Has an awful attitude."

"And you're sure it's not an Asra?" Sloane smirked.

"Very sure."

"Okay." Sloane happened to glance over at Loch and saw he had a bunch of matchbooks in his hands. "What are those?"

"Ah! Evidence!" Loch beamed as he handed them over for Sloane's inspection. "Behold! They are all from the Velvet Plank. I thought it was odd the deacon had so many."

"Hey, nice detective work!" Sloane grinned, turning the matchbooks over and examining the Velvet Plank logo. They seemed normal enough. "Where did you find them?"

"In the master bedroom inside a safe."

"A safe?" Sloane raised his brow. "Kind of a weird place to keep matches."

"Are they valuable?" Loch hummed thoughtfully. "I thought perhaps he was planning to drive the club into bankruptcy by forcing them to reorder more."

"Doubtful."

"Why?"

"Matches don't cost that much." Sloane put them in his pocket. "We gotta figure out why he'd keep them locked up and why he was hanging out at the club."

"He went there to protest, yes?"

"Yeah, but he would have had to go inside to get the matches. I can't imagine Stoker passing them out to the people trying to shut him down."

"You already said you didn't like my bankruptcy theory, so I have nothing to add at this time."

"I wonder why Stoker didn't say anything about it. Why wouldn't he want to tell everyone that the deacon was frequenting his club? Feels like that would be great revenge to rat him out for being a hypocrite."

"The deacon did have his cat," Loch reminded him. "Perhaps he was using that as leverage to ensure Stoker's silence?"

"Maybe. I feel like we're missing something, but I don't know what."

"I also found this." Loch offered out a large knife with a handle made of bone.

"What is that?"

"It was hidden inside a warded chamber beneath the deacon's bed within a vault sealed with twenty-six magical locks and seventeen curses for anyone who dared to disturb it."

"Wow." Sloane blinked. "So, uh, what is it?"

"Oh, it's nothing." Loch balanced the tip of the blade on the tip of his finger. "Mere bone and metal. It has absolutely no magical properties whatsoever."

"Kind of a lot of security for some 'mere' bone and metal, don't you think?"

"Pffft. Not a lot for me."

"What I mean is that it could be some sort of Lucian artifact. There has to be some reason the deacon locked it up like that."

"Well, I can tell you someone has been trying very clumsily to steal it."
Loch switched the blade to his other hand, and the knife spun in his palm.

"Oh?"

"Sixteen of the magical locks had already been disengaged."

Sloane paused to lean against the side of the house. He was out of breath, and he thought he might have to pee again. "Damn."

"Are you all right, my love?"

"I'm okay." Sloane looked around the yard with a miserable sigh. "Didn't expect to be running around chasing a cat."

"Go rest in the car, dear husband," Loch urged. "I am responsible for losing it. I will be the one to retrieve it."

"That's sweet of you. Thank you." Sloane would have normally protested being excluded from any investigative activities, but he really wanted to sit. "Put the knife back too."

"But why?" Loch frowned.

"Because it was obviously very important to the deacon."

"If I put it back, someone is going to steal it."

"You just stole it!"

"I'm the god of thieves. I'm expected to steal, and I do it very well."

Sloane glared. His feet were hurting now, and his shoes felt too tight. "Put the damn knife back."

"Fiiine, my most precious mate. I shall return the knife for some *amateur* to steal."

"Thank you. Good luck with the cat."

"I don't need luck. I'm great."

Back in the car, Sloane leaned his seat as far back as it would go and cranked the engine so he could blast the air-conditioning. Even though he could not actually see his swollen belly through the glamour, he stared down at it anyway.

"Mm, this is your fault, you know," he addressed his unborn child. "My back hurts, my hips hurt, and it's weirdly hard to breathe. I've thrown up more in the last few days than I have in months. Also, I'm pretty sure my damn feet are swollen now too."

Smiling, he rubbed his stomach. The glamour wasn't strong enough to stop him from touching, even though his big belly appeared invisible.

"You're lucky you're gonna be really cute," he mumbled affectionately.

It was all going to be worth it, he knew, to finally hold their child in his arms. Until then, it was pretty damn miserable, and he felt like utter crap. He closed his eyes, sighing as he tried to relax for a few moments.

The deacon wouldn't be the first conservative person to lie about where he liked to spend his free time, but locking up matchbooks was very strange. Sloane suspected this was more than a man of the cloth sneaking around for a lap dance.

Sloane reached into his pocket and pulled out one of the matchbooks. It was blue, shiny, and the logo was metallic. Flipping it open revealed no missing matches, and yet....

Sloane raised his hand for a perception spell, and he was startled to see there was writing hidden inside the cover. It was faint, barely legible even with his spell, but it was definitely a series of numbers.

Money? A phone number?

He checked the others and found they all had numbers hidden inside as well.

What could be important enough to lock up in a safe?

A loud meow drew his attention away from the matches, and he looked up to see Loch marching toward the car with a fluffy cat in his arms.

The cat did not look happy, but at least the knife appeared to be gone.

As soon as Loch sat in the car, the cat leapt into the back seat and hissed.

"Mission accomplished," Loch said proudly.

"And you put the knife back?"

Loch sighed with all the exasperation of a toddler. "Yes, I put it back. I decided that stealing an item so worthless was utterly beneath me."

"Good, thank you. Where was the cat?"

"She was in a tree, and she did not want to leave." Loch turned his head to eye the cat. "She was a worthy opponent."

"Well, I'm glad you caught her." Sloane held up one of the matchbooks. "And I found something. There are numbers hidden in the matchbooks."

"Ah! I did very well!" Loch grinned. "I'm the best at collecting evidence."

"You did great." Sloane put the car in reverse and backed out of the driveway.

"Hugh is watching us from the window." Loch waved.

"Don't wave."

"Why?"

"Because I don't trust him. I think he's hiding something."

"Oh?" Loch cocked his head.

"I can't imagine him killing the deacon, since it eliminates where he was staying. Well, unless he was staying there to do exactly that, but... I don't know. Maybe he's the one trying to steal the knife? You said someone was trying to get it, right?"

"I thought we established that it was worthless?"

"If it's a Lucian artifact, maybe it's valuable in another way."

"But it's not."

"It might be something special for the Lord of Light."

"But he's not real."

"He's real enough to Lucians. Some worshippers might pay a lot of money for a relic they believe is sacred. Reason enough for Hugh to keep squatting here, maybe."

"Perhaps a motive for murder?" Loch perked up.

"Sure, but nothing he said tripped up the truth spell, and he really seems to have cared about the deacon. Ugh." Sloane reached down to adjust the elastic waistband of his pants as he drove. "I'm too pregnant to think."

"You're just the right amount of pregnant," Loch promised, patting Sloane's knee. "We can ask my uncle and Chase about the worthless knife, and we can ask Stoker about the matchbooks in exchange for the safe return of his cat."

"We're already exchanging the cat to talk to Nathaniel." Sloane frowned. "I don't think Stoker is gonna be receptive to more demands."

"I'm simply going to make a very teeny, tiny small adjustment to the terms of our deal." Loch batted his eyes.

"I don't think that's a very good idea, and we should...." Sloane noticed there was now a large golden tome in Loch's lap. "Wait, what's that?"

"A book. Often full of pages whereupon words are written to express thoughts, feelings, sexual positions—"

"You stole that from the deacon's house! I know I saw that in one of the cases!"

"Ah! I reclaimed it. He is a Lucian. He can keep his stupid knife, but he has no right to Sagittarian books."

"You robbed a dead man."

"Yes, I realize it's not very sporting—"

"Twice."

"—but I remain certain it was the right thing to do."

"It's Sagittarian? Really?" Sloane stopped at a red light and looked over to study the book.

It was covered in gold and godstongue scripture, and Sloane could sense strong magic emanating from it.

"This one is by a poet who took a journey to the worlds between worlds," Loch said as he turned the pages. "It details her adventures with the old gods and the various rituals she witnessed that have probably not been seen by mortal eyes for hundreds of years."

"Fine." Sloane sighed. "I guess it's a good thing that you recovered a very special book for future generations of Sages. I mean, it was just the one book, right?"

Loch grinned.

"Oh no."

"Don't look in the trunk."

By the time they arrived at the Velvet Plank, Sloane had managed to convince Loch to turn over most of the books to the city museum.

"They could work with those new covens and translate some of the rituals," Sloane was saying. "Sages have lost so much, you know? It would be very nice to give back if we can."

"I still like my hoarding option better, but for you, sweet Starkiller, I will part with a few of them."

"Thank you. Can you grab the cat?"

"Absolutely." Loch reached back behind his seat with his tentacles to carefully dislodge the protesting feline from where she was hiding. "Come along, furry creature. It is time to use your fluffy little face for extortion, oh yes, it is!"

Sloane opened his door and grunted with effort as he pulled himself out of his seat. He really hoped this would be the last of his physical exertion for the day. He, Loch, and the fussing cat headed inside the club, and Sloane struggled to walk as normally as possible.

Judging by Stoker's quizzical expression when they came in, it wasn't working.

Loch held out the cat, declaring loudly, "We have retrieved your purloined feline, as requested."

"Ah yes." Stoker's confusion gave way to joy. "My darling Sprinkles!" He came around the bar with open arms. "Thank you so much. I never—"

"Not so fast!" Loch held Madame Sprinkles closely against his chest.

Madame Sprinkles meowed.

"Loch," Sloane cautioned. He had no idea what his darling husband had planned, but there were a lot more people here than the last time they visited.

At least a dozen patrons were seated around the stage, while a scantily clad woman danced on the pole and several others crowded the bar. Two waitresses were working the floor, serving drinks and escorting men through the curtains beside the stage.

Way too many potential witnesses for godly shenanigans.

"What?" Stoker demanded impatiently.

"We have a revision to our arrangement," Loch replied. "In addition to allowing us to chat with Nathan, we—"

"Nathaniel," Sloane mumbled.

"—would like you to explain what the numbers in these matchbooks mean. We found them at the deacon's home, and they're most curious."

Stoker scowled. "No."

"Mmm, are you sure?" Loch smiled wickedly. "Is that your final answer?"

"Give me my cat, please." Stoker sighed. "I'm really not in the mood to play right now."

"Ah, I thought you might say that."

There was the pop of a portal opening, and Madame Sprinkles vanished. It happened so quickly that Sloane didn't even see the actual portal, but the cat was definitely gone.

"Really?" Stoker looked annoyed. "This is what we're doing now?"

"Oh absolutely," Loch said gleefully.

"Where did you send my cat?"

"Mmm." Loch scratched his chin. "Seems to have slipped my mind. If only someone could tell us what all those numbers mean, it might run my memory."

Time suddenly froze.

The woman dancing on stage was caught twirling in the air around the pole, and one of the men tipping her was stuck bent over as he ogled her behind. The music had stopped, and a man about to take a shot at the bar was totally motionless.

Everything was still except for Stoker, Sloane, and Loch.

Sloane tried not to react—he'd seen Loch do this before, but never on this scale. He had no idea what Stoker was, but he knew it took a butt load of magic to stop time like this.

"I've had a very long day," Stoker drawled. "I'm not going to bore you with all the gritty details, but let me assure you my patience is razor thin."

"Then tell me what the numbers mean," Loch countered. He didn't seem at all bothered by Stoker's abilities. "There are so many little worlds out there. Who knows where your precious kitty went? Mm, hope it wasn't anywhere dangerous."

"It's not going to help your investigation. Those numbers are meaningless now that the deacon is dead."

"If they're so meaningless, why can't you tell us what they are?" Sloane smiled sweetly.

"I suppose it doesn't really matter." Stoker looked contemplative for a moment. "They're passwords to access wire money transfers from a banking app. You type in the code, you get the money."

"Money for what?"

"Mmm, I can't say."

"Can't say or won't say?" Sloane pressed.

"I am sure you and your little police friends can figure the rest out."

"What friends?"

"Oh, don't sound so surprised." Stoker smiled. "I know you and Azaethoth here were invited to the Sagittarian priest's crime scene. Do they know, I wonder, what you two really are?"

"Nope," Sloane lied, pushing through the pressure of a truth spell he sensed clinging to him. After all, Merrick didn't know Sloane that well, so it wasn't technically a complete lie.

It seemed to work because Stoker shrugged and said, "Follow the money. The end of the world is a mere matter of when, as they say."

"Counting the minutes as it chokes on the avarice of men," Sloane finished the quote. "You know Callisto, the Sagittarian poet."

"I know a lot of things." Stoker held up his hand. "Except what you've done with my cat. Bring her back from whatever world you sent her to, if you'd be so kind."

Loch waited until Sloane nodded, and then he said, "Oh pfft, I didn't actually send your cat anywhere. She's been right here." He held out his hands and there was Madame Sprinkles, wide-eyed and very confused.

She was also neon green.

"What did you do to my cat?" Stoker snatched her away from Loch and hugged her close. "Oh, you poor thing! What did that idiot do to you?"

"Green is a gender-neutral color," Loch declared. "She is fine."

"There, you have your cat back." Sloane's feet were hurting again. "Is there somewhere we can go sit down to talk to Nathaniel?"

"Of course." Stoker waved for them to follow him, and he walked through the curtains at the side of the stage. "After this, our business is concluded. I do enjoy seeing you, Mr. Beaumont, but you've made my life a bit more exciting than I prefer."

"What a shame," Sloane drawled, waddling behind him. It was hard to keep up with Stoker's brisk pace, and Sloane found he could only walk so fast now.

"Easy, my love," Loch soothed, taking his arm to help him. "I've got you."

"Thank you." Sloane gratefully leaned into Loch for support, and they followed Stoker through a dark hallway into a large room.

It might have been an office because there was a desk and some chairs, but there were also big wooden sculptures of tentacled old gods and fantastic creatures crowded around, as if it were meant for storage. The sculptures matched the woodwork of the club, and these must have once been on display.

Like the rest of the decor here, they were worn and dusty, and a few were broken.

Sloane recognized one as Azaethoth's true godly form, grand wings and all, and he smirked when he saw Loch admiring it.

The desk was cluttered with old papers and a phone that didn't appear to be plugged into anything. Stoker sat at the desk with Madame Sprinkles in his lap, and he tapped the phone. "Once you pick it up, Nathaniel will be on the other line."

"That's it?" Sloane took one of the chairs, scooting it up to the side of the desk closest to the phone. "I pick it up?"

"That's it."

"I'm guessing you're staying here to listen?" Sloane frowned.

"Nathaniel is my friend. I have his best interests at heart, so yes, I'm staying here. I don't trust either one of you after that nasty little stunt you pulled with my cat."

"I'm absolutely heartbroken," Loch drawled. "And here I was thinking we could be besties."

"You're an absolute idiot." Stoker snorted.

"You're an absolute dumpster," Loch shot back.

"That doesn't even make any sense. How did anyone ever worship you?"

"Usually on their knees. Which is where I'm about to put you."

"That's enough." Sloane's head was starting to hurt, and he could feel his pulse in his feet.

"My apologies, Mr. Beaumont." Stoker smiled sweetly. "I didn't mean to upset him. I didn't realize gods were so sensitive."

"Do you know what's really sensitive?" Loch growled. "The underside of your skin."

"Shhh." Stoker wagged his finger. "The adults are talking right now."

"Insult me again and you will feel the full force of my godly wrath—"

"Ha!" Stoker laughed. "You can take that pathetic wrath of yours and shove it right—"

"That's it!" Loch snarled as he lunged forward. "I'm eating you—"

"Oh, by all the gods, will both of you shut up?" Sloane snapped. He was done listening to this childish bickering, and his feet hurt like hell, and he had the ridiculous urge to pee again. "We have two fuckin' murders to solve, and this is not helping! Daphne wants to see her brother again, preferably not behind bars, so I need to talk to him and figure out what the fuck is going on! You two can have your stupid fuckin' pissing contest later!"

Stoker and Loch both cowered like little puppies who had just gotten their noses bopped with a newspaper.

"There! Thank you! For fuck's sake!" Sloane snatched up the phone, taking a deep breath as the line rang. He snapped his fingers for a truth spell and rubbed his pounding head.

"Fierce little thing, isn't he?" Stoker murmured, glancing at Loch.

"Oh, you have no idea." Loch grinned wickedly.

"Hello?" a timid voice spoke up.

"Nathaniel Ware?" Sloane asked.

"Yes." Nathaniel's voice wasn't coming directly from the receiver. It sounded like he was in the room with them.

"My name is Sloane Beaumont. I'm a private investigator. I was hired by your sister to find you." He set the phone down since he didn't actually need it. "I know what you are, and I don't believe you killed the deacon. I want to help you prove your innocence."

"Yeah, sure." Nathaniel scoffed. "And how are you gonna do that?"

"By finding the real killers. But I can't do that without your help. I need to know what really happened at the deacon's house. Please. Tell me the truth."

"Stoker?" Nathaniel sounded uncertain.

"Go ahead," Stoker replied. "Tell them what you told me."

"Okay," Nathaniel said hesitantly. "Yeah, okay, I went over to the deacon's place. I ported in to get through the wards. He was already dead when I got there. I rolled him over, I tried to, you know, check for life or whatever. I don't know. I heard someone coming from the back, so... so I ran, okay? I was too freaked to port, so I busted through the front door and ran as fast as I could. That's it."

"Why did you go there?"

"I wanted him to back off!" Nathaniel snapped. "He and those other Lucian bastards were the ones starting all the shit at the protests! He was the one stirring everything up! I knew he was probably warded like the house, so I brought a gun—"

"A gun?" Sloane exchanged a worried look with Loch.

"Yeah, but look, I just wanted to scare him! I was not going to kill him, I fuckin' swear!" Nathaniel exclaimed passionately. "All I wanted was for him to stop!"

"A likely story," Loch sneered.

"What happened after you found the deacon dead?" Sloane asked gently. "Where did you go?"

"I went over to Ziol's," Nathaniel replied. "I didn't know where else to go. He was, he was always a really good friend to me. He tried to calm me down, and—"

"Wait, Ziol was alive?" Sloane blurted out. "But he died before the deacon was killed."

"No," Nathaniel whispered sadly. "No, he didn't. It's my fault... I...."

"Go on," Stoker urged. "You can tell them."

"Ziol took the gun from me." Nathaniel sniffed loudly. "He told me to stay put and he would take care of everything. He went to go take a shower 'cause he'd been working out in his garden, and he…." He sniffed again. "That's when I heard the shot. I found him… I found him dead like the deacon, and I tried to turn it back."

"Turn what back?" Sloane asked.

"Time." Nathaniel sounded even more miserable. "I kept trying to turn back time to stop Ziol from being killed, but it didn't work. I couldn't go back far enough, and I kept seeing him fall down dead again and again! I couldn't even see who shot him."

"Your Faedra abilities," Sloane realized out loud. "You can manipulate time. That's why his time of death was before the deacon's. You kept resetting it, trying to save him."

"And fuckin' failed." Nathaniel snorted back an audible sob. "I'm not strong enough. I couldn't do it. And like with the fuckin' deacon, I didn't see anyone. I didn't… I didn't see shit! I couldn't do fuckin' anything to help him!"

"It's all right," Stoker soothed. "Nathaniel, we talked about this. You're not responsible."

"Still feel like shit anyway," Nathaniel said quietly.

Sloane's mind was reeling. Nathaniel's crazy story hadn't triggered the truth spell, and now he was not sure what to think. "What happened to the gun?"

"I didn't see it," Nathaniel replied. "Whoever shot him must have taken it with them."

"Any ideas who would have wanted to hurt Ziol?"

"Ha." Nathaniel scoffed. "The deacon. Fuckin' prick. That snake that works for him, Hugh. He's just as awful. He tried to get Ziol arrested at the last protest for standing up to the deacon's shit."

"Hugh Barman is the one selling this sob story about finding the deacon dead and clinging to his crest." Sloane grimaced. "They're going to make a martyr out of him."

Nathaniel got quiet for a long moment.

"That would certainly explain why the protests have become so impassioned," Stoker noted.

"What?" Sloane blinked.

"You haven't seen the news?"

"No, we've been busy chasing your damn cat."

"There were multiple arrests made today," Stoker explained, petting said cat, who other than being frightfully green seemed very happy to be home. "A fight broke out. Someone had a magical taser. All very exciting."

"Shit."

"Hey," Nathaniel spoke up. "You want me to tell you guys who killed the deacon?"

"Wait," Sloane protested. "I thought you didn't see anything?"

"I didn't, but I know who did it," Nathaniel said firmly. The truth spell again held. "You want me to tell you and come outta hiding, I will. I swear. But only on one condition."

"Okay, what?"

"You find who killed Ziol first."

CHAPTER 8.

FOR THE first and possibly last time, Sloane let Loch drive them home.

Sloane adjusted the passenger seat all the way back and tried to stretch out his aching body. There was absolutely no way to get comfortable, and he couldn't possibly get behind the wheel like this. He swore his belly was actually getting bigger.

Desperate, he had handed Loch the keys.

"We'll be home soon, my love," Loch promised, swerving through traffic. "I swear I will get us there safely."

"And the car?"

"Yes. The car as well."

Sloane tilted the air-conditioning vents so they were blowing directly on him. Not being the one driving was giving him motion sickness, and Loch's erratic driving was not helping.

"Are you all right, my sweet Starkiller?" Loch asked.

"Feeling a little queasy." Sloane closed his eyes. "Uh, so we know now that the deacon was killed first and then Ziol. So the deacon being murdered in retaliation for Ziol's death is out."

"Mm, it is true I didn't get much of a sense of 'revenge' when we were at the deacon's house. Perhaps Ziol was targeted in response to the deacon's death." Loch paused. "Then again, I did not sense any kind of retribution at Ziol's either. Without having witnessed the murders, I cannot be sure."

"If you had witnessed them, we would know who killed them."

"Ah, true."

"This still means we're looking for two killers who can both move through wards without breaking them."

"Which leaves gods, the Asra, the Absola, the Faedra, and any mortal that can teleport as potential suspects."

"That's not helpful."

"Why not?"

"It doesn't narrow down our suspect list at all."

"Well, it's either someone who really doesn't like Lucians or someone who really doesn't like Sages."

"Oh sure. That's very helpful."

"See?" Loch had clearly missed the sarcasm. "I'm an excellent detective."

"Mm, says the guy who put a bunch of stolen books in the trunk."

"I'm also an excellent thief."

Sloane grimaced when Loch slammed on the brakes too hard, and he grumbled, "Not so excellent on the driving."

"My apologies."

"I need to call Daphne." Sloane inhaled slowly, hoping to soothe his churning stomach.

"Why?"

"Well, I think it would be nice to at least let her know that her brother is alive." Sloane pulled out his phone and scrolled through the screen for her number.

"Fair assumption."

"Hey, Mr. Beaumont!" Daphne sounded tired but hopeful when she picked up.

"Hey! How are you doing?"

"Trying not to watch the news. They're saying, well, they're saying a lot of stuff about my brother. I'm, uh, trying to stay positive. Uh, how are you?"

Nauseated, sore, miserable, experiencing all the joys of being pregnant.

"Oh fine. I wanted to call and touch base with you about what I've found out so far," Sloane continued, keeping his complaints to himself. "I've spoken to your brother—"

"He's okay? He's alive?"

"Yes," Sloane promised. "He's still in hiding. I'm sure you understand, but he's okay."

"Where is he?"

"I can't tell you that right now because I'm not even sure, to be honest. I was able to speak to him on the phone for a little while."

Probably best not to mention it was a magical phone in Sullivan Stoker's office.

"Oh." Daphne sighed.

"He says he knows who killed the deacon, and if I can find who killed Gerard Ziol, he'll tell me."

"If he knows, why doesn't he tell the cops and clear his name?" Daphne was angry now. "That bastard Hugh whatever his fuckin' name is? He's on the news saying what a monster Nathaniel was and how this is what happens when people stray from the Lord of Light's path! It's bullshit!"

Sloane had to pull the phone away from his ear to spare his eardrums as Daphne's voice rose to a shout. "I'm really sorry, Miss Ware. I don't know. He might be worried that once the deacon's killer is caught they might not look as hard for Ziol's."

"You mean because Ziol is a Sage." Daphne's rage gave way to sadness. "They don't care as much about getting justice for a dead Sage. Not as exciting as a dead deacon to put on the ten o'clock news."

"Just a guess," Sloane said quietly.

"Well, I'm so very glad he's so concerned about Ziol. No big deal that all my coworkers won't even speak to me because they all think my brother is a killer. My manager even told me to leave early today, as if I haven't already lost enough hours! I just—!" She cut herself off and sighed again.

"Are you okay, Miss Ware?" Sloane grimaced as the car suddenly lurched hard to the right, and he pressed his hand over his mouth. He was trying to be sympathetic, but it was hard with bile creeping up into his mouth.

He really needed to talk to Urilith about that pregnancy blessing when they got back.

"Yes. Thank you so much for calling me," she replied weakly. "I appreciate it. Uh, what are you gonna do now?"

"I'm going to work Ziol's murder case," Sloane said as clearly as he could while trying not to puke. He was grateful when the car finally stopped at a light, and he took a deep breath. "If that's your brother's price to come out of hiding, then that's what I gotta do."

"Thank you, Mr. Beaumont. Call me when you know more, okay?"

"I will. And if I talk to your brother again, I'll make sure to—" The line disconnected before Sloane could finish. "Well, damn."

"Didn't go well, I take it?" Loch asked.

A horn honked behind them.

"No. She's upset. Saw her brother blasted all over the news about the deacon's murder, and now she's resentful because of how his actions are affecting her." Sloane rubbed his forehead. "It's complicated."

"Family often is."

"Yeah."

The horn honked again, followed by a few more and an angry shout.

"What's going on?" Sloane frowned.

"I thought my driving was exacerbating your nausea, so I decided to stop until you felt better."

"Huh?" Sloane realized they were not actually stopped at a light but right in the middle of the road. "That's very thoughtful of you, but uh, let's go, okay? I wanna go home."

Loch didn't seem to care about all the noise, and he shrugged. "As you wish, my love."

Sloane managed to survive the rest of the ride home with no gastrointestinal disasters, and he didn't complain one bit when Loch carried him inside their apartment.

His damn feet hurt too much.

The apartment smelled wonderful and hazy from whatever Galgareth and Urilith were brewing, and Sloane's uneasy stomach instantly relaxed. "I don't know what that is, but I love you both."

"Oh, you poor thing!" Urilith cooed. "Are you all right? Was being an investigator today stressful? Did my blessing not help?

"I'm afraid my driving was the culprit," Loch lamented, gently placing Sloane on the couch and petting his hair.

"You drove?" Galgareth scoffed. "Wow, Sloane really must be feeling like crap."

"I'm feeling better now." Sloane smiled wearily. Being on his back hurt his spine and his hips, so he tried rolling on his side to relieve some of the pressure.

"It's my own very special blend of ginger and lightning root incense." Urilith beamed. "I'm glad you like it. Do you need anything, sweet child?"

"I'm fine, Mother," Loch replied. "Thank you."

"Not you! Your mate!"

"I'm okay." Sloane grinned. "Your blessing has helped a lot, but I guess it wasn't enough to counter Loch's driving. Just trying to get comfortable now." He took off the glamoured watch and patted his now visible belly. "Not exactly easy with all of this."

"You should visit the Hot Springs of Donatis," Urilith said. "I would go there often when I was with child. A nice soak in those magical waters is sure to offer you relief."

"That does sound nice." Sloane hesitated. "We have a lot of work to do, though. I need to review the case files for the Sagittarian priest's death, probably need to call Chase and ask him about this weird knife Loch sort of stole—"

"I did steal it," Loch argued. "You made me put it back."

"Ah-ah!" Urilith waved a spoon at Sloane. "You need to rest. You might be laying your egg any day now!"

"Besides," Galgareth chirped, "we can help with your detective work!"

"Oh yeah?" Sloane grinned.

"Of course! We were already inviting Uncle Gordoth and Chase over for your Neun Monde tomorrow. We can ask them to stop by early and help us review the case for you! Loch can catch us up on what you've been up to today while you rest!"

"Oh, just you two wait!" Loch exclaimed. "Our adventures today were most grand!"

"I don't know… I mean…." Sloane really couldn't think of one good reason why he shouldn't turn the case over to three gods and one of the best mortal detectives he knew. It was only going to be temporary, after all.

And his feet really did hurt so much.

"Come along, my sweet mate," Loch urged. "Allow us to take care of you."

"It is Sagittarian tradition to revere a pregnant person as a god, you know," Urilith said with a coy smile. "Neun Monde was not always a mere feast. It was once a full nine months of glorious celebration and worship. Giving birth is a sacred act and demands proper tribute."

"Soaking in a magical hot tub definitely sounds like proper tribute," Galgareth agreed.

"Okay, yes, it totally does." Sloane held up his hands in defeat. "I give. I'm totally ready for celebration and worship and magical hot tubs." He pointed firmly. "At least for tonight."

"And tomorrow as well," Loch said smugly. "We still have your feast to look forward to."

"Okay, but after all that, back to work! Murders to solve!"

"Absolutely." Loch turned to Urilith. "We're ready, Mother."

"Take care, sweet ones." Urilith waved a tentacle, and the apartment vanished in a colorful blur.

Sloane instinctively closed his eyes against the strange visual sensation, and he found himself now standing with Loch next to a steaming pool.

They were in a large grotto, and a brilliant night sky glittered above them. An eerily silent waterfall cascaded down over the grotto's dark ledges to feed the pool, and shiny black sand crunched beneath their feet. The water seemed to be glowing, and Sloane thought he saw something move....

"Eels?" Sloane tiptoed to the edge of the pool, and he gasped.

Long slithering eels were swimming through the pool, their luminous bodies lighting up the water around them with a soft lavender glow.

"Those are light eels! Starlupen!"

"Yes. Very good, my sweet mate." Loch smiled. "It's said a single starlupa can travel all the worlds from Aeon to Zebulon a thousand times in the space of a mortal thought by using nothing but moonlight."

"Yeah? Well, they're beautiful." Sloane grinned, reached for Loch's hand, and then gave it a firm squeeze. "This is all so beautiful."

"And right now, it's all yours." Loch gently lifted Sloane into his arms and walked into the water with him. Their clothes vanished, and the surrounding rocks lit up with greenish-blue light.

Sloane saw it was some sort of bioluminescent moss growing on the stone itself, but he was far too distracted by the hot water to spare another thought, no matter how pretty it was. "Oh, by all the gods, that's so *good*!"

"Does this please you, my love?" Loch asked.

Groaning loudly, Sloane nodded. Every ache in his body was leaving him, and his feet—*finally!*—stopped their agonizing pounding. It was absolute bliss. He stretched his legs and wiggled his toes. "Oh yes. Uh-huh. Very pleased. Don't tell your mother, but I think I like the magical hot tub better than her blessing.

"Here." Loch slid his hand down Sloane's back.

There was an odd squeak of plastic, and Sloane laughed as a rainbow-colored inflatable raft appeared beneath him. It was floating just enough to keep his head from dropping beneath the top of the water but still allowed his body to remain fully submerged. "Have I told you how much I love you today?"

"I could always do with hearing it again." Loch leaned in for a very brief kiss. "Mmm, I love you, my sweet mate." He smirked at Sloane's belly. "And you too, my beautiful spawn, even if you are causing your father so much discomfort."

"This is seriously amazing," Sloane praised. "The waterfall, the beach, the everything."

"I'm glad you like it." Loch nuzzled his cheek. "I'm going to entertain Mother and Gal with tales of today's adventures for a little while. You will stay here and relax. I shall return soon."

"Mm, will do." Sloane beckoned Loch in for a kiss.

Loch obliged with a happy smile, but again the kiss wasn't much more than a mere peck. "Can I get you anything else before I go?"

There was something about those teasing kisses and the earnest way Loch was looking at him that left Sloane wanting more.

A lot more.

"Just one thing." Sloane reached up to grab Loch's curls, pulling him down and pressing their lips together in a fierce kiss.

It was hot, deep, and the resulting shudder that ran through Sloane's body made his toes curl. It felt like it had been years since they'd last been intimate, and Sloane was starved for affection.

He drank in every one of Loch's eager kisses, and he moaned when their tongues met. Loch held him close, wrapping him in a tender tentacle-filled embrace as the kiss heated up. Despite the rising passion, Loch kept his touches restricted to chaste caresses.

Being denied the level of swift intimacy he'd grown accustomed to only made Sloane want more. He slid his hands back over Loch's shoulders, feeling for the base of his tentacles where they emerged from his shoulders. This was a sensitive place for Loch, and the resulting moan from Loch's lips made Sloane shiver.

All he could think about was having Loch inside him, his tentacles taking turns filling him, making him come over and over again. He was so hard that it *hurt*, and he wanted to be able to reach down and touch his stomach and feel the bulge of Loch so deep inside him….

But wait, no, the baby!

Sloane suddenly couldn't stop thinking about it—he wouldn't be able to feel Loch through his stomach like he normally could because of the baby in his belly. Oh gods, what if they had sex and the tentacles somehow hurt the baby? What if the baby could feel what was happening?

Sloane broke the kiss, shaking his head as he suddenly withdrew. "Mm, I'm sorry. I can't."

"There is nothing to be sorry for." Loch didn't seem upset at all, and his eyes were full of bright stars. "Was this satisfactory, my sweet mate?"

"No." Sloane huffed. "No, I mean, yes, it was a great kiss." He grimaced when he looked at his stomach. The mood was definitely lost now. "Fuck. I don't know."

"I am concerned about mating." Loch frowned. "I do not wish to engage in any physical pleasures unless you're very sure, and right now you seem particularly indecisive."

"I don't want you to think I'm not interested!" Sloane sighed. "It is very sweet how considerate you're being, and the desire is definitely here! I just, ugh, I feel like I'm being a cocktease because I can't make up my mind. Wait. Tentacle-tease?"

"As I said before, my love, I do not mind. I don't want you to be uncomfortable. I only wish to share pleasure with you if we're both going to enjoy it. I am more than capable of pleasuring myself, after all."

"Oh?" Sloane perked up. The extinguished heat in his loins took a tick up to simmering. "I've never, uh, seen you do that."

"I much prefer the pleasure we obtain together."

"But you have done the other thing." Sloane bit his lower lip.

"Yes?" Loch didn't seem to understand what Sloane was getting at.

"I don't know if I'm up for the full mating gig, but uh, thinking about watching you pleasure yourself makes me want to pleasure myself."

"Oh!" Loch grinned wickedly. He definitely got it now. "You would want to see that, hmm?"

"Oh, very much." Sloane was excited. He couldn't explain why this was turning him on so much, but he wanted to see it so badly. "Show me?"

"Anything for you, my sweet Starkiller." Loch kissed him, soft and slow, and his tentacles shifted out from around Sloane's body. One of the slitted cocks and his monstrous tentacock rose above the water where Sloane could see them, and they rubbed up against one another. "I start off like this...."

The slitted tentacle was much more flexible, and it spiraled around the tentacock, squeezing down in steady pulses. A few coils focused in on the tentacock's bulbous knot, and they stayed wrapped tightly around it as the rest moved up the shaft in a familiar stroking motion.

Sloane watched with wide eyes, entranced by the amazing sight. His hand drifted to mirror Loch's stroking, but he grimaced when he touched his stomach. It was so big he couldn't even see what he was doing, and his thickening cock felt weird brushing against his belly.

Although Loch was still working on twisting his tentacles together, he noticed Sloane's distress. "Would you like me to give you pleasure?"

"That's not really fair, is it?" Sloane swallowed back a needy whine. "It's okay, I can watch—"

"Please," Loch urged. "I have missed the taste of you. I have missed your blissful smile, the lovely sounds you share with me. I want to make you feel good, my sweet love. With your permission, I would gladly pleasure us both."

"Yeah, yes, okay." Sloane made a mental note to find a way to show his utmost appreciation for Loch's selfless attentions later. "Mmm, I've been thinking about this for days. Thinking about you."

"Me?" Loch's other slitted tentacle slid up Sloane's thigh. "About what?"

"Mating with you." Sloane gasped as the tentacle latched on to the head of his cock.

Loch had continued to pleasure himself without missing a beat, twisting and untwisting the slinky tentacle around the shaft of his tentacock, the lower coils still squeezing his knot. The tentacock was dribbling out milky liquid, and it was utterly mesmerizing.

"The way you told off Stoker." Sloane panted. "It was hot. Okay, I don't usually go for any macho bullshit, but wow, knowing that you really could eat him if you wanted to totally did it for me."

"I shall defend your honor by threatening to eat people more often, then." Loch smiled, leaning in to kiss Sloane's brow. "Mmm, I love you."

"I love you too." Sloane groaned as the tentacle on his cock took him deeper, sucking hard at the same steady rhythm Loch was jerking himself off with. The pressure and suction was divine, and the inside of the tentacle was pulsing softly, adding to the incredible sensation.

Loch grunted, his eyes closing as his tentacles rearranged themselves. The tentacock pressed against the tip of the slitted one, rubbing its juices all around before trying to push inside. Loch kept thrusting the two ends together, almost violently, and it didn't seem like the tentacock could possibly fit.

Sloane was overcome by a flash of panic. Those slits always felt tight on his damn dick, and he wasn't packing half of what Loch had going for him. "Loch, I don't want you to hurt yourself."

"Mmm, your concern is sweet." Loch nuzzled their noses together. "Fear not. I've been doing this a very long time." The head of the tentacock suddenly popped inside the slit, and he groaned triumphantly. "Mm, all those eons I was waiting for my mate...."

Sloane's face turned blazing hot. He was the first person to ever experience Loch's tentacock, and he'd always considered it such an honor. Now all he could think about was the countless centuries his husband had spent literally fucking himself just like this.

Loch pushed the tentacock in with short bursts, stretching out his tentacle to take on the massive girth. He kept the tentacle on Sloane's cock relentlessly working away, and he was panting faster, his efforts soon matching the frantic rhythm of his breathing.

"For me," Sloane whispered as he bucked up into the incredible sucking grip. He wished he could see, but he stared at Loch's writhing tentacles instead. "Mmm, fuck yes. Oh, Loch. You were waiting for me."

"Yes." Loch's voice was strained, and he thrusted the tentacock harder, pushing it deeper into his tentacle. He mouthed along Sloane's neck, and his hands tightened down on his hips. "Ah, I fear it's been too long... I'm... I'm close...."

"Me too," Sloane moaned. "Fuck, I'm gonna... I think I'm gonna...."

The thrust of Loch's fat tentacock inside his own tentacle was hypnotic, the sounds wet and utterly obscene, and Sloane was lost to it all. Even the pinch of Loch's brow was sexy, knowing he was focused on fucking himself for Sloane to enjoy as much as he was intent on sucking Sloane's cock until he lost his mind in ecstasy.

It was there Sloane surrendered, caught in Loch's starry eyes as he came, moaning a symphony of praise as he gave himself over to the tentacle writhing on his cock. "Gods! Yes! Fuck, mmm! I'm coming! It's so good! Fuck, you feel so fuckin' perfect!"

"Mmm, my love," Loch gasped, his entire body shaking down to the ends of his tentacles as he climaxed mere moments after.

Sloane was transfixed by the forceful slams of Loch's tentacock within the receiving tentacle, groaning in sympathy at the thick seed spilling out with each thrust. The tentacle's lower coil squeezed the thick knot, and Sloane could see it pulsing. Loch's expression melted in bliss, his lips parting with a gasp, his eyes fluttering.

The stunning visual made every peak of Sloane's climax soar even higher, and every gush of thick come was impossible to look away from. And yet Sloane did, again finding himself staring into Loch's gorgeous eyes.

"Oh, Azaethoth," he whispered, his muscles heavy and sated as he gazed up at him. "I love you."

"Mm, and I love you," Loch whispered in reply, leaning in for a deep kiss. He stroked Sloane's hair and held him close. "My sweet Starkiller."

"That was without a doubt the hottest fucking thing I've ever seen in my life."

Loch laughed. "Was it?"

"Uh-huh." Sloane grinned. "Big fan."

"Perhaps it is something I can share with you more often." Loch's tentacles gently nudged Sloane's belly. "Even after our baby retreats from your body."

"I would like that." Sloane rested his hand on Loch's tentacle.

"Mmm, now I must leave you." Loch stood up straight. "The temptation to attempt further mating is too great."

"We just did it!"

"Ah, but pleasuring myself is nothing compared to the sheer ecstasy of being inside you." Loch kissed him. "I will return soon."

"I'll be right here."

"I can't wait to tell Mother we found a way to be intimate again. Ah, I was getting worried. I know it hadn't been very long, but—"

"Okay, how about you *don't* do that?"

"Why?"

"Because it's weird."

"Weird like when I told everyone you get grumpy when you don't have a helping of my hot seed inside you?"

"Yes. Like that."

"Ah."

CHAPTER 9.

SLOANE COULDN'T be sure that Loch was really going to resist telling his mother the details of what they'd just done, but he decided it was best not to worry about it. Loch meant well after all, and gods didn't have the same boundaries as mortals did.

There were worse things to worry about than his mother-in-law knowing her son-in-law apparently had a bit of a voyeur kink.

Like how he was going to solve Ziol's murder and discover the truth of who killed the deacon.

The wards at Ziol's home hadn't been broken, so the only way in or out was through teleporting or very powerful magic like an old god would have. Chase and Merrick would have already checked into the people holding licenses for teleportation magic, and there wasn't any immediate evidence an old god was involved with this case.

Of course, now that they knew there was a group of people descended from the everlasting races who were all in hiding, there was no telling how many possible suspects were out there who might possess the right kind of magic to do this.

Not to mention how strange it was that Nathaniel claimed to know who killed the deacon. He said he hadn't seen anything, but he seemed so sure that he knew who did it.

The angle of the bullet....

Sloane hated he couldn't figure out what he was missing. It seemed so obvious, and yet it still eluded him completely.

The hot water all around him and the buzz of a spectacular orgasm lulled him into a light doze, stirring only when the baby in his belly kicked or twisted around. He laid his hands over his stomach, and he smiled as he enjoyed the tiny aerobics display.

"You're doing this on purpose," he scolded. "Wiggling around when your other father isn't here."

The baby kicked again.

It was impossible to tell time here, so Sloane wasn't sure how long had passed before Loch returned. Loch was all smiles, still naked, and he dove right into the water to swim on over.

"Hello, my love," Loch greeted cheerfully, leaning in for a kiss.

"Mm, hello." Sloane smiled. "Everything go okay?"

"Fine. Mother and Galgareth are all caught up, as you say. They are equally mystified as we are, especially concerning the true nature of Sullivan Stoker."

"You told them about the numbers in the matchbooks, right?"

"Yes, I told them about all the things. Except the mating thing because you didn't want me to."

"Thank you." Sloane closed his eyes and yawned. "Mm. Sorry. Tired. I really do love it here. Almost as much as my garden."

Loch huffed.

"I said 'almost.'"

"It is all right, my love. This place is sacred, you know. Many gods and goddesses travel here to spawn. I myself was born here, right here in this very pool."

"Really?" Sloane peeked at Loch.

"Yes."

"Would you want our baby born here? To, uh, hatch here?"

"The location matters little to me, but it is very sweet of you to ask." Loch slipped his arms beneath Sloane, and the magical raft vanished. "Come along, dear husband. It is time for you to sleep."

"Mm, no argument here."

Loch carried Sloane up on shore, and a large canopied bed appeared, cradled in the curve of a cluster of rocks. He tucked Sloane in beneath lush blankets and a pile of pillows before cuddling beside him.

Sloane hadn't felt this good in days—no aches, no pain, no overwhelming urge to spill up his guts. It was wonderful.

"Happy, my love?" Loch asked.

"Hmm?"

"You're smiling."

"Yeah, I am happy. Feel good." Sloane's smile grew as Loch's tentacles curled around him. He snuggled closer. "Thank you. For everything."

"You're my mate. It's my duty and my honor to take care of you." Loch kissed his forehead. "Sleep now."

"Mm, good night."

"I love you."

"Love you too."

SLEEP CAME fast and hard, and Sloane didn't stir once. When he woke up to the quiet rush of the magical waterfall, he was completely refreshed.

Surrounded by cozy blankets and tentacles, he sighed contentedly. He was comfortable, happy, and... oh no.

He rolled over, frantically pushing Loch's tentacles away so he could promptly vomit off the side of the bed all over the sand.

"Good morning, my dear husband!" Loch smiled, and one of his tentacles rubbed Sloane's back. "Ah, so, breakfast?"

"Ugh...."

Loch cleaned the mess and got them dressed before they returned to the apartment. Sloane much preferred getting sick in his own bathroom over spewing all over the beach of a sacred grotto. After round two ended in dry heaving, he trudged out to the kitchen to find Loch and the others.

He stopped short, staring in bewilderment.

Sloane almost didn't recognize his own apartment.

There was a large table with chairs in the living room, and all the other furniture like the couch and television were gone. Sweeping garlands of flowering vines were draped along the walls, and a great assembly of food had been gathered on the table: roast beef, chicken, fruit, puddings, tiny sugary cakes, and more.

Despite the morning purge, Sloane's mouth watered.

"Holy shit," Chase blurted out. He was staring at Sloane's stomach.

Sloane sighed.

"You look beautiful," Merrick said politely. He and Chase were in the kitchen, helping Urilith and Galgareth. Loch was also in the kitchen, but he didn't seem to be helping as much as he was stealing food.

"Yeah, no, seriously!" Chase grinned. "You're glowing. Really. Sorry. Just, you know, wasn't expectin' all of that."

"It's okay," Sloane grumbled.

"He is very beautiful, and I have the urge to mate with him even more often," Loch announced cheerfully, snatching a piece of food from one of the pans and popping it in his mouth.

"Thank you." Sloane smiled wearily.

"That's great. Wonderful." Chase held out his hand to Loch. "Now gimme."

"Give you what?" Loch cocked his head.

"Loch." Chase narrowed his eyes and didn't back down.

"Fine!" Loch groaned as if in deep agony and produced Chase's badge with one of his tentacles, handing it over.

"Good morning!" Urilith swished away from the stove to greet Sloane with a kiss and a steaming bowl of soup. "How are you feeling, dear child?"

"Better, thank you. The springs were amazing, and wow, the house looks incredible." Sloane hesitated. "Totally not being ungrateful, but where's my couch?"

"Oh!" Galgareth spoke up from where she had been rummaging around the fridge. "Everything is right outside in the hallway! We'll put it all back as soon as the feast is concluded, promise!"

Sloane resisted the urge to facepalm.

"I know how much you enjoy the couch. I will not let anything happen to it." Loch came over to kiss Sloane and give him a tentacle-filled hug. "How is your stomach, love? Do you need to be sick again?"

"No. It's still kinda gross but much better, really." Sloane looked at the bowl Urilith gave him. "I have no idea what this is, but it smells freakin' delicious."

"Bone broth with ginger, chicken, and seaweed." Urilith smiled, returning to the kitchen. "It should rest easy on your tummy, and I've imbued it with another blessing."

"Think of it as godly chicken noodle soup," Galgareth suggested.

Sloane waddled over to the table to sit, moving some of the food out of the way so he could put the bowl down. "Is there anything I can do to help?"

"No." Urilith waved a tentacle at him "You are to sit, rest, and eat your soup!"

"And listen to the awesome dope me and Merry got on our boy Stoker," Chase chimed in. "Mama Suckers over here and Gal told us what was up, and we did some digging."

"Oh?" Sloane slurped at his soup. It tasted even better than it smelled, and his uneasy stomach relaxed almost immediately.

"Get this. Stoker was the middleman for a nasty little deal between the city council and, drum roll please, Deacon Douchebag."

"What?" Sloane blinked.

"Oh yeah," Chase confirmed. "So we know that the city wants that big-ass tree gone to make way for new shit."

"A very sophisticated playground and a large water feature," Merrick clarified.

"Two of the city council members have a stake in the construction company that was gonna do the work," Chase said, "so they were way invested in making the tree go bye-bye. But here's the thing. The city doesn't even own that land."

"No?" Sloane raised his brow. "Then who does?"

"Sullivan Jacob Stoker," Chase declared.

"Huh?"

"He purchased the land from some cat named Jacob Pick, and ol' Jacob had been leasing it to the city for the last fifty-some-odd years to use as a park. Stoker kept up the lease agreement, but when the city wanted to fuck up the tree?"

"He told them that they would have to purchase the land outright from him," Merrick continued. "Before the deal could be confirmed, the public learned of the tree's imminent destruction. The city did not want to purchase land they could not build on because of the protests."

"So now we got Stoker and some pissed-off city council guys, and nobody is getting paid." Chase grinned. "Well, except for the deacon."

"How does he fit into all of this?" Sloane asked.

"Stoker was arranging for those very invested members of the city council to, ahem, donate to the Lord of Light's damn church so the deacon would withdraw his people from the protest."

"The numbers in the matchbooks?"

"Bingo. They're passwords for an anonymous money exchange app. Seems like donating to the church wasn't enough for the deacon, and he wanted the cash sent right to him. Ol' Stoker would get the codes and pass them along to the deacon on those matchbooks."

"That's a really dumb way to pay someone."

"I'm guessing Stoker insisted on it. What better way to make the deacon squirm than forcing him to come to the club he tried to get shut down?"

"Fair. Still pretty risky just to be an asshole. Okay, no, I can totally see Stoker doing that. Right, so the deacon is being paid off to get his people to leave the park. Why didn't they leave?"

"Best as we can figure, it's 'cause nobody expected the Sages to suddenly show up."

"And then the Lucians didn't want to leave, no matter what the deacon said, probably," Sloane mused. "None of them had any idea that there was going to be a huge religious pissing contest over the tree."

"That was our assumption as well," Merrick confirmed. "We are checking into the council members who were involved, but we have not yet uncovered anything useful."

"What about the Sages? Gerard Ziol?" Sloane asked. "Were they involved?"

"My guess is that Stoker probably tried, but they didn't bite," Chase replied. "Could be motive for why Ziol was killed. For not playing nice."

"If that is why the deacon or Ziol were killed, it is ironic, because their deaths have only increased the strength of the protests." Merrick sighed. "Neither side is showing any signs of leaving, and more show up every day. We have stationed men there to keep a vigilant watch and ensure the protests remain peaceful."

"And meanwhile, Stoker and the city council guys aren't making any money." Sloane stirred his spoon around the bottom of his empty bowl.

"What is wrong, sweet mate?" Loch crowded behind Sloane at the table, leaning down to nuzzle his cheek. "You look concerned."

"It's kind of a big mess, you know?" Sloane replied. "I'm worried what's going to happen with that many people who don't like each other in a relatively small area."

"We'll handle that," Chase promised. "We're doing our best to root out all the assholes who are only there to start shit, and the rest of 'em can stay there forever for all I fuckin' care. Stoker and his goons will have to suck hind-tit until the protesters decide to leave."

"Did you guys find out anything about the knife Loch found?"

"The knife I *stole*," Loch gleefully corrected.

"Not much." Chase grimaced. "The church ain't exactly bein' cooperative."

"They did not wish to share what possible relics the deacon may or may not have been in possession of." Merrick's brow wrinkled. "They did, however, make it clear that everything in his estate was to be donated to the church upon his death."

"Of course." Sloane sighed. "Which means they probably know exactly what it is, but they don't want anyone else to know."

"Does that mean it's valuable?" Loch snuggled Sloane's cheek. "Should I go steal it again?"

"No, 'cause if the church is looking for it, then they'll definitely notice that it's missing."

"Hmmph. Fine. I'll let the amateur steal it, then."

"It's gotta be Hugh, right?" Sloane shrugged. "I mean, he's having money problems. If he didn't kill the deacon, he still might be the one trying to steal the knife."

"Someone should tell him that he's doing a terrible job of it," Loch quipped.

"We got guys watching the deacon's place," Chase promised. "As far as we can tell, Hugh is squatting there illegally, but this way we can keep an eye on him. If he so much as sticks a pinkie toe off the property, knife or no fuckin' knife, we'll know."

"Good. In the meantime, we need to go back to Ziol's house." Sloane braced himself on the edge of the table and stood. "There has to be something there we missed." He looked to Chase and Merrick. "I'm sure they told you about that part, right?"

"The part where the only suspect you have wants you to find who one of the killers is so he'll tell you who the other one is?" Galgareth grinned. "We did."

"I'd say the suspect list grew a bit," Chase said. "We got Hugh, the dumb pricks on the city council, plus Stoker's got a wicked strong motive."

"I agree, but why would Stoker be sheltering Nathaniel if he did it?" Sloane shrugged. "Doesn't make sense to protect someone who could turn you in for murder. Plus, he told us about the matchbooks. I mean, kind of. But he didn't have to."

"Touché."

"Should you discover anything of interest at Ziol's house, call us at once," Merrick said firmly. "We will be here making...." He glanced to Urilith.

"You're going to be making raspberry goat cheese tarts!" Urilith exclaimed.

"That. We're doing that."

"Ah, this is so nice!" Urilith leaned in to curl some of her tentacles around Merrick. "Our little family celebrations keep growing!"

"You and Loch go investigate your murder house, and we'll take care of everything here!" Galgareth said. "The rest of our partygoers are supposed to show up at five o'clock! So try to be back before then."

"I promise we will return soon," Loch swore. "I'm hoping to take Sloane to bed again before the party—"

"Loch," Sloane warned.

"Oh? Were you able to find a satisfactory way to mate?" Urilith asked. She might as well have been asking about the temperature outside.

"Yes! It was wonderful, very sensual." Loch paused, and he grinned sheepishly when he saw how Sloane was glaring at him. "But I am not going to talk about that. We are going to leave now."

"Now," Sloane confirmed.

"Right now?"

"Yes."

They managed to exit the apartment without Loch spilling any juicy details from their sex life, and Sloane considered that a win. The furniture in the hallway was less of a win. After some coaxing, he got Loch to stash the furniture in their private garden world so as to not upset their neighbors. He made sure to put the glamoured watch back on, and he was again grateful for the maternity pants.

Damn if they weren't comfortable.

Ziol's house was locked when they arrived, but that was no problem for the god of thieves.

"Merrick told us the code to get the key out of the little padlock thing." Sloane gestured to the device hanging from the doorknob.

"Where's the fun in that?" Loch grinned and strutted into the house.

Shaking his head, Sloane followed him inside and shut the door. He took a deep breath and looked around. It looked the same as before, untouched and no immediate sign of anything amiss.

"Okay. Now let me think."

"Back to the bathroom?" Loch guessed.

"Yeah?"

"Scene of the crime, all that." Loch magically transported them into the bathroom in a blink. "Ah, they cleaned up the blood. That's nice."

Sloane looked over the pristine bathroom and tried to focus. He waddled over to the shower and did his best to imagine Ziol's final moments standing there. He couldn't get his thoughts to settle, and he decided to step into the shower.

"What are you doing?" Loch whispered loudly.

"Working." Sloane grinned. "Look, I know it's a little crazy, but I can't picture it in my head like I usually can."

"Ah, it's the pregnant brain. Mother warned me of this."

"Whatever it is, I figured this might help. Trying to put myself in Ziol's shoes. Couldn't hurt anyway."

"Yes, but he was murdered and not wearing shoes."

"It's okay." Sloane took a deep breath. "Okay, Ziol is standing here, no water on, but he tilted his head back before he got shot."

Loch leaned against the doorway. "Perhaps he was looking at the ceiling?"

"Hmm." Sloane checked the ceiling with a perception spell. "Nothing there. So, if he wasn't looking up…."

The angle….

"Maybe he was looking down." Sloane stared at the drain at his feet.

It couldn't be that easy.

Could it?

Grunting, Sloane fought to get on his knees. He had to brace himself against the sides of the shower, and Loch's tentacles quickly slithered over to help him.

"My love, what are you doing?" Loch frowned.

"The angle of the bullet was crazy, right? We kept thinking Ziol's head had to be tilted way back for him to have been shot through the window or whatever, right?"

"Yes."

"What if we were wrong?" Sloane popped open the drain, finding the cover was hinged and quite loose. "What if his head was tilted forward and down?" He snapped his fingers to summon a beam of light so he could stare into the drain.

The drainpipe went down about a foot, and there was a glimmer of something metallic at the bottom.

"Would you be so kind?" Sloane gestured to the hole.

"What's down there?" Loch asked suspiciously.

"Evidence."

"Is it filthy?" Loch stepped closer to peer at the drain with a scowl. "It looks filthy. And wet."

"Come on. I can't reach it!"

"You want me to put my tentacles, my sacred godly appendages, down there?"

"If you ever want to put them anywhere else, ahem, yes."

"Ah." Loch nodded. "You mean inside your body?"

"Yes."

"Including your mouth?"

"That's still part of my body, Loch."

"That's very mean of you." Loch reached down the drain with one of his tentacles, griping, "It's very cold. And it feels slimy. Your evidence had better be incredible."

"I have a feeling it will be awesome."

"Huh." Loch pulled his tentacle back out, and he was holding a small revolver. "A gun? Well, why would anyone put it there? That's silly."

"I think Ziol was trying to hide it," Sloane replied excitedly. "Maybe he—"

"Wait, wait, wait!" Loch raised his hands. "Is this going to be the spectacular moment in which you crack the case and name the killer?"

"Uh... I guess?"

"We must wait." Loch grabbed Sloane and pulled him to his feet.

"Huh?" Sloane blinked.

"There is no audience here to appreciate your reveal." Loch stared at Sloane as if it was obvious. "We must wait until you have several witnesses so they can all gasp at the same time and possibly fight."

"You're serious? You don't want me to tell you?"

"No." Loch shook his head. "We must wait until the maximum level of drama can be achieved."

"Well, okay." Sloane shrugged. "We've gotta call Chase and Merrick. Put the gun back."

"Why?"

"So they can be the ones to find it. I don't want them to have to explain why we were here while they were busy baking tarts with your mother."

"I already reached down there once, and now you want me to do it again?"

"Loch."

"But it's so gross."

"Please?"

"There was *hair*. Stringy, disgusting hair down there. I could feel it."

Sloane grinned. "You've literally braided intestines, but a little hair grosses you out?"

"I do not like how it feels as a singular entity clinging to my tentacle. It does not belong there," Loch grumbled. "But for you, yes, I will return the evidence as we found it, and then we can have our dramatic reveal later."

"Thank you very much."

Loch continued to mumble as he carefully lowered the gun back into the drain. He visibly shuddered and closed the drain cover. "The things I do for you."

"And I appreciate them, every single one." Sloane kissed his cheek. "So, we'll call Chase and Merrick, and then we can go see Stoker. Once I tell Nathaniel who killed Ziol, he'll have to tell us who killed the deacon."

"I expect lots of gasping." Loch went to the sink to wash off his tentacle. "Maybe someone will even faint. Hmm. Think we can accomplish all that before your feast?"

"Yeah, it's not even lunchtime. We've got this!"

The very mention of lunch made Sloane's stomach audibly growl.

"Food first?" Loch smiled.

"Oh definitely."

CHAPTER 10.

LOCH WAS able to convince Sloane to get a salad, but how healthy that selection was got canceled out when it was followed up with three ice cream sundaes. Loch didn't complain too much; after all, he got to eat the third one.

Sloane ate his ice cream on the way and parked around the back of the Velvet Plank to finish his salad. He called Merrick and Chase to tell them what they'd found, though Loch covered his ears to make sure that the dramatic reveal wouldn't be ruined for himself, and Chase assured him they would take care of it right away.

As soon as the tarts were done, anyway.

When Sloane was done eating and his stomach appeared to be in little danger of rejecting his lunch, he and Loch headed inside the club.

It had the same light daytime crowd as before, and Stoker was again tending the bar. He looked surprised to see Loch and Sloane, but he waved them over all the same.

"I know who killed Ziol," Sloane said.

"Well, hello to you too," Stoker drawled.

"I need to talk to Nathaniel. I know who did it."

Stoker raised his brow expectantly.

"Let me talk to Nathaniel."

"Why don't you just tell me and I will tell him, hmm?"

"Oh, lots of reasons." Sloane narrowed his eyes. "Because I need the name of the person who killed the deacon, and I don't trust you as far as I can throw you."

"You wound me, Mr. Beaumont. When have I ever given you any reason not to trust me?"

"Seriously?" Sloane glared. "You lied to us about the matchbooks."

"How so?"

"You were the one passing them to the deacon!"

"But they were exactly what I told you, were they not?"

"Withholding information is as good as lying," Sloane snapped. "Quit screwing around and let me talk to him."

"If he doesn't want to cooperate, there's always time for arts and crafts," Loch said cheerfully. "I saw this *adorable* one of an octopus made from a paper plate and pasta shells strung together with yarn. I'm thinking about trying it with a paper plate and, oh, let's say all of Stoker's finger bones. What do you think, my love?"

Sloane plopped at the bar to give his feet a rest. They were already hurting again, and at that moment, he honestly didn't care what Loch did.

He just wanted the bullshit to end.

"Fine!" Sloane threw up his hands. "I'll get some glitter so they're really sparkly, and we can hang it on our fridge!"

"You two are so violent." Stoker, as usual, did not seem at all bothered by the threat. He leaned on the bar in front of Sloane, fixing him with a flat stare. "You know my poor cat is still green. If anyone should be making threats, it should be me."

"Nathaniel."

"Someone is awfully grumpy today." Stoker smirked. "Trouble in paradise?"

"*Now.*"

"As you wish." Stoker shrugged and finally came around the bar to lead them to the office they'd met in before.

"I love it when you get so aggressive," Loch purred in Sloane's ear. "It's riveting."

A tentacle teased around Sloane's hip, and he scolded affectionately, "Behave."

Riling up an immortal being was still pretty thrilling, and Sloane waddled into the office with his head held high.

It was still full of sculptures and junk, but there was someone else here.

It was Nathaniel Ware.

He appeared human and was standing in front of the desk, coiled as if he was about to pounce.

"Ah!" Loch pointed triumphantly. "There! I found him. Another case closed."

"Mr. Ware!" Sloane blinked in surprise. "Uh, hello. It's nice to—"

"Tell me," Nathaniel snapped, wringing his hands. "Who did it?"

Stoker patted Nathaniel's shoulder as he brushed by to take his seat at the desk.

"Please." Nathaniel relaxed somewhat and leaned back on the desk. "Please tell me who killed him."

Loch's expression was absolutely gleeful, glancing between Nathaniel and Sloane expectantly.

"Ziol did."

"Huh?" Nathaniel gasped sharply.

Loch clapped. "There. Yes. That was lovely." He eyed Stoker. "Could have used a little more excitement from you, but eh, I suppose that stupid look on your face will have to suffice."

Stoker, predictably, rolled his eyes.

"What happened?" Nathaniel demanded. "What do you mean it was Ziol?"

"It was an accident," Sloane explained gently. "I found a gun in the drainpipe of his shower."

"I don't understand." Nathaniel looked over his shoulder to Stoker and whirled back on Sloane. "How did it kill him?"

"I believe he was trying to hide the gun." The pounding in Sloane's feet had now reached his ankles, and he sat down. "Maybe he was worried you had actually hurt the deacon or might change your mind and try again. Whatever he was thinking, he wanted to stash the gun in the drain.

"He dropped it in there, but the hammer of the gun must have hit a curve in the pipe. It went off, and when he fell over, his body landed on the cover of the drain, closing it back up. So, even when you tried to turn back time, that's why you never saw the gun or another shooter."

"It's… it's all my fault…." Nathaniel grimaced miserably and held his face in his hands. "If I hadn't given him the gun… no, I should have never even gotten the damn thing! Fuck!"

"Nathaniel." Stoker's tone was firm, but his expression was surprisingly sympathetic. "This is not your fault. You're not responsible for his actions."

"Even if they're a direct result of my actions?" Nathaniel sighed.

Before Stoker could reply, there was a rush of a movement at the doorway.

"Nathaniel!" It was Daphne, staring wide-eyed at her brother.

"Daphne?" Nathaniel gasped. "How did you…?" He glared at Loch and Sloane. "Did you guys tell her I was here?"

"No!" Sloane said quickly.

"Hey, they didn't tell me anything," Daphne confirmed. "I waited for them to leave their house, and then I followed them here."

"How rude." Loch snorted. "Also, it's not a house. It's clearly an apartment."

"Nathaniel," Daphne pleaded, taking a few steps closer toward him. "The police are looking all over the city for you. They've come to the house twice already. I need you to do the right thing and turn yourself in."

"I didn't do it!" Nathaniel insisted. "The deacon was already dead, okay? I tried to—"

"Your fingerprints are all over the kitchen, the door, even his crest—" Daphne's eyes filled with tears.

"Of course they are! I put that stupid crest in his pocket after it fell out of his hand when I rolled him over! I was trying to help him!"

"Do you have any idea how much shit I'm in right now because of you?" Daphne sobbed. "I might lose my job because no one wants to work with me! I can't get any hours! You're so selfish—!"

"You're the selfish one!" Nathaniel barked back. "Are you even hearing yourself right now? You don't care about anyone else but yourself, and I see that now!"

"Oh, fuck you! You asshole!"

Loch sat and scooted his chair closer to Sloane's while Daphne and Nathaniel kept on arguing, whispering, "Would it be inappropriate to summon popcorn at this time?"

"Very," Sloane hissed.

"This is much more exciting than even your magnificent reveal…. Are you very sure I cannot summon popcorn?"

"Yes."

Stoker was watching the siblings fight with a sort of fond annoyance, like an owner whose new puppy had chewed up his favorite shoes. He did, however, nothing to stop it.

Sloane, on the other hand, was getting a damn headache. He clumsily got out of his chair with a groan, huffing, "Hey! Will you guys stop?"

"Not until he turns himself in!" Daphne tearfully replied. "This has to end!"

"He knows who really killed the deacon! He doesn't need to do that!" Sloane exclaimed. He turned to Nathaniel. "Please tell us who killed him, and I promise we can help you."

Nathaniel shook his head. "No."

"What?"

"I can't do that."

"We had a deal, Mr. Ware," Sloane protested. "I found out who killed Ziol for you!"

"It's better if I don't tell you who it is!" Nathaniel argued with a sudden burst of passion. "It's safer. Okay? For all of you. I see that now. I've already gotten too many people involved." He took a deep breath. "I should have never run away. Hey, Daphne? I'm so sorry."

"Nate, what are you doing?" Daphne demanded worriedly. "Please don't go. If you really know who it is, tell them and the police can take care of it!"

"I've gotta fix this myself. Don't worry. I know what to do now!" Nathaniel hugged her. "I love you."

"I love you too, but… no!" She gasped and tried to hold on to him. "You idiot! Don't you dare!"

Nathaniel vanished.

"I'm going after him!" Daphne cried, and she too suddenly disappeared.

"Loch?" Sloane urged. "Can you follow them?"

"Yes." Loch remained seated.

Sloane sighed.

"What?"

"Will you please go follow them? Now?"

"Oh, of course." Loch grinned and blinked away.

Sloane sagged in his chair, wishing his feet didn't hurt so much, and wow, this cushion was not helping his back.

"Couldn't wait to get me alone, could you?" Stoker teased.

"I'm going to vomit on your desk." Sloane rolled his eyes, knowing Stoker had no idea how real that threat was.

"We could be such good friends, Mr. Beaumont. I can be very helpful."

"Your help isn't that helpful."

"No? And what if I knew where Jeff Martin was hiding?"

Sloane froze.

Jeffrey Martin was the leader of the Salgumel cultists. He was a career criminal who, among his many crimes, had nearly killed Chase's nephew, Ollie, in a ritual to awaken Salgumel.

Okay, technically, Jeff *had* killed Ollie, but Chase had been able to stop Ollie's soul from leaving Aeon while Merrick and Loch healed him.

The ritual ultimately failed because of some fine print that made Ollie an imperfect candidate, but the hunt for Jeff was still ongoing.

It was only a matter of time before he tried again. If not the ritual that nearly killed Ollie, he was undoubtedly searching for some other way to wake up Salgumel.

"And what do you know about Jeff Martin?" Sloane asked casually.

"I know he spends a lot of money on rare healing artifacts, and he's a big fan of Salgumel. It's said he's gathering quite a following. Maybe even enough to attract the attention of like-minded gods trapped in the dreaming."

Sloane's stomach sloshed. "Oh?"

"Merely a rumor." Stoker flashed a charming smile. "If we were friends, maybe I would be inclined to let you know if I heard anything else."

"If you actually know anything about Jeff Martin and you're not telling me, I swear I will summon a sword of starlight and stab you right in your freakin' eyeball," Sloane growled as he forced himself to stand. "I don't know what you are, but I'm damn sure I can make you bleed."

"Such fire," Stoker purred, shamelessly scanning over Sloane's body. "All of that fury inside such a delicate little mortal body. It's quite beautiful. No wonder Azaethoth fell in love with you."

"Do you actually fucking know something or not?" Sloane's palms crackled with starlight. He wouldn't dare actually summon the sword. It was an intense strain on his body, and he was worried it might hurt the baby.

But Stoker didn't know that.

"No." Stoker propped his elbows on the desk and steepled his fingers. "It is merely a rumor I was gifted by the man who sold him the healing artifact. Jeff can be quite chatty, apparently."

"Did he happen to mention that he almost killed a good friend of mine?" Sloane narrowed his eyes. "He's a monster, and if you know anythi—"

"If I know anything, I have to tell you or sword of starlight in the eyeball," Stoker drawled. "Yes, I got it the first time. I may not be a dedicated fan of following the letter of the law, but I certainly don't want to see the world end."

"No?" Sloane scoffed.

"No profit." Stoker winked. "Should I hear anything substantial, I'll give you a call. What's your number?"

"Well, aren't you smooth." Sloane rolled his eyes and fished a business card out of his pocket. "Here."

"Thank you." Stoker smirked at the little stylized arrow on the card. "The Sage's Cross, hmm?"

"Yup." Sloane waddled back to his chair and sat.

"How cute."

Sloane would have been happy to sit in silence until Loch's return, but the mention of healing artifacts got him thinking. "I don't suppose you know anything about the deacon's collection? His Lucian relics, books... maybe an old knife?"

Tapping the business card against his chin, Stoker pursed his lips. "A knife that perhaps he keeps sealed beneath his bed in a ludicrously complicated vault?"

Sloane couldn't hide his surprise. "And how do you know that?"

"There is not much about the deacon that I do not know." Stoker winked. "Except who killed him, of course." He set the card on his desk, balancing it on a single corner. "The knife is believed to be an ancient Lucian blade blessed by the Lord of Light himself."

"Is it?"

"The Lord of Light certainly walked Aeon, if that's what you're asking. If he's the one true god destined to give peace to all of mankind by bringing us into his holy light, well, I think we both already know that's not true."

"So the knife is worthless?"

"I didn't say all that." Stoker smiled. "Everything has value, Mr. Beaumont."

"You just need someone else to believe it's valuable. Like maybe the Lucian church?"

"Mmm. Such a clever brain in a delicious mortal package."

Sloane grimaced. "Is it possible for you to actually answer a question without flirting with me?"

"Yes, but where's the fun in that? And you are so very beautiful when you're flustered."

Sloane was about to tell Stoker exactly what he could do with that beautiful comment—wow, maybe he really was grumpy today—when Loch reappeared in the chair next to him.

"Now, don't be upset," Loch said carefully, "but you see... I may have lost them."

"How did you lose them?" Sloane complained.

"Well, they did have a bit of a head start."

Sloane paused to inhale deeply, trying to keep a hold of his temper. He was not feeling well, and he didn't want his bad mood to cause him to say something he would regret. "So, we solved one murder that wasn't even a murder, and you let the person who could solve the second murder escape?"

"Yes, that is precisely what happened."

Sloane hung his head.

"Very impressive," Stoker said dryly.

"I don't suppose you'd be willing to call me if you hear from Nathaniel?" Sloane got out of his chair, bracing his hands against his aching back with a grunt.

"Any reason to hear your voice, Mr. Beaumont."

Loch reached over and snatched the phone off the desk. "I'm taking this. Consider it tribute so I won't eat you for making sexual advances on my mate again."

"Whatever." Stoker snorted. "Ah, behold, the mighty god of thieves and his magnificent purloining skills."

Sloane was afraid the taunt was going to start another fight, but Loch only smiled.

"Take care, Mr. Beaumont." Stoker waved, a quick twirl of his fingers. "We'll be in touch soon, I'm sure."

"Farewell, Stoker!" Loch waved back. "Enjoy your green cat!" He offered his arm to Sloane and marched out of the club, dragging the phone behind him by the receiver.

Sloane's crankiness eased, and he was unable to resist a laugh at the awful sound of the phone clanking behind them. It was especially ridiculous when they hit the sidewalk.

"I am sorry I was unable to locate Nathaniel," Loch fussed as they rounded the corner into the parking lot. "I got a bit turned around with all the jumps. To be quite honest, I'm not even sure I was following the right sibling."

"It's okay. We'll let Chase and Merrick know what happened. Maybe they have some ideas as to who Nathaniel might be going after."

"Am I driving?" Loch asked hopefully.

"Gods, yes." Sloane groaned. His shoes seemed to be cutting into his ankles now. "I might actually ask for some of that magical seed of yours, because I feel spectacularly awful right now. I think your mom's blessing has worn off again."

"It would be my pleasure, my love." Loch opened the passenger door of the car for Sloane and helped him sit. He gingerly shut the door and walked around to the driver's side with a little bounce in his step, the phone clanging away.

Sloane waited for Loch to join him in the car before saying, "I'm really proud of you, by the way."

"Oh, I know." Loch cranked the car, cocking his head as he passed a slitted tentacle over. "Any particular reason right this moment?"

"Mmm." Sloane sucked the tentacle into his mouth, and a quick swirl of his tongue coaxed out a load of hot seed. He swallowed it, sighing as the aches drained away. "Thank you. And I was gonna say for not taking Stoker's bait when he made fun of you for stealing his phone."

Loch's tentacle wiggled back into his sleeve, and he grinned slyly. "Look in the back seat."

"What?" Sloane turned his head.

Propped up in the back was the wooden statue of Azaethoth the Lesser from Stoker's office. It took up the full seat and was neatly strapped in by the seat belts.

Sloane laughed. "Oh no. You didn't."

"Oh, but I did." Loch sent a tentacle over to pat Sloane's thigh. "No one messes with my mate."

"Wait, what's that silky thing?" Sloane couldn't turn his head far enough to make it out, but there was a bit of fabric wrapped around the statue's legs. "A handkerchief?"

"Those would be Stoker's underwear." Loch snorted as he backed the car up, pulling out of the parking lot with a cackle. "My purloining skills are indeed magnificent!"

Sloane could not agree more.

It was only when they got home that he saw the Azaethoth statue was actually wearing the stolen underwear, and Loch considered donating his prize to his personal shrine at Dead to Rites since he'd found it so lacking.

Even though Sloane was feeling better from having a dose of Loch's godly seed, he still let Loch carry him inside, and they were greeted by a chorus of shouts and cheers.

Urilith and Galgareth were stacking more food on the already overflowing table, and Chase was finishing up icing some chunky cupcakes while Merrick watched. Sloane couldn't immediately explain the warmth surging through him at the sight of them all, and then it hit him.

Family.

He was home to feast with his family.

That was about the time he started crying again, and he clung to Loch with a loud sob.

"What's wrong, my sweet husband?" Loch asked worriedly, cradling him close against his chest.

"I'm, I'm just so happy!" Sloane sniffed. "Ugh, now I can't stop crying!"

"Aww, dear child," Urilith cooed as she came over to wrap her tentacles around Sloane and kiss his brow. "Today is your special day, as is every one that follows this. You may cry as much as you wish."

"I just might!" Sloane sniffled, smiling despite the tears.

"We still have some time yet before the feast. Why don't you go rest, hmm?" She patted Loch's shoulder. "Go mate with him. Sharing seed is always good for easing the troubles of being with child."

Sloane blushed, saying quickly, "No, I think I'm good. I mean, resting sounds nice. We can go do that. And only that." He looked to Chase and Merrick, eager to redirect the conversation. "Uh, so, how goes the stuff at Ziol's?"

"Fine!" Chase replied. "We didn't even leave. Just told Milo to go back over there and get the gun out of the drain. They'll check to make sure it's the one that killed Ziol."

"In our defense," Merrick grumbled, "the tarts were still in the oven."

"What happened at Stoker's?" Chase asked. "Did Nathaniel tell you who killed the deacon?"

"I stole a statue and his underwear," Loch said proudly.

"Wait, whose underwear?"

"Stoker's!"

"Nathaniel said he didn't want to endanger any of us, and he took off to handle it himself." Sloane rolled his eyes. "He didn't tell us crap, and Loch couldn't find him. So, unless you guys have any ideas who might want the deacon dead, we are back to where we started."

"Not quite." Merrick smiled. "Thanks to you, we are only searching for one killer."

"See?" Galgareth cheerfully chimed in. "Even all knocked up, you're a fantastic investigator!"

"I'll let you know when I start feeling fantastic again." Sloane buried his head in Loch's chest and let out a little laugh. "I'm totally exhausted."

"Go rest. Get your godly bang on. You know, whatever works for you." Chase grinned. "We got your party tonight, and hey, we can all start fresh tomorrow, okay?"

"Sounds good."

"Come along, my love." Loch snuggled Sloane close. "You are in need of a nap."

"Let's go." Sloane could not agree more.

The world shifted around them, and Sloane found himself back in the sacred grotto. Loch was still carrying him and took him over to the bed they'd slept in before, lovingly tucking him in under the covers.

"There you go," Loch cooed. "Do you need anything, my sweet mate?"

"No. Not right now." Sloane smiled softly. The glamour watch was gone, and he was wearing baggy flannel pajamas. "I actually feel pretty good. Magical seed and all. Just tired."

"This is the part where I normally offer you more of my seed, but I will decline for now."

"I don't want you to decline." Sloane sighed. "I want to take your seed and do all the normal non-pregnant things. I feel fine, and then I don't. The blessings work for a while, and then I want to puke again. My shoes fit, and suddenly they're cutting off circulation to my feet because both of my ankles have swollen up like sausages."

Loch frowned and stroked a loving hand through Sloane's hair. "I am sorry that carrying our child is so taxing on your body. I promise to spend the rest of our lives making it up to you."

"That's very sweet of you. I'm sorry for bitching. I'm frustrated. I feel like this weird little alien thing has taken over my body, and my body isn't even mine anymore. I'm just this thing for making a baby."

"I believe you have effortlessly described being pregnant, dear mate."

Sloane snorted out a short laugh. "Yeah, I guess I did."

"It will be over soon, and we will be able to hold our beautiful child in our arms."

"And it will be worth it." Sloane inhaled deeply. "So very worth it."

"Rest now." Loch kissed him. "I will awaken you when the feast is ready to begin."

"Mm, I love you."

"I love you too."

The soft lull of the waterfall was enough to send Sloane off to sleep, and he dreamed of green cats and silk underwear. It was a little weird, especially the part with the cat wearing a crest for the Lord of Light with the aforementioned underwear.

When Sloane woke up, it was because Loch was hovering over him and carefully placing a crown of branches and lavender on his head.

"Hello, sweet mate," Loch chirped. "I hope you are refreshed and excited."

Sloane reached up, reverently touching the crown. "Ah, is it what I think it is?"

"Yes, that's a crown."

"No, I mean is it time for the feast?"

"Ah, yes. That as well."

"I am ready." Sloane sat up, holding his crowned head high. "Let's go."

CHAPTER 11.

WHEN LOCH brought Sloane back to their apartment, he was swarmed by a joyous crowd of their family and friends. The air was a sweet mix of lavender and chamomile, and he knew the Neun Monde feast had truly begun.

Milo and his girlfriend, Lynnette, were the first to greet him, and Lynnette was eager to compare their growing bellies. She was almost six months pregnant now, and she was happy to trade war stories about vomiting and crying.

Fred and Ell brought some sort of pickled eggs, and the very aroma made Sloane's mouth water. He also couldn't help but notice how very not dead Fred looked, and he made a mental note to ask Ell about his healing techniques later.

Lochlain and Robert cooed over Sloane's big belly, and Lochlain was already promising to teach the new baby how to pick locks. Loch was very proud of his favorite disciple and gladly accepted the lessons.

It was all so wonderful, thoughtful, and equally overwhelming. Sloane managed to survive saying hello to everyone and waddled over to the head of the table to escape for a few moments.

Urilith didn't let him linger for too long, bringing him a large jar and a happy smile. "This is for you, sweet child."

"Honey?" Sloane guessed, peering at the dark orange goop inside.

"Ah, but not just any honey," she said proudly. "This is from Babbath's orchard. He kept a small hive there and tended to them for thousands of years. Gordoth mentioned they'd been there and there was a fire of some sort—"

"Just a small one!" Loch griped.

"—and I thought to look in on the bees! They are thriving, and I helped myself to some of Babbeth's sacred honey just for you."

"Wow!" Sloane grinned. "Thank you so much!"

Loch brought him a platter packed full of an assortment of food from the feast and a big mug of tea. "Here, my love. Make sure you get enough to eat."

"Thank you." Sloane had barely taken a bite before Galgareth was there, offering another gift. "Mmm, what is this?"

"It's a blanket made of starlight, like the one I made you and Azaethoth for your wedding," she replied. "But this one is special. It will grow with your child as they do! I also gave it a blessing of good luck, of course."

"Thank you so much, Gal." Sloane smoothed his hand over the soft, glittering lavender fabric. "It's beautiful."

Loch took the chair next to Sloane and scooted close, a tiny porcelain bell in his tentacles that he offered out reverently. "This is hardly new. It's used, in fact. And I technically stole it since I had to snoop through your belongings to find it."

"That makes it all the more fitting, doesn't it?" Sloane held the little bell close to his chest. It was the same one from his own birthing ritual, rung by his mother the day he was born. "Thank you. I'm so glad you found it."

Loch snuck a quick kiss. "Mm, a bell so our child's first sound will be music."

"Honey so their first taste will be sweet. Herbs so their first smell will be calming, and blankets so their first touch will be tender." Sloane smiled. "Everything is perfect."

He still couldn't believe he and Loch were getting gifts for a Neun Monde, much less for a child that Sloane himself was carrying. It was beautiful, magical, and he knew he was going to end up crying again.

"And a crown," Loch declared, using his tentacles to adjust the crown on Sloane's head, "so when our child looks upon you, their first sight will be your beauty as their father."

"Shouldn't that technically be 'mother'?" Sloane grinned.

"Why? Fathers can give birth. Mine did."

"Fair." Sloane pulled Loch in for a hug. "Thank you. Thank you so much for finding my bell and for helping put all of this together. Seriously, just... wow...." His voice cracked. "Oh, Azaethoth."

"What is it, my sweet mate?" Loch frowned and rubbed Loch's back.

"I'm really, really happy," Sloane whispered. He could hear a collective chorus of "awwing" from their guests, and he hastily pulled away so he could wipe the tears from his eyes. He laughed, teasing, "Don't you guys have food to eat or something?"

Chase was the only one actually seated, and he was already eating. Merrick glared at him, prompting a muffled, "What?"

Merrick rolled his eyes.

Chase mumbled and went back to his food.

"I have something for you and your spawn as well." Merrick's smile was shy as he approached Sloane, and he offered what first appeared to be a large charm bracelet.

It was a long string of chunky beads and charms, like a bell and a hollowed piece of glass that had small pebbles inside. It had a large ring at one end, and when Sloane gave it a shake, it made the most delightful racket.

"Indestructible," Merrick promised. "At least it was when Azzath played with it."

"This was mine?" Loch stared in awe. "When I was a little spawn?"

"Yes." Merrick beamed. "You used to play with it for hours, little Azzath."

"How did you ever find this?"

"He had some help," Lochlain chimed in proudly.

"You stole this?" Now Loch looked like he might cry. "For our child?"

"Yes, but he also had some help." Robert grinned. "Someone else stole it, and then it made its way through some not-so-legal channels until it wound up getting picked up in a police raid."

"I may have maybe told somebody about it being in evidence," Chase said between bites. "Since a certain godly somebody has some issues with breaking the law and all, I helped."

"It was a group effort," Lochlain confirmed.

"Did you know the museum it came from said it was a totem for summoning rain?" Robert chuckled. "Can you believe it?"

"And it's Loch's old baby rattle?" Sloane laughed. "That's amazing. Seriously! And wow, thank you, everyone who helped! This is incredible."

Loch slipped a tentacle through the ring and gave the rattle a good shake. "Ah, good, still works."

Lynnette and Milo were sitting down to eat now, and Fred and Ell soon joined them, though Fred still did not try any food. Galgareth whisked away the presents for safekeeping in the nursery, and Urilith took it upon herself to fuss over everyone and make sure they had enough food, especially Sloane, and soon he was sure he was going to burst.

Chase got a second plate of food, but only once everyone else had a chance to eat. Merrick nibbled off of his plate and occasionally offered Chase a bite with his tentacles.

"So, okay," Milo was asking, "the birthing ritual is actually done right after the baby is born, not during the actual... birthing?"

"Be a little weird clanging a bell away while someone's trying to push out a baby," Lynnette replied with a little laugh. "But yes, as soon as the baby is ready, the birthing ritual is done. Sooner the better. And then comes the naming."

"See! I remember that!" Milo beamed. "It's the welcome ritual, right? Welcoming into the faith."

"Exactly," Sloane confirmed. "It's a little different for a baby, since that's when you give them their name."

"I'm so ready to meet little Luke or Mara Organa!" Milo exclaimed, bowing his head to smooch Lynnette's belly.

"You guys still don't know what you're having?"

"Nope!" Lynnette smiled. "We wanted it to be a surprise. Thought it would be fun! I mean, the last time we had a big surprise, a naked cat man stole all the Parmesan cheese."

"Asta the Asra," Sloane recalled fondly. "Ah, kinda hard to top that, huh?"

"I think Jay tried," Milo teased.

"Oh yeah? What happened? Is he still working at the department?"

"Yeah, he's over in that janitor's closet doing IT stuff, and we never fuckin' see him. When he came back from Xenon, he told me, 'Don't ever fall in love with your cat,' and then he wouldn't say shit else."

"Poor guy." Sloane frowned. "I can't imagine Asta being an easy person to date."

"Because he's a vile, evil Asran fiend?" Loch suggested.

"No, because he seems... sort of flighty."

"Like a *fiend*."

"Well, he sure did a number on Jay." Chase laughed. "Poor guy is real beat up over it. I poke my head in there, like, once a week to make sure he's still alive."

"He also had some kinda drama with his old roomie," Milo went on. "Not like bad drama, but like, roomie had to come back from Xenon to sign some papers so Jay could take over the lease kinda like drama."

"What was his name again?" Sloane rubbed his belly thoughtfully. "Kicker of Cats. Ted something."

"Ted Sturm."

Ell's fork clattered on his plate, and he quickly cleared his throat as he picked it back up. "Oh. Sorry."

"Ell, isn't your last name Sturm?" Sloane realized.

"Oh yes." Ell stared at his plate and shrank. "Right. It is."

Sloane waited for Ell to say something else, and when Ell didn't, he asked bluntly, "Are you related to Ted?"

"Uh…. He's my brother."

"The cat kicker is your brother?" Loch wrinkled his nose. "No accounting for taste, seeing as how he's set to marry the Asran king."

That was apparently news to Ell, judging by how big his eyes got.

"Why didn't you ever say anything?" Sloane asked gently.

"I haven't talked to him in a really long time." Ell's sweet face suddenly turned sad, and he looked back at his plate. He'd apparently lost his appetite, because his gloved hands dropped into his lap, his food abandoned. "Family is… complicated."

Fred draped a thick arm around Ell's shoulders and pulled him in close.

It was obvious whatever had happened between Ell and his brother was personal.

And painful.

"Oh, trust me, I know all about family problems." Loch sighed loudly. "My father will destroy the world if he wakes up, which is exactly what every single one of my idiot brothers seem intent on doing."

"Not all of them!" Urilith huffed, shooting a yellow tentacle over to bop Loch on top of his head. "Xhorlas is still dreaming as sweetly as ever!"

"Ow!" Loch tried to duck.

"I prefer to think of you guys as my family," Ell said with a little smile. "Fred and all of you. You guys have always been very kind to me."

"That's very sweet of you, Ell." Sloane reached over to pat Ell's shoulder, and he didn't miss how Fred glared at him. "Thank you. You're definitely part of the family now."

When Sloane pulled away, Fred relaxed, though he kept his arm around Ell and practically dragged him into his lap.

Wow, and Sloane thought Loch could be possessive.

"Thank you, guys." Ell perked up again. "This is really awesome. I hope, well, I hope Ted is happy."

"How could he be?" Loch lamented. "He's marrying the king of the Asra. Have you ever met one? Just awful."

"The two dicks are probably fun, though," Lynnette said.

"Wait, the what?" Milo blinked.

While Lynnette went into vivid detail about what she'd seen of Asta's anatomy, Sloane could have sworn he saw Robert and Lochlain exchange a worried look.

He was missing something.

Sloane could hear a faint whisper of words coming out of nowhere right into his ear. It was a warning, some kind of message, it was something about Ell—

"Oh! Cake!" Loch exclaimed.

The mysterious whisper forgotten, Sloane looked to see Urilith bringing a large cake toward them.

"Urilith! Wow! That's your Dhankes cake!" Sloane frowned at Loch. "I thought you didn't want her to make it?"

"I know how much you like it." Loch curled a tentacle around Sloane's hips. "I only ask that you please keep your moaning to a minimum."

"Thank you," Sloane gushed, leaning over for a kiss.

"You are most welcome, my beautiful mate."

They feasted long into the night, and Sloane only moaned once over the cake, as promised. Fred and Ell were the first to leave, and Milo and Lynnette were gone shortly after. Lochlain and Robert stayed to help clean up, and Merrick wanted to spend more time with his family.

Chase had gone back for another plate.

Sloane was beyond full, near dozing in his chair. His crown was askew, and he could not even be bothered to lift his hand to fix it. His body was relaxed, nothing hurt, and he was too damn comfortable.

"There is still no word on this Jeffrey Martin who is leading the cultists?" Urilith was asking, using her hands and tentacles to tidy up the table.

"No, but you can bet your ass every cop in the city is still lookin'
for him since he blew me and Merry up." Chase took a big bite. "If he's
dumb enough to show his face, he's gettin' got."

"Gettin' got?"

"He will be arrested," Merrick clarified.

"He attacked two cops," Chase went on. "We're not real happy
with him."

"Stoker mentioned something about Jeff," Sloane mumbled
sleepily. "Something about him needing rare healing totems. Some
rumor he heard."

"Probably for his messed-up face," Chase muttered.

"What's wrong with his face?" Galgareth asked.

"He's got a big-ass rotten handprint in the middle of it," Chase
replied. "But not like a ghoul, like somethin' else."

Lochlain and Robert exchanged another worried look like before,
and Sloane wasn't letting it go now.

"What's up?" Sloane asked bluntly. "You two don't like Ell or
something?"

"No, please don't think that." Lochlain grimaced. "It's just a little
weird sometimes... you know, with what he is."

"What...?" Sloane didn't understand. "With what who is? Ell?"

"You don't remember." Robert stared flatly. "The Galmethas party."

"Well, him and Azaethoth were both a little drunk." Lochlain
grinned. "Maybe more than a little."

"Right." Sloane rubbed his eyes. "Because I told Ell about the
Starlight Bright book, and that's why him and Fred got it for us as a
wedding present."

"I strongly believe we had a wonderful time," Loch cheered.

"What else happened?" Sloane had experienced strange feelings
being near Ell before, but he couldn't explain what it or he was. Ell
seemed so sweet and harmless; what could it possibly be?

"Ell is part Eldress," Lochlain replied. He must have been expecting
more of a reaction because he huffed, "What? Did we already know that
was a thing?"

"Nathaniel Ware and his sister are both descended from Absola,"
Merrick said. "There are apparently a great number of beings who are
descendants from the everlasting peoples who were left behind when the
gods went into the dreaming."

"Oh well. Shit." Lochlain laughed with what seemed to be relief. "Any of 'em got horns?"

"Tusks and tails." Sloane smirked. "They don't look like full-blooded Absola. More like half-human and half-Absola squished together?"

"And glamour to hide it?" Robert ventured.

"Yeah. Daphne mentioned that not everyone who carries the blood will look like them. A lot of them are totally normal." Sloane tilted his head. "Wait, does Ell have horns?"

Lochlain nodded. "Yeah. Saw 'em once after that job at the auction got nasty last year."

"The auction where you guys stole one of the Lord Collins crazy cultist paintings, right?" Sloane clarified.

"Yeah, that's the one," Lochlain confirmed. "Ell's got some crazy powers."

"Can't be silenced, for one thing," Robert added.

"And the healing he does? That's part of it?" Sloane asked. "Being part Eldress, I mean."

"Think so."

"Well, awesome." Sloane beamed. "I think it's great so many of the everlasting people were able to survive and live on like this."

"Do you know what else is great?" Loch asked as he cuddled in close, curling his tentacles all around Sloane.

"Mm, lemme guess. Is it you?"

"All this fantastic mortal beauty and a sharp intellect to match it." Loch sighed dreamily. "I am truly a lucky god. Who is also great."

"Yes, you are."

"You're both adorable." Galgareth leaned in to hug them. She smirked at Sloane. "Get enough to eat, or do you want more?"

"No, thanks. I'm so good." Sloane stroked his stomach. "I think we're both happy for now. And thank you, everybody, for all of this. This feast has been amazing."

"It is our pleasure, sweet child." Urilith came over to give Sloane a hug and kiss his hair. "Oh, I just can't wait to meet the little one!" She looked over Sloane's belly. "Mmm, should be ready to hatch soon."

"And you're sure it won't hurt? I mean, not that I'm afraid of pain. I get it. Childbirth ouch, got it. Ring of fire to get my crown. But what exactly is going to happen?"

"He or she will pass from you as an egg, and then they will hatch!"

"It's the passing part, that bit, that I'm worried about." Sloane grimaced.

"All will be well," Urilith promised. "You should experience little discomfort. You will know when it's time. You will feel it."

Sloane frowned at his belly. Other than a few kicks and wiggles, everything else he'd felt so far hadn't exactly been pleasant. He had no idea what to expect, but he hoped Urilith was right.

Passing through a ring of fire to accept your crown of stars....

Sloane would gladly do it all to hold their child in his arms.

It would be worth it a thousand times over.

"Hey." Chase came over to shake Sloane's hand. "We got all the leftovers in the fridge, although I think Merry is taking some of that donkey cake with us."

"Dhankes," Merrick corrected with a fond smile.

"Them too."

"Thank you, guys, for everything," Sloane said. "As scary and weird as all of this has been, especially with all the crazy surprises—" He gestured to his belly. "—I had all of you here with me. Really. This has seriously been awesome."

"And hey, you look beautiful." Chase grinned. "I mean, I guess that's cool to say, right? That's what we always tell pregnant chicks, and you're, like, super pregnant."

Sloane's enthusiasm fizzled. "Thanks, Chase."

"You have grown magnificently," Merrick said with a solemn nod of his head. "I wish you and Azzath a lifetime of joy with your spawn."

"Aw, thank you, Merrick."

"Magnificently and gorgeously," Loch purred in agreement, snuggling in close to Sloane's side. "So much that I must whisk you away now to do unseemly things to your lush naked body."

"Oh, it's that time, huh?" Sloane laughed.

"On that note, we're gonna get going too," Lochlain said. "We may go check out those protests at the Xenish Sprig."

"Maybe we'll hear something about Nathaniel or anybody else who might have a strong enough motive to kill the deacon." Robert shrugged. "It's worth a try."

"Be careful," Chase cautioned. "They've been getting a little rough."

"Don't worry." Lochlain grinned and winked at Loch. "I've already been murdered once. I don't plan on doing it twice."

They said their final goodbyes to everyone, exchanged hugs and tentacles, and Sloane was secretly relieved to see them go. The party had been great, but he was tired. He was ready for bed.

Maybe not for all the unseemly things Loch had in mind, but a solid nap sounded awesome.

"We'll finish cleaning up." Galgareth gestured to the living room. "And we'll put the furniture back—"

There was a knock at the door.

"Who could that be?" Loch batted his eyes.

Urilith answered it. "Oh! Chase? Back so soon?"

"Yeah." Chase held out his hand expectantly. "You. Loch. Gimme."

"Fine. Here." Loch stretched out a long tentacle, handing Chase his badge back. He gave his rattle a stubborn shake. "You're no fun."

"Yeah, just the worst." Chase took his badge back and rolled his eyes. "Good night, guys! Again!"

"Farewell!" Urilith waved and then shut the door.

"Why do you keep doing that?" Sloane asked. "You know he's gonna know it was you."

"Because it's fun," Loch declared. "Now, are you ready for bed, my sweet mate?"

"Only if you're gonna behave and put a rain check on unseemly things being done to my body."

"Oh, I only said that to make sure everyone would leave quickly."

"That is weirdly thoughtful of you." Sloane kissed his cheek. "Thank you."

"Go rest now," Urilith came over to hug them both with a sweep of thick tentacles. "We'll be here if you need us."

Galgareth hugged them, too, leaning down to smooch both Sloane and Loch on top of their heads. "Love you guys."

"I love you, sweet Sister," Loch said, turning to nuzzle his mother's tentacles. "And I love you, dear Mother."

"I love you both very much," Urilith said. "Sleep well, hmm?"

"Thank you again." Sloane smiled. "Love you guys too!"

Loch whisked them away to the grotto with the waterfall, Sloane cradled in his arms as he stood on the beach. He used a tentacle to straighten Sloane's crown. "Now, do you wish to soak in the hot springs? Or to bed?"

"Bed," Sloane replied. "I'll soak tomorrow. Right now I just want you, bed, and lots of snuggles."

"I'm happy to satisfy your every request." Loch tucked him into the lush bed and cuddled up beside him, curling his tentacles all around him.

Sloane could feel them coiling around his thighs and belly, but it was Loch's hand that he searched for, lacing their fingers together. "Mm, that was an awesome party."

"We can keep on celebrating if you wish." Loch gently removed the crown from Sloane's head and hung it on the headboard. "Every day until the baby is born."

"One night is plenty for me." Sloane wiggled around and stretched his legs, trying to get comfortable. He sank into Loch's embrace and squeezed his hand. "Mm, besides, we have work to do."

"We do?"

"Yes. We gotta figure out where Nathaniel went. Maybe Daphne will turn up soon, and she can tell us what he's doing." Sloane yawned.

"Boring."

"We could try talking to Stoker. If he was working with the deacon on this tree deal, I bet he knows who Nathaniel is going after."

"He may be displeased with us, since I stole my statue and his underwear."

"Maybe. But those are the only leads we have right now." Sloane closed his eyes. "Mm, we gotta try."

Loch moved their hands over Sloane's belly. "Right now, we 'gotta' rest. You, me, and our beautiful spawn."

"Hmmph."

"Sleep well, my sweet mate."

"Good night, Loch. Love you."

"And I love you, my beautiful Starkiller."

CHAPTER 12.

SLOANE WOKE up to the quiet rush of the magical waterfall and a savory aroma that immediately made his stomach rumble. Loch wasn't in bed, but he was still close, judging by the tentacles petting Sloane's hair.

"Good morning, sweet mate," Loch said. "How did you sleep?"

"Mm, good." Sloane opened his eyes groggily. His back distantly throbbed and he was a bit nauseated, but overall not too bad. "Did you sleep?"

"No. I watched you rest for a while, and then I went to make you breakfast. Now I am back. With breakfast. That I made."

Sloane smiled at Loch's obvious excitement. "What is it? Smells good."

Loch's tentacles pulled a tray from behind his back and proudly presented Sloane with a puffy pastry in a big ramekin. "I have made you a cheese soufflé! I have conquered this culinary mountain with no magic, and—"

The top of the puffy soufflé began to sink and then completely deflated.

Loch's eyes turned jet black, and his tentacles trembled. He lifted the entire tray as if he was going to throw it.

"Hey, hey, what's wrong?" Sloane grunted, sitting up. He rubbed the sleep out of his eyes and tried to wake up.

There was a dull throb between his legs, but he ignored it. He'd just woken up after all, and he had to deal with an angry god who looked like he was ready to go full dragon and torch a soufflé.

"It *collapsed*!" Loch wailed.

"Hey, it's okay!"

"No, it is not!" Loch's mortal body collapsed onto the ground, and his true godly form appeared. He was a giant horned dragon with a long neck, slick skin, and bulging muscles all over. Though his arms were small, his tentacled tail and twisted hind legs were especially thick.

His wings, however, were by far the most impressive feature.

They were massive, clawed with awesome talons, and their thin webbing shimmered like a jewel. Each glittered fantastically as Loch flapped them in frustration, his long tail whipping around and smacking the tray into the air.

It flew up so high that Sloane couldn't even see it, now lost in the twinkling sky above them.

"I made sure there were no egg yolks in the mix. I separated them all perfectly!" Loch continued to rage with his great wings flapping. "I jiggled the dish as instructed to ensure proper form before removing them from the oven!"

Sloane watched, totally enraptured. Seeing Loch so enraged and powerful was doing nothing to dissuade his hard dick. In fact, it was doing quite the opposite.

"I even placed the dishes on a cookie sheet to ensure a smooth transition when it was time to remove them!" Loch turned his head up as the tray and ramekin came flying back down. He roared, spraying out a blast of prismatic fire that reduced it all to smithereens.

Sloane's hand went right to his hard cock, and he pulled the sheets out of his way. He didn't even think twice about his belly or how sore he was. The very sound of Loch's ferocious roar made him shudder in his very core, and he scooted clumsily to the edge of the bed.

Loch was stomping on the burned remnants of the soufflé, and he gave it another blast of fire before he seemed satisfied. He sat on his haunches and huffed.

"Loch," Sloane said. "Come here."

"I wanted to make you moan." Loch pouted, his wings folding back as his shoulders drooped. "It is all I wanted. I'm sorry my meager culinary skills have failed again."

"Well." Sloane licked his lips. "I know another way you can make me moan."

"I will make the soufflé again. I will make it right this time, and I will not set it on fire."

"Loch."

"Perhaps some of the yolk did make its way into the mix.... It could be a much more nefarious substance than I first thought."

"Azaethoth!"

"What?" Loch finally turned to look at Sloane, naked on the bed. "Oh." He visibly shivered, all the way down to the tip of his tail. "What do you need, my love?"

"Fuck me. Right now."

Loch bolted right over, still in his big dragon body and looming over Sloane.

The speed at which Loch moved startled Sloane, and he scrambled back on the bed. He reached up to touch Loch's long neck and then stroke the smooth skin there. "Come on. Please. Now."

"You... you wish to mate with me like this?" Loch tilted his head.

"Yes," Sloane whispered. He was so empty, his cock was hard to the point that it was pounding, and he had never wanted anything so much.

Dragon monster with tentacles or smoking hot redhead, Loch was his mate, his husband, and the father of his child. Sloane didn't care how they made love.

He wanted him.

Badly.

"I will need to adjust my size." Loch immediately shrunk, now less than half his original mass. He still towered over Sloane quite a bit, but he was much more manageable. "All of my reproductive organs will scale to an appropriate girth, though they may still be... large."

"You've done this before, right?" Sloane scratched his nails down Loch's chest. "Like this?"

"Yes, many times." Loch shifted and bowed his head, his snout nudging Sloane's legs apart. "You're still the only person to enjoy that one particular part of my anatomy, but yes, we can mate like this. I will be so gentle, my love."

"Just come on." Sloane shoved Loch's head down insistently. "Whatever you're gonna do, just go ahead and—oh!" The tip of Loch's long tongue pushed inside his hole. "Ah, fuck!"

Loch chuckled low, his front claws kneading the mattress as he licked and thrusted his tongue into Sloane's ass. The tentacles of his tail swung around to curl around Sloane's thighs and keep them spread wide. "Oh, how I've missed the taste of you...."

One of Loch's slitted tentacles slipped out from somewhere, unfurling as it snaked its way up to suck Sloane's cock. Though it frustrated Sloane that he couldn't see anything because of his belly, he closed his eyes and gave himself over to the incredible sensations.

The tentacle sucking his cock was amazing as always, but wow—Loch's tongue like this was new and thrilling. It was bigger than a human man's cock would be and infinitely more dexterous. He could feel it curling inside of him, twirling around his prostate with flawless precision.

It was thick, wet, and was stretching him open inch by tantalizing inch. Loch's magic ensured there was never any pain, only the intense feeling of being opened up and filled. His hot breath was an added thrill, and Sloane could smell the ever-present aroma of mint as Loch growled.

"Ah, f-fuck, mmm! So close!" Sloane rolled his hips, grinding on Loch's tongue eagerly. The little tentacles on Loch's chin were probing around his slick hole now, and he moaned as one wiggled inside of him. The urge to come was burning deep within, and he was certain he was going to lose his mind if he didn't bust soon.

Sloane was hot, his skin buzzing, and he didn't think he had been this pent-up since he was a damn teenager. He couldn't be bothered to worry about if this was weird or not. He was making love to a god—an immortal being of unimaginable power, beautiful and strong, with wings that shone like diamonds and tentacles that went on and on and encircled every inch of his tiny mortal body.

There was an excited tingle in his lips as his neck and face flushed, and he pushed down on Loch's tongue with a loud cry. The tentacles around his arms were keeping his upper body pinned, and he loved the wicked thrill of struggling against them. He wanted more of it, so much more.

Loch's touch was slippery, firm, and there, it kept hitting that same spot, mmm, right there, there was so good, it was—*yes*! Fuck!

Sloane threw his head back, groaning as he came in the tight tentacle wrapped around his cock, thrusting up into it with a needy whine. Loch's tongue curled inside him, dragging out the ecstasy of every searing pulse. The pleasure sated Sloane but for a moment, and the desire for another orgasm was already winding up again.

It really hadn't been that long since they'd been intimate, but Sloane was totally ravenous for physical affection. And horny. Fuck, he was so damn horny that getting off again was his only focus. He knew Loch could go all night and then some, and he was ready to fuck until he couldn't move.

Loch withdrew his long tongue and licked over Sloane's hole with a soft purr. He nuzzled Sloane's big belly as he made his way up Sloane's body between his legs. Loch's tentacle remained attached to Sloane's cock, its suction gentle and pulsing now. "You should roll over on your hands and knees... it will be much more comfortable."

"Yeah?" Sloane petted Loch's snout, dragging his fingers through the long tentacles hanging from his chin. "Mm, I might need a little help—"

He'd barely spoken before Loch's strong arms and tentacles had embraced him and gingerly flipped him over.

"Yeah, this works," Sloane breathed, arching his ass back with a happy sigh. Being on his hands and knees took a lot of pressure off his hips, and he didn't have to deal with staring at his belly.

Loch was right on top of him, his warm body pressing against Sloane's back as he grinded against his ass. One of his clawed hands slid over Sloane's hip, and he licked the side of his neck. "I'm going to leave you quivering, my sweet mate."

"Bring it on." Sloane gasped when something thick and hot bumped his asshole. He didn't have to see to know exactly what it was.

The tentacock.

Loch's claws dug into Sloane's skin as he slowly pushed the fat head of his massive tentacock in. "Mmm, there you go, love... yes... open up for me... I will give you such pleasure."

Sloane panted, frantic and loud, willing himself to relax as Loch's tentacle breached him. There was a flash of pain, but it was quickly swallowed up by the bliss of being absolutely stuffed. Loch definitely felt bigger now, and the prick of his claws was new, exciting, and Sloane shuddered.

"Ah.... Azaethoth...."

It didn't feel right to call him by any other name, not when he was like this.

Sloane was being mounted by a god, and all he could do was moan and take every incredible inch being driven into him. The lazy thrusting was driving him crazy, and Loch was hitting nerve endings inside of him that he didn't even know he had, his skin lit up with little goose bumps.

Sloane had to see, and he turned his head to watch Loch fucking him. He admired the flexing muscles of Loch's thick thighs as he pounded his ass, and the flap of his glittering wings as he really got going was especially beautiful.

Deeper and deeper Loch went, pushing in and out until his knot was bumping against Sloane's ass. He rested his head on Sloane's shoulder, his hot breath tickling Sloane's ear as he growled. "You feel so good, my sweet mate... my husband... mmm, I can't wait to knot you...."

"Yes," Sloane gasped. "Please. Give it to me. Come on, baby. I wanna come, I wanna fuckin' come!"

"Oh, and you shall," Loch promised, his hips slamming forward with more intent. His claws and tentacles held Sloane right where he wanted him, as he fucked him harder and faster. "Many, many times!"

Sloane gritted his teeth, his body awash in intense sensation as the fat knot popped inside. His thighs shook, and he had to drop onto his elbows as he screamed.

He was coming, hard and fast, and he moaned as Loch's tentacles coiled tightly around his legs. Loch was lifting him right off the bed, fucking him ruthlessly. Sloane couldn't believe the angles Loch was hitting like this, and he was totally helpless in the embrace of so many tentacles.

His orgasm wasn't stopping, and his cock was still pulsing even as it went soft. The bliss was coming in waves, leaving him shaking down to his bones. Loch's come dripping between his thighs only added to the intense pleasure, and he was achingly full.

Sloane lost count of how many times Loch filled him, his knot swelling over and over again until all Sloane could do was sob. His mouth was dry, and he cried out as his cock gave one final squirt.

"Mmmm, Sloane," Loch murmured, all of his tentacles squeezing around him like a hug. "You are magnificent."

"Oh, Azaethoth," Sloane whispered, blinking away the tears clouding his eyes. "By all the gods, I love you."

"And I love you, my beautiful mate." Loch sighed contentedly, and he licked Sloane's cheek. "With all that I am."

"Big fuckin' ditto."

Loch's sharp claws seamlessly morphed into strong human hands, gently laying Sloane back on the bed on his side. His tentacock was still buried inside of Sloane, but he had assumed his mortal body once more.

Cuddling up behind Sloane, Loch smooched his shoulder. "Do you require any additional physical pleasure, my love?"

"Mmm, gimme a minute." Sloane's thighs were still shaking, and he was nearly exhausted. His muscles were shivery and tired, and he clenched down on Loch's tentacock to earn himself another intense shudder. "Fuck."

"Are you all right? Was it too much?" Loch sounded worried. "I'd not thought to offer my true form to you before. I didn't know if we were... hmm. What's the word? Kinky! Yes, I didn't know if we were that kinky."

"Don't worry. We definitely are." Sloane laughed, and he touched his stomach. "Oh shit." He stroked more worriedly. He'd been so desperate to get laid that he'd actually forgotten his very obvious condition. "The baby! Do you think we hurt the baby?"

"No, my love." Loch put his hand over Sloane's and shook his head. "They're absolutely fine."

Sloane could hear the sweet thumping heartbeat of their child, and he let out a relieved sigh. "I'm sorry. Wow. I don't know what got into me."

"I did," Loch said gleefully. "And I will again, as many times as you'd like."

"Which is very appreciated, and I may take you up on it, but... mmm...." Sloane ducked his head, inhaling sharply as Loch pulled out of him. "All I could think about was, well, getting some of your godly goods."

"It is a good look on you. I enjoyed it very much."

"I enjoyed it too." Sloane closed his eyes and kept listening to their baby's heartbeat. There was a fluttery little kick, and he gasped. "Ha! Did you feel that?"

"Yes!" Loch eagerly wrapped a flurry of tentacles over Sloane's belly. "Finally! You devilish little spawn! I am being allowed to feel your prenatal aerobics!"

The baby twisted and kicked, maybe even punched, and Sloane knew he would never recover from the weirdness of having another being moving inside of him like this. He loved how Loch cooed and fawned over his belly, and there was a warmth bubbling inside Sloane's chest that rivaled the passionate heat they'd shared mere moments ago.

He turned his head to look at Loch, and he smiled when he saw his eyes were full of stars. "It's amazing, isn't it?"

"Truly," Loch agreed. "That is our little one. Our baby. Right there."

"Uh-huh."

"Would it be inappropriate of me to mate with you now?" Loch leaned in for a kiss. "I want... mm... I am filled with such joy, and I want to be inside of you, my love."

"I think that would be okay." Sloane grinned. "I know I was kinda freaked out about my body and how I looked and all that, but right now... wow." He grinned. "When you look at me like that, I don't really care."

"Like you are the most beautiful creature in all of creation and my every thought is consumed with filling your tight bodily chasms with my thick seed?"

"Yeah. Just like that." Sloane kissed him, reaching back to slide his hand through his curls. He could feel one of Loch's slitted tentacles slithering back between his legs, and he arched expectantly into the—ow!

Sloane jerked in pain.

"My love?" Loch frowned.

"I'm okay." Sloane held his stomach, breathing through a particularly sharp cramp. "I'm, I'm not sure what that was, but…." He took a deep breath and tried to will the feeling to pass. "Shit."

"Should I get Mother?" Loch was sitting up now, and he held Sloane close. "What is wrong?"

"Cramps." Sloane grimaced. It was similar to gas pains, very uncomfortable, and he had no idea what was happening to him. "Fuck. I think it's okay. I don't know exactly if this is normal or bad or… ah *fuck*!"

One final shooting pain rocked his abdomen, and then….

The baby was gone.

Wait, his *entire* bulging belly was gone.

"Loch?" Sloane frantically patted his magically flat stomach. He was empty and terrified, looking all around in a panic. "The baby! Wait! Where is our baby?"

"I don't know, my sweet mate!" Loch tried to soothe him. "Calm down—"

"Don't you tell me to fucking calm down! Our fucking unborn baby vanished, and—" Sloane gasped as *something* dropped into his lap, and he swore he heard a faint giggle.

It was a sac, dark purple in color and shimmering like the inside of a geode. It was rubbery but firm, long and tubular, and it filled Sloane's arms. He knew immediately it was their child, and he cradled it against his chest.

"For the love of all the gods!" Sloane rocked it back and forth, smothering it with kisses. "What the fuck? Like, seriously! What the fucking fuck just happened?"

"It's our little one," Loch whispered, quickly wrapping both the child and Sloane in a big hug with his arms and tentacles. "They are almost ready to be born!"

"Wait, I did it?" Sloane blinked in shock. "I laid the egg? That's it? Some stupid little cramps?"

"Mother did say the discomfort would be very minimal," Loch reminded him. "Congratulations, my sweet mate! It's a...! Hmm, well. It's an egg."

"We have an egg." Sloane cuddled it close and instinctively reached for the bedsheets to wrap it up. "What do we do now? We wait for it to hatch?"

"Exactly so, my sweet mate." Loch petted the egg adoringly. "It will be very soon, I should think."

Sloane strangely missed his big belly, but he found it was much easier to move now. He did his best to properly swaddle the egg, and he was grateful for Loch's magic to clean them up and put them in fresh pajamas.

"Do you think it was the sex?"

"Huh?" Loch cocked his head.

"That made the baby come out!" Sloane frowned, fussing over the swaddled egg in his arms. "I mean, I heard that having sex could start labor. I didn't really think it could jumpstart me laying an egg, though."

"Perhaps. We could ask Mother. If we describe the position we were in and how I was inside of you, she might be able to—"

"Nope. On second thought, I'm totally good."

"As you wish."

"Should we take her to the nursery? Is it going to be, well, messy when she hatches?"

"Not too much, I would think." Loch grinned. "You said 'her.'"

"I did?" Sloane hadn't even realized. "I guess it just kinda slipped out."

"We shall soon see if you are right."

"Wow." Sloane let out a long sigh. The aches in his body were fading, and his stomach was back to normal. He should have been happy he wasn't carrying around their spawn now, but he found that he missed it already.

"What is it?" Loch nuzzled Sloane's cheek. "You have that funny wrinkle in your brow."

"I was just thinking... I was really eager to get her or still possibly him out of me, but I kinda wish they were still hanging around in there." Sloane smiled sheepishly. "I know it's silly, but—" A jolt of pain seized his head. "Oh fuck! What now?"

"My beautiful Starkiller?" Loch held him tightly. "What is happening?"

The pain increased until Sloane thought he might puke, and he couldn't muster out a single word. His head was throbbing miserably, and he could hear a voice screaming at him, but it was from very far away.

Mr. Beaumont! Help! I found my brother!

"Daphne," he hissed. "It's Daphne!"

Help! I found my brother.... Daphne's voice was getting weaker, and it was more difficult to hear her... *being held... he did it... he killed the deacon... he did it... he killed the ... he's gonna kill us too... if we won't... if we won't... if we won't....*

"She found Nate," Sloane quickly said, unsure if Loch could hear her or not. "Being held by someone, it's whoever killed the deacon. Says he's gonna kill them both." He waited, hoping for more, but then only silence followed. "Shit!"

"That was it?" Loch scowled.

"She sounded like she was yelling at me across a football field. I couldn't make out everything she was saying, but she definitely said that she and Nathaniel are in danger."

"Mmm... so this would be a bad time to ask if you're still interested in the additional mating?"

Sloane glared.

"Right. Bad. Got it."

CHAPTER 13.

"So, I just had my egg, and Daphne Ware tried to telepathically contact me to tell me where her and her brother are being held prisoner," Sloane said urgently. "She said this person is going to kill her and Nate, so if we want to save them, we have to figure out who the killer is."

"Well, uh, congrats on your egg," Chase replied through the phone, "but we ain't got a fuckin' clue who killed the deacon. We were pretty damn sure it was Nathaniel!"

"I know." Sloane gently laid the egg in the crib, trying again to swaddle it properly in the blanket of starlight Galgareth had given them. "With their teleporting abilities, it's kinda hard to imagine either one of them being trapped anywhere."

"We'll keep an eye out. Heading over to have a little chat with our buddy Stoker. He was hiding Nathaniel all this damn time… maybe he knows who killed the deacon too."

"Good luck." Sloane grimaced.

"Oh!" Urilith came bounding into the nursery, so excited that at least a dozen tentacles popped out to wrap around the crib as she cooed at the egg. "Little one, look at you! Aww, you're so very beautiful!"

Loch was right behind her, and he walked over to Sloane's side to nuzzle his cheek. "My mate did wonderfully. He was only slightly panicked."

Sloane took Loch's hand, still addressing Chase on the phone as he said, "If you get anything from him, please give us a call."

"Will do," Chase said. "Later."

"Bye." Sloane hung up and sighed.

"Anything?" Loch asked.

"No. They're just as lost as we are. They're gonna go try and talk to Stoker, see if maybe Nathaniel told him anything that might help us. Ugh." Sloane rubbed his forehead. "Lemme think."

"Congratulations on laying your first egg!" Urilith declared, one of her tentacles patting Sloane's arm.

"Thank you." Sloane stroked the egg. In spite of the danger he knew Daphne and Nathaniel were in, he allowed himself to enjoy this moment. "It happened so quickly, it was all over before I even realized what was happening."

Urilith smirked.

"You were right." Sloane chuckled. "I will never doubt the gods again, especially my mother-in-law."

"Most wise." Loch's tentacles crept forward to join his mother's, and one or two went inside the crib to pet the egg. "Our little spawn... right here. It is truly magical. And ah! I finally got to feel it move while it was still gestating inside Sloane!"

"Aw, how wonderful!" Urilith smiled sweetly. "I'm very happy for you both. It should hatch soon. Oh, I can't wait to hold them in my arms!"

"Me too." Sloane's heart clenched. He could only imagine how excited his parents would have been to meet their grandchild. Sure, the godly impregnation would have been a bit weird to explain, but he was sure they would have been happy for him.

Loch hugged Sloane, sighing contentedly. "Oh, my sweet mate. This is wonderful."

"It really is." Sloane rubbed Loch's forearm. "Now if we could just crack this damn case. I'm worried about Daphne and her brother."

Galgareth came in then, and she charged right over to the crib to gush over the egg. "Oh! Look at them! They're so little and adorable and agh! The cuteness is killing me!"

"Perhaps you should step away?" Urilith frowned.

"She doesn't mean literally," Loch said.

"Ah."

Loch's tentacle slithered over to retrieve his ancient toy rattle, giving it a little shake before tucking it into the crib. He also grabbed another blanket, a plush octopus, and a shiny gold necklace.

"What are you doing?" Sloane asked. "I don't think they need all that quite yet."

"I want to be ready." Loch sniffed.

Sloane smiled, and he wished he could enjoy this more. He couldn't help it. He was worried about Daphne and Nathaniel. He toyed with the plush octopus's arm, and then he reached for the necklace. There was a Lucian crest dangling from it, encrusted with jewels.

"Loch, where did this come from?"

"I wanted to show our little one the awesome spoils of being the god of thieves. The naming of a little god or goddess is a very special rite, and I wanted to provide adequate inspiration. I know it is some years away, but—"

"Okay, wait. They'll have two namings?"

"Of course." Loch snorted. "You really didn't think my uncle was called 'the Untouched' from the moment he was born, did you?"

"Right. Okay, we will revisit all that later because I don't want our child's first impulse to be seeking out a life of crime—"

"Ah! It's only a crime if they get caught!"

"—so *please* tell me. Right now." Sloane shook the necklace. "Where did you get this?"

"Oh that. I stole it."

"From the deacon's house?"

"No." Loch fidgeted. "Technically I stole it while we were there, but I did not take it from the house itself."

Sloane sighed. "You stole it from Hugh, didn't you?"

"Maybe."

"You did." Sloane looked over the fancy necklace with a frown. "But why did he...."

It didn't seem like something such a low-ranking member of the church would own, especially one who had been recently fired and supposedly had to squat at a dead man's house because he had nowhere else to go.

Maybe Hugh had taken it. He was most likely the one trying to steal that knife from under the deacon's bed.

No, well, the necklace could have been a gift.

But maybe....

"The crest!" Sloane exclaimed. "That's it!"

"Of course it is!" Loch looked very pleased, but then he frowned. "Wait, what is it exactly?"

"Hugh was telling everyone how the deacon died with his crest in his hand," Sloane replied excitedly. "Don't you see?"

"No."

"Nathaniel told his sister that he put the crest in the deacon's pocket because it fell when he moved the body. That's why his fingerprints are on it."

"Still not following."

"If Hugh says the crest was in the deacon's hand when he died, it's because he put it there. He said he found him lying facedown, remember? How did Hugh know where the crest was?"

"X-ray vision?"

"No. He lied." Sloane grinned triumphantly. "Or should I say, he told us the truth."

Loch shrugged at his equally confused family. "He's very cute when he gets like this, but I have no idea what he's on about."

"The day we went over there to get the cat!" Sloane groaned. "Hugh told us the deacon died with the crest in his hand. Which was totally true according to the spell I cast... because that's where it was when Hugh killed him."

"I get it now!" Galgareth exclaimed. "If Hugh had found the deacon after Nathaniel ran out of the house like he said he did, the body should have been on its back and no crest in sight."

"Ah, but since he says he found him facedown with the crest in his hand, we know he is actually lying, murdering scum who possibly has x-ray vision." Loch nodded wisely.

"Get off the x-ray vision thing." Sloane smirked. "It's thin, but I think this is more than enough of a reason to go visit Hugh." He took a deep breath and patted his stomach.

Right, wait. No baby.

He approached the crib and gave the egg a kiss. "You be a good little spawn while your daddies are gone. We have to kick some butt." He smiled at Urilith and Galgareth. "I guess I should ask first, but—"

"Go!" Urilith urged. "We will take care of the little one while you unfork this mystery."

"Unravel, Mother," Galgareth gently corrected.

"That as well."

"Here!" Galgareth bopped Sloane and Loch with a tentacle. "A quick blessing of my serendipity. Happy accidents, right? Here's hoping it helps!"

"Thank you," Sloane said. "We'll be back as soon as we can."

"Take care, little spawn," Loch cooed, leaning down to hug the egg and kiss it. He reached for Sloane's hand. "I am informing Uncle Gordoth of our discovery and telling them to join us as soon as possible. There is no time to waste."

"I'm ready." Sloane squeezed Loch's hand. "Let's go. I hope it's not too late."

"We shall save the day, my sweet husband. We always do."

The world shifted around them, and they were standing right in front of the deacon's front door. Right away, Sloane could hear screaming, but it wasn't only the high-pitched wail of terror that was so alarming.

The scream kept starting and stopping, as if it was caught on a loop.

"What the fuck?" Sloane hissed. "Come on, let's go!"

Loch shattered the door with a thought, and he raced inside the house with Sloane right behind him. Sloane summoned a shield of starlight, his heart pounding. He had no idea what to expect, and nothing could have prepared him for what they walked into.

Hugh had Daphne on the floor in the living room with a rope around her neck and a giant knife poised over her chest. She was in her Absola form, and so was Nathaniel, currently bound to the sofa by some kind of magic.

Just as the knife sunk into Daphne's chest and the life left her eyes, the image of her and Hugh flickered and replayed like a scene skipping on a movie. It happened every few seconds while Nathaniel screamed repeatedly, and Daphne continued to die right before their eyes on a loop.

Time, Sloane realized. Nathaniel was resetting time over and over again to keep Daphne alive. The area of effect for the spell appeared to be limited to only Nathaniel, Daphne, and Hugh since Sloane and Loch were still moving at normal speeds.

"Loch!" Sloane shouted. "Go get Daphne!" He bolted forward, swinging his shield back right as the loop started again and cracked Hugh right in the face.

Hugh teetered backward, blood dribbling over his lips from a busted nose. "Agh! You fools!"

"I've got her!" Loch swept in to grab Daphne before she could hit the ground, and the rope around her neck vanished.

She wheezed weakly, limp in his arms but alive.

"Daphne!" Nathaniel shouted as he continued to struggle to free himself.

"You fiends!" Hugh waved the knife, and he snarled, baring his bloodstained teeth. "You have no idea what power I have awakened! This blade has been blessed by the Lord of Light himself, and it only took but one taste of corruption to awaken him! He will be here to reveal himself in all of his holy light!"

The very tip of the blade had managed to pierce Daphne's skin, and Sloane could see a faint glimmer of blood.

"You're all about to be incinerated by his holy fires!" Hugh screamed, holding the knife above his head. "Heathens, all of you! Abominations in the eyes of the Lord of Light! He will come, judge your worthless flesh, and burn you into ash!"

Sloane watched the knife, and his heart pounded with dread. He'd never heard of any Lucian artifact having such power, but he didn't put down his starlight shield. "Hugh, stop this! Now! Before anyone else gets hurt!"

"No!" Hugh wailed, swinging the blade around wildly. "The Lord of Light is coming! I've given him the sacrifice of blood that the blade requires! Yes! He is coming! I can feel it! When I killed the deacon, my path was made clear!"

"Oh! No!" Loch suddenly gasped, and he clutched at his chest. He almost dropped Daphne as he panted haggardly, wheezing in agony. "I can feel it! It's… it's burning me! My skin is on fire! What magic is this?"

"Loch?" Sloane's stomach twisted, and he rushed toward Loch. "What's wrong?"

"Stay back, my sweet love!" Loch squeezed his eyes closed. "This fire, this horrible burning… it might… it might be contagious! I must have caught it from touching Miss Ware!"

"Feel the wrath of the Lord of Light, you heathen scum!" Hugh screamed triumphantly. "Yes! I can feel his power flowing through me! All of you are going to suffer the consequences of your unjust lives! All of you will cower before his greatness!"

"Loch!" Sloane screamed, immediately in a panic. He couldn't believe this was happening, and he didn't know what to do. He was terrified to see Loch in such pain, and he racked his brain trying to come up with a spell to combat this strange holy fire—wait, why was Loch smiling?

Not just smiling, no, now Loch was *cackling*.

"Whew!" Loch kept on laughing, clearly struggling to catch his breath. "Oh, the looks on your faces!"

"No, no!" Hugh shook the knife angrily. "Why isn't it working?"

"Because the Lord of Light isn't real, you silly man!" Loch laughed so hard he almost choked. "Ah! Can't breathe!"

"You deserve that, Loch, you jerk!" Sloane's temper flared. His annoyance with Loch was interrupted by Hugh swinging the knife at Nathaniel, trapped on the couch.

"No! No! It has to work!" Hugh was hysterical. "I must need more blood! More corrupted blood!"

"Fuck! No!" Nathaniel screamed.

Sloane swung his shield of starlight as hard as he could, smacking Hugh in the back of the head and sending him to the floor. The knife clattered away, Hugh didn't move, and Sloane kicked Loch in the side repeatedly. "Oh, I'm so freakin' mad at you right now!"

Loch cleared his throat, still laughing as he teased, "But aren't you really glad that I'm all right?"

"I'm too pissed off at you to think!" Sloane stomped over to Nathaniel and kneeled beside him. "Hey, are you okay?"

"Fuck me! What about Daphne? Is she okay?" Nathaniel groaned. He was clearly exhausted, and his greenish skin was sweating and pale. "I've been trying to save her for hours!"

"She is all right," Loch promised, being quite sincere for once.

Sloane could sense the power still holding Nathaniel immobile and felt for the edges so he could break it. "You kept resetting time like you did with Ziol, right?"

"Yeah." Nathaniel nodded. "She said she tried to reach out to you, but I didn't... I didn't know if you heard her or if you would actually come for us. Hugh used this ward to trap us, and then he stripped our glamour. He kept on ranting and raving about what fuckin' abominations we were and how he was going to cleanse us with that stupid knife!"

"Typical." Loch rolled his eyes and laid Daphne on the floor with one of the cushions from the sofa.

Having found the edges of the ward, Sloane twisted his fingers and focused on breaking it. "Yeah? Lemme guess. He had to kill you to purge the earth of your evil and all that?"

"He said the Lord of Light would appear and bless him if the blade tasted our corruption," Nathaniel said bitterly. "He's been trying to break it out of this magical safe here at the house—"

"See? I told you I should have stolen it!" Loch chimed in.

Sloane looked over at the knife, and he recognized it as the very same bone-handled one he had made Loch return. "This is why Hugh was staying here at the house? To get that knife?"

"Yeah. After killing the deacon, he thought it was his fuckin' mission to take it and start purging more evil or whatever from the world." Nathaniel sighed miserably. "Fuck. I should have known this was going to happen."

"Look, this isn't your fault," Sloane began.

"But it is," Loch interjected. "Had he gone ahead and told us the true identity of the deacon's murderer, he may not have had to spend the last few hours exhausting himself manipulating time to stall his sister's demise."

"Loch!" Sloane scolded sharply.

"No, he's right." Nathaniel's shoulders sagged. "If I had told you guys the truth instead of trying to come handle this on my own, this wouldn't have happened."

Sloane flicked his wrist, and the ward broke.

Nathaniel stood from the couch, his tail swinging around as he hurried over to check on his sister.

"She is all right," Loch promised. Sloane saw a glimpse of a tentacle slithering back up Loch's sleeve. "I have healed her, but she must rest."

"You didn't...?" Sloane stared at Loch expectantly since his favorite way to heal people involved that special nectar of his.

"No." Loch turned up his nose. "We're married now. That belongs to you."

Nathaniel touched her hair, and his eyes filled with tears. "I couldn't go back far enough to stop it. I tried. All I could do was try to hang on to those precious seconds right before she died, and I could feel them slipping away every time I went back."

"Ughhh...." Hugh was up. "No, no, this cannot be. I must... purge... I must purge all of this evil...."

"You fuckin' bastard!" Nathaniel snarled, his tail flicking angrily and cracking across the floor like a whip. "The only evil thing here is you!"

Loch cleared his throat.

Hugh suddenly fell back, gurgled, and did not move.

"Archersville PD!" Chase's booming voice called out as he and Merrick came charging into the room with their weapons drawn. He looked disappointed when all the action seemed to be over, scoffing, "Really?"

"They did have a head start," Merrick pointed out.

"Only because you insist on driving instead of using you-know-what!"

Nathaniel cowered back as if he could hide his true appearance, and he stammered, "L-look, I can explain. I'm, uh, I'm… uh…."

"It is all right." Merrick put his gun away and held up his hands. "We are not here to hurt nor arrest you."

"Yeah, but uh, the backup that's on the way might not be as understanding," Chase said. "You and your sister may wanna do somethin' about—" He gestured around his face. "—all of this."

"Hugh broke our glamour charms." Nathaniel scowled. "I don't see any choice for me and my sister except to run. Unless one of you happens to know those spells…?"

"Uh… oh, here." Sloane spotted a familiar but broken watch on the floor. He knelt beside Daphne and clapped his hands, restoring the watch and the glamour spell he'd cast on it before.

As soon as he fastened it on her wrist, her human visage appeared once more.

"Quick!" Sloane said. "I need something for Nathaniel."

"My charm was a bracelet, but I don't see it anywhere!" Nathaniel began to frantically search the room.

"It doesn't actually have to be jewelry, does it?" Chase asked.

"It has to be something he can put on," Sloane replied. He tensed when he heard sirens approaching. "Shit!"

Loch lifted a single pillow on the couch and seemed to be done looking after that. "Well, I suppose it's time to run, then."

"Here!" Chase had pulled the hair tie out of his hair and handed it over to Sloane.

Merrick stared at Chase with a sort of funny expression as his long hair tumbled over his shoulders, but Sloane didn't know what it was about.

"Thanks." Sloane held the hair tie between his hands and quickly cast the spell. "I don't know how long it will hold, but it should be long enough to get through tonight."

"Thank you." Nathaniel slipped the hair tie over his wrist and morphed into a normal-looking human being.

"So, what the hell happened here?" Chase asked. "Sleeping Beauty over there killed the deacon?"

"Yes. He found out the deacon was involved with that deal," Nathaniel replied. "You know, taking the bribes to make sure the congregation left the Xenish Sprig alone so the city could plow it the hell down deal. Hugh didn't think it was right for the church to be led by someone so corrupt."

"It's a fair point," Loch noted.

"After he killed the deacon, he wanted to get his hands on that stupid knife and cleanse more corrupt people. I guess he felt like it was his new holy mission or whatever. Which, of course, includes abominations like me and my sister. He trapped us, broke our glamour, and he was gonna…." Nathaniel trailed off, looking over at his sister sadly.

"I'm guessing you already knew about the deal from Stoker?" Sloane guessed, hoping to distract him. "But you weren't totally sure it was Hugh until I mentioned him talking about the crest? Is that when you knew?"

"Yeah." Nathaniel nodded. "I was already pretty sure. He's a fuckin' creep, and the worst part is that he felt fuckin' justified doin' it. Just like trying to kill my sister. He really felt like he was doing the Lord of Light's work."

"Charming." Chase picked up the knife and nudged Hugh with his foot. "Hey, you. Shitbag. Wake up. We gotta arrest you."

"Language," Merrick scolded.

"Douchebag?"

"That is… marginally better."

Hugh gurgled again.

"Two old gods, a Starkiller, and a Chase," Loch mused. "Seems a bit like overkill for one hateful little mortal, doesn't it?"

"Gods?" Nathaniel blinked. "Did you just say…."

Sloane facepalmed.

It was that very moment the first wave of responding officers came barging in, and Sloane had never been so thankful for Galgareth's lucky blessings. Had they arrived a mere few minutes earlier, they would have had to explain Daphne and Nathaniel's unusual appearance.

Chase and Merrick took charge of the scene, arresting a still dazed Hugh and hauling him away while the rest of the cops secured the house.

Sloane flopped over on the couch to get out of the way. Even without carrying a child around, saving the day was exhausting. He smiled at Loch when he sat next to him. "So. Here we are."

"Yes." Loch beamed. "Another dastardly case cracked. I didn't solve this one, but I think it is fair that you have some of the glory occasionally."

"Mmm, that's very thoughtful of you."

"Are you all right, my sweet love?"

"I'm okay." Sloane shrugged. "Is it weird that I'm… I'm almost disappointed that it really was just one crappy guy?"

"And not one of my godly brothers?"

"Yeah." Sloane reached for Loch's hand. "I guess we've been so busy fighting gods I almost forgot how crappy mortals can be too."

"I could have told you. I would have gladly recounted the great injustices my catalogues suffered at the hands of our weepy mailman."

"Mm, an absolutely heinous crime."

"The most heinous."

Medical personnel arrived and helped Daphne while Nathaniel watched like a hawk. She was weak, but she was able to sit up with assistance. She happened to catch Sloane's eye from across the room, and she smiled.

Thank you.

Sloane waved in reply.

After getting the okay from Chase and Merrick, Nathaniel was allowed to stay with his sister while the medics checked her out, provided he answered Merrick's questions while they did so.

Loch was quick to point out she shouldn't need anything after he healed her, and Sloane patted his shoulder to console him.

"Hey." Chase came over to check on Sloane and Loch, asking, "You guys good over here?"

"Yeah. Just tired." Sloane smiled.

"I am in need of some cake," Loch replied. "I would like chocolate, but I would also accept carrot or spice cake."

"I wanna run somethin' by you, see what you think." Chase was clearly ignoring Loch's request for cake. "We know our ol' pal Hugh killed the deacon 'cause he found out he was takin' bribes and shit, right?"

"Yeah." Sloane frowned. "What is it?"

"I'm wonderin' how did Hugh find out?"

"Well." Sloane paused for a moment. "He was living here with the deacon. He could have overheard something. Seen something. Not to mention he used to work for him. Maybe that's why he got fired from the church? Snooping around, learned too much?"

"Could be, yeah." Chase scratched his beard. "Also could be I thought of somebody who has a great reason for ratting out the deacon."

"Who?"

"Stoker!"

"Huh?"

"With the deacon out of the way, he don't have to fuck with the bribes now, right? They can move ahead with this tree-plowing crap and Stoker can get fuckin' paid."

"How could he know that Hugh was gonna go crazy and kill the deacon, though?"

"Maybe he didn't. Maybe he thought Hugh would go public with it and ruin him."

"I don't know, Chase." Sloane grimaced. "It's kind of a stretch."

"The stretchy theory does have merit," Loch said. "Stoker was in a position where he could not attack the deacon directly. He would be an obvious suspect. Setting up someone else to do it alleviates him of suspicion. The method is not guaranteed, but the result remains the same."

"How is dead and not dead the same?"

"Because either way the deacon is out of the photo."

"Picture."

"Picture what?"

"Okay, strong maybe." Sloane leaned back and sighed. "I don't trust Stoker any more than you guys do, and yes, I agree that it's possible... but."

"But what?" Chase scoffed.

"But you're gonna have a hell of a time proving it." Sloane shrugged. "Good luck."

"That's it? Come on!"

"I'm not a cop anymore, Chase." Sloane smirked. "I did what I was hired to do, which was help find Nathaniel. My part in all this is over. If you guys would like to hire me, I'll be sure to give you a good discount."

"We have coupons," Loch said cheerfully,

"No, we don't."

"Okay, we will *get* coupons."

"Fine, fine." Chase snorted. "I get it. World's not ending, you ain't gettin' involved, huh?"

"Something like that." Sloane chuckled. "You know, it might be worth looking at the wards Hugh used to trap Daphne and Nathaniel. They were pretty powerful. And well, Stoker maybe used something similar on me and Loch when we first met him."

"Think Stoker was goin' around teachin' Lucian creeps magic?"

"I think you wanted a connection to look into." Sloane grinned. "There you go!"

"That will be nineteen ninety-five," Loch said.

"Check's in the mail," Chase promised.

"Then it shall arrive shortly... though there is a risk of wrinkling."

"Thank you, guys. Seriously." Chase took off his hat and ran a hand through his hair. "Now if we could only get those protests around the damn tree to stop, this would be a really super week."

"I wouldn't be surprised if that tree suddenly isn't a problem soon," Sloane mused.

"What do you mean?"

"If you're right about Stoker trying to eliminate anything stopping him from getting paid for that land, the only thing left is that tree. No more tree, no more reason to protest, right?"

"Mmm, my ears are burning," a familiar voice purred.

Sloane turned to see—who else—Sullivan Stoker walking in.

Gone was the dingy Velvet Plank T-shirt and jeans, and in its place was a dark three-piece suit perfectly tailored to his broad frame. He looked sharp, dangerous, and....

Okay. Maybe a *tiny* bit attractive.

"Why is your mouth open?" Loch complained.

Sloane quickly clicked his teeth together and cleared his throat. "Stoker."

"Hey! We were lookin' for you! What are you doing here?" Chase demanded. "This is a closed crime scene! Who let you in?"

"Your officers did," Stoker said as he strolled up to them. "I was coming by to return a book I'd borrowed from the deacon before his unfortunate passing." He smiled. "They were very accommodating once I explained the situation."

"I bet." Chase grimaced. "Let me guess. You just happened to be in the neighborhood when you had this overwhelming urge to return a book to a dead man?"

"Spot-on detective work."

"Where's the fuckin' book, huh?"

"It's the funniest thing. I seem to have forgotten it."

"Why are you here?" Sloane asked. "Really?"

"Maybe I just wanted to see you again, Mr. Beaumont," Stoker replied coyly.

"Oh yeah? And how would you know I was here, huh?"

"Magic." Stoker winked.

"Braiding is magical," Loch hissed hatefully.

"Ah, I'd almost forgotten you were here. Hello there, my thieving friend." Stoker smiled at him. It was not a very nice smile. "You think you're very clever, don't you?"

Stoker was naturally referring to the recent theft of the Azaethoth statue and his underwear.

"I know I am." Loch scoffed, as if this was obvious.

"How did you get through my personal wards?"

"Because you might as well have written them in crayon. Because that's what children use to write things. Crayons."

"I'm surprised you could even read them."

"Oh, you are about to feel wrath of a godly nature—"

"Stoker," Sloane cut in. "Seriously. What are you doing here?"

Stoker glanced at Chase. "My apologies if I'm not comfortable speaking candidly."

Sloane gave Chase an imploring look.

"Fine. Okay, speak whatever way you want, Stoker." Chase made a face. "Off the record."

"How kind of you, Detective." Stoker looked back at Sloane. "Off the record, I was worried about Nathaniel and his sister. I had my suspicions about Hugh, and I followed my gut. Imagine my surprise when I found myself not only at the deacon's house, but also as the current topic of conversation."

"Off the record, I think you had somethin' to fuckin' do with this." Chase scowled. "I can't prove shit, but my gut is tellin' me you're involved."

"Are you sure it's not telling you to have another donut, Detective?"

"Watch it, smartass." Chase grinned. "I'm just lookin' for a reason to drag you downtown."

"You really came down here to check on Nathaniel?" Sloane asked, eager to defuse the rising tempers. "That's almost nice of you."

"I'm very nice when I want to be." There was a twinkle in Stoker's eye, as if he wanted to say something else, probably flirt again, but he only said, "But yes, that's why I'm here. Also to offer my sincere gratitude."

"For what?"

"I spoke to Nathaniel outside. You saved him and his sister. Thank you."

"You're welcome."

"That'll be one thousand nineteen dollars and ninety-five cents," Loch chimed in.

"No," Stoker said flatly.

"You will receive a bill."

Stoker ignored him and addressed Chase. "I assume that any statements Hugh makes about what Nathaniel and Daphne are will be kept... quiet?"

"You mean about them being Abfola abominations or whatever?" Chase asked. "Yeah, don't worry. The little hidden world of people will stay nice and hidden. Even if Hugh's testimony does get out, nobody will believe him."

"I hope not." Stoker clapped. "Well, since I was so silly and forgot that book, I suppose there's no reason for me to linger. I'm going to check in with Nathaniel and his sister again, and then I'll be on my way."

"Oh, I've got plenty of reasons for you to linger," Chase cooed. "Like this lil' theory I'm working on about you and our buddy Hugh."

"And I'm sure my lawyer would love to hear it. Please give them a call, Detective." Stoker bowed his head politely to Sloane. "Mr. Beaumont." His upper lip twitched. "Azaethoth."

"Enjoy your gender-neutral cat," Loch said with syrupy sweetness.

"Goodbye, Stoker." Sloane waved.

Stoker turned to leave, but he paused and sighed loudly. "Return them. At once."

Loch snickered.

With a shake of his head, Stoker left.

"What did you do?" Sloane accused.

"Me?" Loch batted his eyes.

"Yeah." Chase frowned suspiciously. "What did you do, Loch?"

"I may have stolen his underwear again."

Chase cackled. "Oh fuck."

"But you gave them back, right?" Sloane tried not to smile too hard.

"I gave him underwear, yes." Loch smiled.

"Wait. You gave him back *his* underwear, didn't you?"

"That's not what I said." Loch's smile grew.

"Oh, Loch." Sloane tried not to laugh. "What did you do?"

"I gave him mine."

"I love you."

"And I love you, my beloved mate."

"Damn, I wish I could do that kinda shit." Chase snorted. "Next time, give him a pair of mine after I've been on a stakeout for twelve hours."

Loch nodded. "That can be arranged."

"No, none of that." Sloane chuckled. "We're going to behave. Don't poke the bear."

"I am still uncertain of what he is, but I am confident he is not a bear. I would have noticed."

"He's a fuckin' criminal, and one of these days I'm gonna catch his slick little ass," Chase said grumpily. "God or Fabfola or whatever, he's going down."

"Good luck." Sloane made a face. "He's definitely not human, you know."

"Hey, neither is my partner." Chase tipped his hat. "I ain't worried."

"My love," Loch said suddenly. He seemed to be listening to something only he could hear. "It is time to go."

"Hang on," Sloane said. "I wanna go say goodbye to Nathaniel and Daphne before we leave. They haven't left yet, right?"

"Nah," Chase replied. "Merrick is still out there talkin' to them. I'm sure he's super excited Stoker is here. You know, now that you mention it, we should probably go check on 'em."

"She is fine." Loch huffed indignantly. "I healed her. Even without using the thing you don't like me sharing, she is healed beyond those medics' meager mortal skill."

"I was more thinkin' that Merrick ain't exactly a fan of Stoker's. We don't need any explosions of godly wrath, you know?"

"Gordoth the Slut does not have explosions of godly wrath. He is a patient and clever god. There would be no witnesses. Now, my love, we really must go."

"Hold on a second," Sloane griped. "Are they going to the hospital, Chase?"

"Doubtful." Chase shook his head. "After Daphne gets checked out, I think they're goin' home."

"Good," Sloane said. "I'm sure they could both use some rest. Home is probably the best thing for both of them right now."

"Yes!" Loch exclaimed. "And that is exactly where we should be going!"

"Where?"

"We must go to our home. For the thing."

"What thing?"

"The very important thing." Loch wagged his brows purposefully. "Because it is time."

"Oh!" Sloane gasped. "Baby time?"

"Yes!"

"Well, why didn't you just say so? Let's go!"

CHAPTER 14.

"Is it happening? Did we miss it?" Sloane shouted, immediately rushing over to the crib.

Loch had taken them around the back of the deacon's house so they could blink away without any witnesses, and those few moments they had to wait were excruciating.

Was the baby hatching without them? Did the baby need to see Sloane first to imprint on him like baby birds?

Wait, was that even really a thing?

"No! It's okay!" Galgareth promised. "You guys are good!"

"Close, but not yet!" Urilith rubbed Sloane's back. "The first one is always so stressful, hmm?"

The egg was still an egg, but the rubbery surface was moving and wiggling.

"Okay, okay, this is fine." Sloane took a deep breath. "Totally fine."

"Ah! Look at them go!" Loch gasped excitedly as he joined Sloane beside the crib. "They're sure to break through any moment!"

"I've already prepared everything for all of you at the Donatis Springs," Urilith said. "Now! Hurry!"

"Wait!" Sloane blinked. "We're going? Why are we—" The nursery vanished, and he was now standing back in the beautiful grotto with the very wiggly egg in his arms. "Oh!"

The bed was here as before, but now there was a crib and piles of blankets and pillows. There was also a table, but Sloane didn't pay much mind to what was cluttered on top of it.

The very wiggly egg had his full attention.

Loch was with him, and he was gently guiding him to the edge of the hot springs. "Come, my dear mate. It's almost time."

"Shit." Sloane clung to the egg, but then he was worried he was holding it too tightly. "Ah, shit. Wait, just, just take two seconds to explain to me what the hell we're doing?"

"We are here having our baby," Loch soothed. "It is important for us to bond with our child, and we will stay here, the three of us, for a little while so we will not be disturbed."

"What's going to happen now?"

"You're going to come into the water with me, and then our child is going to hatch," Loch said, leading Sloane into the pool. As they stepped into the water, their clothes transformed into breezy purple robes. "All will be well, my love. I am right here."

"We're doing this? Just the two of us?" Sloane's heart was pounding, and his nerves were fried. He wasn't sure if the egg was vibrating or if that was his hands shaking. "This is all happening way too fast, and I thought your mom was gonna be here—"

"She is a call away if we need her." Loch faced Sloane and urged him to lower the egg so it was right above the surface of the water. He wrapped his arms and tentacles all around Sloane and the egg to help hold it, and he kissed Sloane's brow.

Sloane's breathing was rapid, his pulse was skyrocketing, and he fought to calm down. It was going to be okay. Everything was okay. Loch was right here. Everything was fine.

A split appeared in the side of the egg.

"Fuck, fuck, look!" Sloane squeaked.

"It's happening!" Loch laughed. "Yes! Come along, little one! Come on!"

Another crack opened up the top of the egg, and a small foot popped out.

All of Sloane's trepidation melted away as joy washed over him. He couldn't stop smiling, staring in awe at the little foot trying to wiggle its way to freedom.

"Our baby," he whispered. "That's, that's our baby!"

The egg convulsed, several pieces shattering all at once, and the rubbery shell began to fall away. There was a faint cry, and Sloane immediately pulled the egg away. He didn't know what he was doing, not exactly, but he knew he had to get to the baby.

The shell fell away beneath Sloane's quick touch, and there they were, a beautiful and bright-eyed baby with little red curls. A little girl, Sloane saw, and he immediately picked her up, cradling her against his bare chest. "Oh! Hi! Hello there!"

"Hello, my spawn!" Loch wrapped himself all around Sloane and the baby, laughing excitedly. "Oh! Look! We have a baby!"

The baby fussed and sniffled, but she calmed down when Sloane rocked her. She cooed, looking up at Loch and Sloane with those pretty, bright eyes.

Ah, bright because they were so full of stars.

Sloane's cheeks hurt from smiling so hard, and his heart had never felt so full as it did in that sweet moment. "Pandora," he said. "That's your name, pretty girl. You're Pandora."

"Pandora Azaethoth the Lesser Junior," Loch said happily, reaching for her hand with one of his tentacles. "She's perfect."

Pandora squeezed Loch's tentacle and giggled.

"She really is," Sloane gushed. "And wow, uh, big? I mean, she doesn't look like a newborn. She's like... bigger. And she's not all wrinkly."

"Egg babies are clearly superior."

"Maybe." Sloane noticed there was a little bit of eggshell still clinging to Pandora's leg, and he carefully washed it off. "There we go."

Pandora kicked and laughed again, tugging on Loch's tentacle until her hand turned into an identical slithering appendage.

"Okay, and newborns definitely can't do that."

"Ah, look!" Loch cackled. "Isn't that amazing?"

Pandora's little tentacle morphed back into a normal human hand, and she grinned proudly.

"Wait, she already has some teeth!" Sloane gasped.

"Egg baby. Vastly superior."

"This is incredible. Seriously." Sloane bowed his head to kiss Pandora's curls. He was overflowing with joy, and his chest was about to burst from so much love surging through him. "I can't stop smiling. Look at her. She's beautiful."

"Mmm. She looks like you." Loch grinned. "She will grow to have your same luscious eyebrows."

"Poor thing!" Sloane laughed.

Pandora wiggled around and tried to pull Loch's tentacle into her mouth, fussing quietly.

"That is not food," Loch scolded, tugging his tentacle away.

Pandora whined and started to cry.

"Oh fine." Loch let her have it back with a huff and narrowed his eyes. "I'm onto you, little one. Using my emotions to manipulate me already... clever child."

For a baby, Pandora managed to look pretty smug.

"She's gotta be hungry, right?" Sloane turned to head out of the pool. "Milk? I mean, shouldn't we give her milk?"

Pandora seemed happy to mouth on Loch's tentacle for now, and Loch followed them onto the beach over to the bed as he said, "Mother provided us with sustenance for her. I believe Galgareth said it was godly level formula?"

"Okay, perfect." Sloane sat on the bed, his robes magically drying. "Let's get some of that. Could you pass me a blanket and—"

Pandora was now dressed in a purple polka-dotted onesie and swaddled in her starlight blanket.

"Thank you." Sloane grinned. "You know, having a god for a husband is sure gonna make raising a child pretty easy."

"I'm wonderful, it's true. Your life would certainly be miserable without me."

"Very true."

Loch smiled confidently as he sorted out putting a bottle together and then filling it with a green sparkly powder. With a snap, it turned liquid, and he gave it a little shake to mix it up.

Pandora gurgled quietly, staring at Sloane as she continued to gnaw on Loch's tentacle.

"Here, my sweet love." Loch handed Sloane the bottle and cuddled up next to him, wrapping his tentacles back around them both.

"Thank you." Sloane cradled Pandora in one arm, trying to get a feel for what would be the best way to hold her as he offered the bottle. "Are you hungry? Hmm?"

Pandora fussed but took the bottle, finally releasing Loch's tentacle in favor of eating. She was alert, and her eyes darted around curiously.

"I still can't believe it." Sloane smiled. "Wow. We're parents."

"Yes, because I am a very irresponsible god," Loch said proudly.

"I'm actually really glad you are, because this...." He beamed at their daughter. "Well, I wouldn't trade this for anything."

"Nor would I." Loch kissed Sloane's cheek and leaned down to nuzzle Pandora.

"Do you know what I just realized?" Sloane quickly continued before Loch could say something smart, "Today is the summer solstice. We have a solstice baby."

"Oh! We need a fire."

"I can't believe I forgot." Sloane cringed. "I'm a terrible witch."

"There are literally four gods on Aeon right now, and we all forgot, my sweet mate." Loch smiled gently. "We've been a bit busy, wouldn't you say?"

"Okay, fair. And I don't feel as guilty now for missing a sabbath."

"We've missed nothing." Loch raised his hand and created a large bonfire on the beach a few yards off. "There. It's not as impressive as the one I stole that first Dhankes, but it will do." He touched Pandora's forehead, and a small crown of violet flowers appeared there. "See? Sabbath traditions have been observed. You are a great witch."

"Yeah?" Sloane smiled.

"Of course. This day is all about celebrating the light in the world, yes? I cannot imagine a better way to celebrate than the birth of our spawn because she is already the light of our lives." Loch winked. "Plus we have a very big fire."

"Thank you." Sloane glanced over to the table. "What all did your mom bring? I don't suppose she brought a bowl to collect the ashes from the bonfire, huh?"

"Oh, but I can certainly provide that. She brought us godly formula, bottles, blankets and other baby-type things. Oh, and the supplies for the naming ritual."

"She didn't want to be a part of it? Not even Galgareth?"

Such events were traditionally family affairs for Sages, and Sloane was surprised that neither of the goddesses wanted to participate.

Loch smiled. "Being gods, this time is usually for the parents. Or the *parent*, as many gods spawn alone. They will join us when we pick her godly title."

"Yeah, when does that happen? The second naming?"

"When the time is right."

"Which is when?"

"We'll know. Trust me." Loch smirked. "Would you like to name our child now, sweet mate?"

"Yes." Sloane hugged Pandora a little closer. "I would love to."

"Stay here with our little spawn, and I will ready everything." Loch could have easily used magic to bring everything over that they needed, but he seemed too excited to sit still. He bounced off the bed and hurried over to the table, tentacles swirling.

He returned with a handful of objects, and he laid them across the bed for Sloane's inspection. "The incense bowl that reminded you of your mother's—"

"That you stole," Sloane noted affectionately.

"—a very shiny rock from the temple with the erotic murals, a candle from Lochlain and Robert's home—"

"That you also stole."

"—and we can use water from the hot springs here. Is that sufficient, sweet Starkiller?"

"Perfect. Do we need to cleanse the space here?"

"No, this is a blessed place." Loch took Sloane's hand, and all the objects magically floated right above their heads. "We have but to create a circle. If you would do me the honor of calling the first corner, my beloved."

"Hail to the guardians of the south, I call on the element of fire." Sloane held out his hand, lighting the floating candle. "We seek your passion and your strength for our circle. As above, so below."

"Hail to the guardians of the west, I call on the element of water." Loch summoned a floating blob of water from the pool. "We seek your creativity and healing to come to our circle. As above, so below."

"Hail to the guardians of the north, I call on the element of earth." Sloane touched the hovering rock. "We seek your discipline and your focus for our circle. As above, so below."

"Hail to the guardians of the east, I call on the element of air." A twirl of Loch's fingers lit the incense in the bowl. "We seek your knowledge and your clarity to bless this circle. As above, so below." He smiled at Sloane. "Will you complete the circle now, my sweet mate?"

"Of course." Sloane took a deep breath. "As above, so below. As within, so without. We call on all the elements of sky and planet to bring us starlight, the light to summon that which has no face, to bless and keep safe this sacred space."

There was a sensational spark of magic in the air, and a faint glittering aura drizzled over them. The circle was blessed now with starlight, but there was something else here too.

The new energy was old, endless, and it made Sloane's breath catch. He was filled with an awesome warmth that made him tremble deep inside, and he immediately knew this magic.

He'd felt it every time he summoned a sword of starlight.

"Great Azaethoth," he whispered.

"Yes." Loch embraced Sloane and Pandora. "See? I am his favorite."

As awesome as it was to experience the presence of the oldest and most powerful god, he had not come alone.

Sloane, oh, our sweet boy....

We love you so much....

She's so beautiful... we're so proud....

"Mom? Dad?" Sloane's voice cracked, and he trembled, tears falling down his cheeks.

His parents were here too.

Their warmth and love were showering over Sloane, and he closed his eyes as he basked in the incredible glow. He had missed his parents so dearly, especially now with the start of his own family, and he wanted to enjoy every second of this gift.

Pandora pulled off the bottle and giggled loudly. She wiggled one of her arms out of her blanket and waved, her hand morphing into a tentacle as it reached up into the air.

We love you....

We love you all so much....

"I love you guys too." Sloane sniffed back a sob, and he smiled through the overwhelming emotions. "So damn much." He closed his eyes, still sensing Great Azaethoth's lingering power. To him, he said, "Thank you."

"Keep going, my love," Loch urged. "Finish the ritual."

"Within this sacred circle and in the sight of all the gods, we name you Pandora Azaethoth the Lesser Junior Beaumont." Sloane looked deep into her bright eyes with a grin. "We ring a bell so that the first sound you hear is music, to remind you of the music of the gods' words and the music you must seek in yourself."

Loch rang the bell from Sloane's mother, and one of his tentacles brought over the jar of honey.

"Honey," Sloane said, dipping his finger inside and rubbing a dab on Pandora's bottom lip, "so your first taste will be sweet, to honey your words and thoughts so you never forget how powerful they can be." He smiled as Loch lit a thick sachet of incense. "Incense, so your first smell will be calming, to teach you finding peace is a fulfilling and sacred act. And a blanket." He snuggled her close. "So your first touch will be tender, and you will know love from the moment you are born."

Scooting close, Loch hugged them both, curling his tentacles around them and kissing Sloane's cheek.

"My beautiful daughter." Sloane took a deep breath, emotion threatening to take his voice. "With this name we charge you to follow the will of the gods even as they slumber, to keep all of the sabbaths sacred, to seek balance in the world and within yourself, and above all else, harm none in what you do."

"Unless they're dillholes," Loch whispered.

"Don't listen to your father."

"No. Definitely listen. Just not when your other father is around."

Sloane laughed and kissed Loch. "You're a mess. Wow. We really did it, huh?"

"Indeed." Loch's tentacle stroked Sloane's cheek. "Are you ready to close the circle now, sweet mate?"

"Absolutely."

After thanking the elements for their power, Sloane dismissed them one by one and closed the circle. The magical aura faded away, as did Great Azaethoth and Sloane's parents, but not before he felt the touch of a hand on his cheek.

He didn't know how, but he knew it was his mother.

The urge to cry again bubbled up Sloane's throat, and Pandora's little tentacle wrapped around his fingers. He smiled, wiping off his tears on his shoulder with a halfhearted laugh. "By all the gods, any other surprises waiting for me that'll make me cry?"

"None that I'm aware of." Loch kissed his brow and snuggled in close.

"That was beautiful. Seriously. Thank you and Great Azaethoth." Sloane sighed wistfully. "I miss my parents so much."

"I know, my sweet mate." Loch curled his tentacle around Sloane's hand and Pandora's little coil, holding them both. "You'll see them again one day."

"I know." Sloane smiled at Pandora, and he tried to give her the bottle back. "Moments like that, though… makes it easier. Knowing they're so close."

She gurgled and latched on to the bottle, both of her hands now little tentacles and wrapping around it as she ate.

"Mmm, that's a very nifty trick," Sloane said, "but maybe no public outings for a little while, hmm?"

"Why?" Loch frowned.

"Well, unless you find a more secure way to swaddle her, the tiny adorable tentacles might be a little too much?"

"Ah, mass panic inducing?"

"Yup." Sloane smiled. "Besides, I think we could both use some time off. No cases, no drama, no crazy godly shenanigans or chasing a gangster's cat. Just us."

"Truly?"

"Yeah. We need to bond with our new beautiful little girl, and we totally deserve a break!" Sloane rocked Pandora. "Just look at her. I wanna spend every second with her."

"And we will," Loch promised. "Except when we're mating. I don't think you'd like that."

"How fast is she going to grow? She already looks like a really big baby. Is she gonna, like, start walking tomorrow?"

"Calm down, my sweet Starkiller." Loch nuzzled Sloane's cheek. "She will grow however she is meant to. She is still half mortal, you know. She can only mature so quickly."

"So we don't have to worry about baby-proofing the apartment yet?"

"Probably not."

Pandora lifted her tentacle, and the appendage grew and stretched until she could swat at the shiny rock still floating overhead.

"Ah-ah," Sloane chided, gently pushing her tentacle back down. "No touchey, baby girl. That's not yours."

"I stand corrected." Loch hummed as he brought down the rest of the items and sent them over to the table. "Maybe we should begin the baby proofing."

Pandora went back to her bottle, but her tentacles remained quite wiggly.

"Oh, I'm gonna say definitely," Sloane agreed.

The bottle was nearly finished, and Pandora pushed it away with a gurgle.

"Aww, good girl! Look at you, eating your first bottle!" Sloane handed it off to Loch and very carefully draped Pandora over his shoulder. "I think I'm doing this right. I mean, you burp godly babies, yeah?"

"Yes?"

"Why did you say that like a question?"

"I don't know?"

"You did it again!" Sloane huffed and patted Pandora's back, relieved when he heard a tiny belch. "There, okay. See? Fine. I did it."

"Excellent work, sweet Starkiller," Loch praised, stretching out a tentacle to put the bottle on the table. "You're a natural."

"Yeah?" Sloane tucked Pandora back in the crook of his arm and adjusted her little flower crown, grinning down at her. "I think she's making it easy for me."

Pandora's bright eyes fluttered, closing slowly, and she smiled.

That smile warmed Sloane's very soul. He was full, happy, and all of this was so surreal. He was in a magical grotto with his daughter, a child that he carried for months inside his own body, fathered by his eldritch dragon husband.

He could remember the lonely days of being an orphan, and now he had a family of his very own.

It was magical, incredible, and....

But wait, what was that smell?

"Ah, already?" Sloane laughed when he heard a soft fart that confirmed his suspicion. "Seems we are in need of our first official diaper change."

"What's that?" Loch cocked his head.

"Huh?" Sloane pulled the blanket open and sighed loudly. "You didn't give her a diaper?"

"Ah, is that what those funny little paper things are? I thought they were sanitary napkins. Weird since she's so young, but I was thinking Mother was just excited and making odd assumptions—"

"Here." Sloane passed Pandora over to Loch. "This first one? All yours."

"As you wish, my beautiful mate." Loch smiled at her. "She really is perfect. A bit stinky right now, but otherwise very perfect."

"Yeah." Sloane smirked. "She gets that from her father."

"The stinky part or the perfect part?"

"Both."

CHAPTER 15.

THE FIRST thing Sloane learned about raising a newborn demi-goddess was that sleeping for more than two hours at a time appeared to be entirely optional, just like any other newborn.

Fortunately, he was married to a god who did not need to sleep at all, which made the next few weeks much more pleasant.

While Sloane slept, Loch tended to their little one's every need. Every late-night feeding or diaper change was taken care of, and Sloane was enjoying being spoiled. He only woke up once to Loch teaching Pandora how to pick a lock at three in the morning, and he considered that a pretty fair trade for being able to sleep.

Urilith and Galgareth visited for a few more days to gush over the new spawn, and Pandora loved the attention. She was bright, happy, and Sloane loved the sound of her little laugh more than anything. It was all so magical that it still felt like a dream, and he loved waking up to the sounds and smells of whatever new breakfast adventure Loch was attempting with his new mini sous chef.

Life was pretty damn good.

Mysteriously, the Tree of Light in the city park was destroyed. It burned down in a single night with no witnesses. Nothing was left behind except a few tiny chunks of burned wood. Since there was now nothing to protest, the crowds soon left, and the city was able to begin construction.

Sloane suspected Stoker was involved, but he couldn't prove anything.

Daphne and Nathaniel returned to their normal lives, but Nathaniel stayed active with the coven and wanted to continue Ziol's work. Sloane gave him some of the old books Loch had stolen from the deacon's house, though he did keep a few of the rare ones to hopefully pass along to Pandora someday.

Lynnette was both happy and equally furious that Sloane's labor experience had been so easy. She still had a few months to go, and both she and Milo were excited to visit and play with Pandora to get a preview of what was to come.

Not that their baby would be able to magically grow tentacles and get into absolutely everything, but still.

Milo brought her a big plush panda to play with on one such visit, and it immediately became her favorite toy. It wasn't long after that they started calling her "Panda Bear," and she seemed to respond to that better than her own name.

Merrick and Chase officially closed the case on the murders and continued their search for the Salgumel cultists. They promised to keep in touch like always, and Sloane offered to do the same if anything else came up. Not that they had any leads.

The Salgumel cultists, including Jeff Martin, had all but vanished into the worlds between worlds. Sloane wasn't waiting around to see if Stoker's gossip about healing totems was true, instead giving the info to Chase and Merrick and asking Lochlain and Robert to keep an ear out.

After all, Robert was a fence for illegal goods, Sagittarian items in particular. Maybe Jeff Martin would end up coming to them without even knowing it.

Even with the fear of knowing the cultists were out there probably searching for a new sacrifice or other gods were likely plotting some other way to awaken Salgumel, Sloane was happy.

No matter what happened, he had his husband, an immortal who loved him.

Together, they could do anything.

Like managing to get their now one-month-old daughter to lay down for a nap so they could enjoy some quality time together as a couple.

"And you're sure she's asleep?" Sloane asked as he stripped off his shirt, kissing Loch fiercely.

"Mmm, yes," Loch promised, kissing Sloane back as he led him toward their bed. "She has her panda bear, her bottle, and her shaky rattle toy. She should be very content."

"And her blanket?"

"What sort of amateur do you take me for?"

"Sorry." Sloane grabbed Loch and turned, shoving him on the bed.

"Oh!" Loch grinned. "Hello."

"I'm really, really into us mating right now." Sloane crawled on top of Loch. "But we have to be quick, okay?"

"So quick."

"'Cause she woke up last time."

"I promise I will leave your body shaking with sweet sensation from my sensuous sizzling slamming long before our spawn awakens."

"Fuck yeah, gimme some of that." Sloane kissed him hard, the rest of their clothes vanishing away until they were both naked and tangled together.

Loch opened Sloane's body up smooth as ever, spreading his legs and immediately shoving one of his smaller tentacles inside. It was almost too fast, and the intense stretch made Sloane gasp excitedly, his cries growing louder as Loch thrusted.

"Good?" Loch growled, pinning Sloane to the bed and sucking at his throat. "Does this please you, my gorgeous mate?"

"Fuck yes, it pleases the fuck out of me!" Sloane moaned. "Don't stop, don't stop!"

Loch's tentacles kept Sloane firmly in place while the slitted one pounded away at his hole. Loch could go so deep, so much that it made Sloane ache and writhe in ecstasy. It was almost too much, and he gritted his teeth as he fought to breathe through the incredible onslaught of feelings.

The tentacle in his ass was hot, slick, and the ones holding him down were strong and firm. Loch kept sucking and kissing all along Sloane's neck and shoulder, and his hands possessively squeezed his sides and slid over his body, grazing his nipples until they were hard at attention.

"I wanna feel, fuck, let me," Sloane pleaded. "I need to feel you there."

Loch let one of Sloane's hands go, urging, "Go on. Feel what I'm doing to you, my sweet mate."

Sloane pressed his palm against his stomach, and he groaned when he felt the bulge of Loch's tentacle slamming away inside of him. "Oh fuck... oh, Loch... there... you're so deep, you're so fuckin' deep...."

"Mm... yes." Loch was smiling. "Your body is pure perfection. I want to give you more...."

"Yes...."

"Until you're moaning...."

"Yes."

"Until you're begging for me...."

"Yes!"

"Until you're screaming my name to Zebulon above...."

"Fuck! Yes!" Sloane reached around and popped Loch's ass. "Come on, then! Give it to me!"

"Oh, my beautiful Starkiller." Loch slammed their lips together in a passionate kiss as he forced the second of his slitted tentacles inside Sloane's hole.

Sloane sobbed, his body torn between pain and pleasure, every nerve throbbing to be so full. It was exactly what he wanted, what he needed, and he rocked down to meet the thrusting tentacles. The discomfort was brief and faded quickly, and Sloane knew he was going to come soon.

He wanted relief from all this building pressure, and he found himself fighting against Loch's grip for the sheer thrill of being held down. He loved how rough Loch was being, his godly husband usually far too reserved with his vast strength. This, however, was the pounding of the century, and Sloane was ecstatic.

They kissed, breathless and hot, and Sloane moaned. "Yes, just like that, fuck, just like that! I'm gonna, I'm gonna come!"

"Go on," Loch growled low. "Let yourself go, let me take care of you... come along, my love!"

"Loch!" Sloane screamed, his entire body locking up tight before melting in bliss, his cock pulsing across his stomach and chest. He was so damn full, and he couldn't stop coming now. It was one wave after another, and his hips weakly thrusted as the pleasure overtook him.

"Mmm, you're so good," Loch praised. "You're always so good for me." He moved onto his back, his tentacles easily lifting Sloane with him and putting him on top. "I'm going to give you more, my beautiful mate. So much more."

If it wasn't for Loch's tentacles holding him up, Sloane would have fallen flat on his face. He was weak, but he tried to muster the strength to rock back on the tentacles still inside of him. In this position, he could ride Loch, but he realized he couldn't move.

"No, no." Loch shook his head, and he smiled up at him. "Allow me to give you your pleasure."

Sloane shivered when Loch stroked his thighs, moving to touch his stomach. Although his body had returned to its normal proportions before being pregnant, silvery stretch marks had been left behind on his belly and inner thighs.

He hadn't been a fan of them at first, but the way Loch always seemed so drawn to them, touching them so worshipfully, made him not mind so much now. He was proud of them, thinking of them as stripes earned from the part he played bringing their child into the world.

Loch traced each one until his eyes turned black, and he kept fucking Sloane ruthlessly with his tentacles. He bent Sloane forward so they could kiss while he fucked him, and he grabbed his ass and spread him wide as his tentacles kept going at it.

Sloane whimpered, his face scalding hot and his mouth dry from moaning so earnestly. Loch was hitting his prostate at this angle, and each thick tentacle pushed and stroked and pounded until Sloane had no choice but to surrender once more.

He came, helplessly writhing, grinding his cock against Loch's stomach to work himself through each shuddering wave. There, finally, Loch was coming too, and two full loads of hot come left him positively stuffed and his hole throbbing.

"Oh, Loch." Sloane tilted his head back and moaned luxuriously. "Ohhh, fuck. Yes. Fuck yes. You feel so good. So fuckin' good. Fuck, I'm so full."

"As you should always be," Loch purred, nuzzling Sloane's cheek and holding him close. "Full of my seed and trembling in the wake of the ecstasy I have bestowed upon you."

"Sounds good to me." Sloane laughed deliriously, and he stretched out as Loch released his arms and legs so he could move again. He was warm and happy, and yet there was still a lingering fire deep within. "Fuck, I feel, I feel like I could come again…."

"I will gladly bring you to climax again." Loch grinned and laid Sloane back against the pillows, withdrawing his tentacles and bringing his giant tentacock up between his legs. "As many times as you desire."

Empty and gaping, Sloane groaned loudly as Loch's come dripped out of him. He was too horny to feel an ounce of shame, and he reached down to thrust a few fingers inside his tender hole. It was so wet and hot, and he bit his lip as he fucked himself. "Please, Loch… I need you."

"I'm here," Loch soothed, pushing Sloane's hips back. His tentacles tucked Sloane's knees against his chest, Loch's tentacock taking the place of his fingers and sinking into his stretched hole.

Sloane moaned happily, grabbing his cheeks to pull them apart and hold himself open. He could see Loch's massive tentacock thrusting slowly into his slick hole, and he had to touch it. He had to run his fingertips along the wet shaft and feel it moving as it slid inside of him.

He could barely believe his body could take such a massive thing, as he rubbed his thumbs around his stretched hole. He clenched down, groaning at the added depth and how the tight ring of muscle clamped around Loch's cock.

Loch liked it too.

"You feel utterly divine," Loch moaned, his lashes fluttering as he thrusted faster. "Your hole is the most wonderful thing I've ever felt. I want to lay my seed in you every minute of every hour. Oh, my love. My beautiful mate. My perfect mate...."

"I love you," Sloane murmured breathlessly, squeezing his fingers around the thick knot on Loch's tentacock. He gasped as he felt his hole stretching wider, opening up for it, and he cried out as it popped inside of him. "Ah, fuck! I love you so much!"

Loch held Sloane close, keeping his legs high as he plunged into him with long, deep strokes. He kissed him, breathless and grunting, all of his tentacles wrapping around Sloane as he sank into him over and over. "Oh, Sloane... my love!"

It was quicker this time, both of them still on edge, and Sloane wailed as he came again. His thighs shook, and he cried as Loch filled him once more. They rocked together, trading wet kisses and soft murmurs, riding out the beautiful feeling until it finally faded.

Sloane sighed, tired and deeply satisfied, fussing as Loch withdrew all of his tentacles. He was an absolute mess, but that had been totally worth it. "Fuck, that was good. It was—"

From the other side of the apartment, Pandora cried.

"Ah shit."

"Well, at least we got to finish?" Loch grinned sheepishly.

"Barely." Sloane laughed.

"Stay here," Loch commanded. "I am going to make sure she goes down for that nap because I plan on pleasuring you many, many more times."

"Mm, I'll be right here. Eagerly awaiting your return."

"Stay naked." Loch smooched his cheek and left to go check on Pandora.

Sloane stretched out in bed, looking at the ceiling and smiling. His heart was still pounding away, and his body was indeed shaking with the promised sweet sensation.

Pandora's crying stopped, and Sloane expected Loch wouldn't be gone for too much longer. Just a few more minutes and they would be able to get right back to—

There was a small flash of light, and a young man with white hair wearing a long black coat was suddenly standing in front of the closet. He was accompanied by a translucent beast with a massive upper body like a gorilla's and spikes cascading down his back from the top of his head. The lower half was a thick tail of tentacles, but it, along with the bulk of its chest, was currently hidden in the walls and floor of the room.

A flurry of shimmering tentacles from the beast moved around the young man, flickering with immense power as they tore at the magical seals on the door.

"Alexander?" Sloane gasped.

Alexander turned his head and scowled. His red eyes glowed brightly. "Oh, it's *you*."

Quickly pulling the covers up over himself, Sloane snapped, "Of course it's me! Did you not know whose place you were breaking into?"

"No."

Hello, Starkiller, Rota's voice said inside Sloane's head. *It's nice to see you again.*

Rota was an old god whose very soul had been forced from his body and bound to Alexander's in a twisted experiment carried out by Gronoch, Loch's godly brother. Alexander was Silenced, a mortal without magic, but he had full access and control over all of Rota's powers.

The situation was complicated, but Alexander and Rota were desperately searching for Rota's body so he could be restored to his godly glory.

They were lovers who had been through unimaginable horror and, as far as Sloane knew, had only ever shared—with Sloane's help—one kiss. Alexander could use Rota's powers to make him materialize in a physical form, but it was only for brief spurts of time.

As Loch had once pointed out, that couldn't be very satisfying for either of them.

Drawn by the noise, Loch appeared in the bedroom doorway with a very not napping Pandora in his arms. "Oh! It's the angry one." He squinted. "Is Rota with you?"

"Hello, Azaethoth." Rota laughed in delight, using his voice out loud now so Loch could hear him as well. "Oh! And who is this?

"You spawned?" Alexander grimaced. "And why are you naked...?" He glanced at Sloane. "Oh. You both are. Gross."

"Yes, thanks, awesome." Sloane rolled his eyes. "This is our daughter, Pandora."

"She is beautiful," Rota praised.

"Thank you. Now, you guys wanna tell me what you're doing in our house?"

"It's not a house. It's an apartment," Loch mumbled. "You keep getting that confused."

"We mean you no harm," Rota promised, "but we need this book, please."

"Book? What book?" Sloane asked.

"The one I've been trying to find for weeks and have now finally tracked down to your closet," Alexander said. "It was in the private collection of some priest and mysteriously went missing after his death." He eyed Sloane. "You kill him?"

"What? No!" Sloane's face got hot.

"Never know with you."

Loch didn't seem to mind that Alexander was trying to break into their closet. He calmly plopped right next to Sloane in bed with Pandora between them.

She gurgled and waved at their new visitors.

Rota waved back, even though she couldn't see it.

It was a nice thought anyway.

Alexander did not wave.

"It's a book about a mortal's travels to the worlds between worlds," Rota explained. "We've been having some difficulty navigating them, and we are in urgent need of this book to help us."

"I'm guessing you haven't found the Fountain of the Kindress?" Sloane asked quietly.

Gronoch, the god who removed Rota's soul, claimed to have hidden his body at the Fountain. It was a mystical place where the Kindress was said to be born and die in an endless cycle, a legend of mythological proportions even to many Sages.

"Wow, do you think we would be here getting an eyeful of your *National Geographic* special if we had?" Alexander turned his attention back to the closet and focused Rota's tentacles on removing the rest of the seals.

"We have been to thousands of worlds." Rota sounded tired. "We've found nothing."

"Don't suppose you guys stumbled across any Salgumel cultists?" Sloane asked.

"No." Alexander was irritated, still struggling to break through and open the door.

"Ah, try hooking your tentacle a bit to the left," Loch taunted. "You may find that part of the seal a bit stubborn."

Pandora gurgled approvingly while Alexander continued to scowl.

"Look, stop." Sloane shook his head. "Loch, open the closet for them."

"Aww, but why?" Loch pouted.

"Just let them take it."

"But I stole it."

"They need it."

Loch groaned. "I suppose, if I must." He waved his hand and the closet doors opened.

I almost had it, Alexander thought sullenly.

Be grateful, Rota scolded.

They should be grateful I didn't blow it up.

"You guys do remember I can hear you when you do that, right?" Sloane drawled.

Alexander scowled again. He sent Rota's tentacles into the closet and pulled out the gilded tome, passing it into his waiting hands.

Alexander.

"Thank you," Alexander grumbled.

"You're welcome." Sloane smiled. "See! Was that so hard?"

"Excruciating." Alexander held the book close. "Now, if you'll excuse us. I would say it's been fun, but Rota hates it when I lie."

Brat.

"You know it's all written in godstongue, right?" Sloane asked.

"Duh." Alexander scoffed. "Let me guess. You just so happen to know someone who can translate it?"

"I do, actually."

"Is it someone you trust?" Rota asked warily.

"Rota!" Alexander snapped. "I can translate these myself. We don't need Starkiller's help."

Yes, we do, Rota argued through their bond. *The key we found only has twenty words, and we don't even know if this book is actually written in Babbeth's tongue.*

We work better alone.

My love, we need this. I need this. Please.

"They're doing that talking in their heads thing, aren't they?" Loch fussed. "I'm sure it's all very dramatic, but when you can't hear it, it looks like Alexander is making faces at the ceiling."

"They're saying they don't need help with the translation," Sloane explained, bringing Pandora over in his lap and kissing her hair.

"Because we don't," Alexander griped. "In the interest of saving time, however... tell us about this translator you know."

"He's a friend, definitely trustworthy, and he's the best translator I know. He's worked with a lot of godstongue before."

"Name?"

"Not so fast. I want you to do something for us in return."

"Ugh." Alexander groaned. "What? Save kittens from trees? Help old ladies across the street?"

"There's a group of Salgumel cultists we believe are hiding in the worlds between worlds."

"And if I find any of them, you want me to what? Strongly encourage them to turn from their evil ways?"

"Just let us know where they are. Please."

"Fine."

"You have our word, Starkiller," Rota promised.

"Okay." Sloane smiled. "Thank you. So, the guy's name is Ollie Logue, and he's—"

Alexander and Rota were gone.

"Well then." Sloane sighed.

"Are we sure that was wise?" Loch asked. "Giving Ollie's name to that angry little child?"

"It'll be fine. Rota will keep Alexander in check. All they want Ollie to do is read a book for them. No big deal."

"Really?"

"Okay, so we should probably text Ollie and tell him to expect company. And probably Merrick and Chase too."

"And you really think they'll help us, hmm?"

"I do. I don't believe Alexander is as heartless as he pretends to be. He cares about the world as much as we do. He wouldn't wanna see it get destroyed by Salgumel or anyone else."

"It's because you made out with Alexander, isn't it? That you have such faith in him?"

"No. I just… I know why they're doing it. Looking for the book, I mean. They're doing it for love." Sloane shrugged. "Maybe that's what I believe in."

"Hmm." Loch mulled that over for a moment. "I suppose love is a powerful enough force. So is french kissing, but love, yes, I suppose it could be that as well."

Sloane wasn't going to bother correcting Loch on whether or not there was tongue, smiling at Pandora as he cooed, "On that note, it's now nap time for little demi-goddesses."

"Yes." Loch ruffled Pandora's hair. "We must rest for tonight, and after dinner we will learn how to make crème brûlée, oh yes we will."

"Loch?"

"Yes, my gorgeous husband, my stunning mate, my most beloved Starkiller?"

"You cannot use crème brûlée as an excuse to teach the baby how to summon fire yet."

"You're no fun."

"Just the worst, right?" Sloane grinned.

"Oh absolutely." Loch chuckled as he leaned in for a kiss. "Mm, I have no idea how I'm going to stand spending eternity with you."

"I'm sure we'll be able to come up with something," Sloane teased. "Somehow, some way…."

"Lots of mating?"

"I was thinking maybe a gag."

Loch grinned slyly.

"For you."

Loch pouted.

"Kidding, I'm kidding." Sloane chuckled. "I love you."

"I love you too, Sloane." Loch's eyes sparkled as he claimed another kiss. "My sweet mate."

"Forever?"

"And always."

Pandora cooed inquisitively.

"Yes," Loch confirmed, "and we love you too, forever and always, our sweet spawn."

Keep reading for an exclusive excerpt from
Our Shellfish Desires
Book Six of the Sucker for Love Mysteries
by K.L. Hiers

CHAPTER 1.

"OLEANDER LOGUE," Alexander read the name off the computer screen with a smirk. "There he is. Home address, bank statements, last credit card purchase, and ah, he renewed his video streaming subscription. Registered magic user under a water discipline. What else...." He clicked around. "Family calls him Ollie."

It's a little worrying how easy it is to find someone's personal information online. Rota's voice mumbled inside Alexander's head.

"More reliable than magic."

Mm, true.

"Let's go."

Right now?

"Yes." Alexander stood up from the computer he'd been using. It so happened to be the computer in Sloane Beaumont's office, the private investigator and Starkiller who had given them Ollie's name.

Considering Alexander and Rota had just spoken to Sloane at home with his husband and child, Alexander had known the office would be unoccupied and they wouldn't be disturbed.

They'd visited Sloane's apartment to take possession of a very rare book, and now they were in need of a translator because it was written in godstongue, the language of the old gods.

The situation was complicated.

Rota was the living soul of an old Sagittarian god, one of many ancient deities worshipped by mankind ages ago before their following faded in the wake of a new monotheistic religion. Rota had been forced by the god Gronoch to leave his physical body and have his soul bound to Alexander, a Silenced mortal. Though he had no natural magic of his own, Alexander could channel Rota's immense godly powers through his body like an antenna.

There were a few limitations, but the one plaguing Alexander in particular was that he could not touch Rota nor Rota him for extended periods of time.

That made things especially difficult when two people were in love.

Rota slid a shimmering tentacle over Alexander's cheek, soothing, *Why don't we rest tonight and go over there in the morning?*

Alexander experienced Rota's physical touch like a cold shiver. Other times it felt like dipping himself into a cool bath. It was always fleeting and all too brief.

Rota's physical manifestations varied between these simple ghostly caresses or mere stationary support like acting as a wall or shield. Anything particularly acrobatic risked unleashing the brunt of his full godly might. There was no in-between. Attempting even a simple hug exhausted Rota from trying to hold himself back, and there was a high chance of hurting Alexander.

They'd tried.

Oh, how they'd *tried* over and over again, and the result had always been the same.

Disappointment and heartache.

It was why the translation was so important. The book was a collection of poems written by Wilhelmina Pickett, a Sage who was said to have traveled all the worlds between worlds created by the gods. Alexander's research strongly indicated this book could guide them to the location of the Fountain.

Where Rota's body was supposed to be.

"Tonight," Alexander insisted.

Are you sure?

Alexander could feel Rota's hesitation. "You're worried about me."

You haven't stopped in months.

"This is important."

So are you. You're exhausted.

It was very strange to have a staring contest with a soul, even more so being on the losing side. It was more of a sensation than a physical act since Alexander didn't see Rota so much as he sensed him. There was a vague outline of the giant beastly god and his big spikes and tentacles, but it was only a shadow of Rota's true self.

Alexander already knew he wasn't going to win. Not when Rota was being this stubborn.

Well?

"Fine!" Alexander scowled. "We'll go home, sleep, and go see him first thing in the morning."

A side effect of their unique bond was being connected psychically. They could feel each other's emotions, hear every thought and subconscious impulse, and at first it had made for a very stressful existence.

As time went on, they learned to tune one another out and each tried to give the other privacy even if it was only an illusion.

I want to get this over with. I'm tired of living like this. One kiss isn't enough. It's not enough. Not after all these years, not after everything! Alexander hated he had lost control of his thoughts, and he hoped Rota would ignore them.

Rota did, thankfully, but he still reached out to touch Alexander's cheek again.

Alexander shuddered. *Not nearly enough.*

Let's go home.

Alexander directed Rota to teleport them away with a thought. One moment they were in Sloane's office, and then they were gone.

They were puppet and puppeteer, Alexander long having since become a master of commanding Rota's magic. He could use his thoughts to control it or his physical body for a bigger boost. The latter option was dangerous since Alexander was mortal and his body couldn't handle the strain of channeling a god's power for very long.

For those fleeting moments when Alexander did take on Rota's full power, however, he knew they could make the whole world tremble before them.

But Alexander didn't care about that.

His desires were very simple, practically base, and achievement of them was so close now that he could almost taste it. He was going to be with the god he loved, no matter what.

Home was the name for wherever they were holing up at the moment, and it was currently the penthouse suite of an abandoned hotel. It was a large space once overflowing with old mattresses, broken furniture, and forgotten trash bags. They'd cleaned it up, made it livable, and Alexander reflected that they'd lived here longer than anywhere else.

Except for Hazel, he thought bitterly, heading to the kitchenette to find something to eat. *That fucking hellhole.*

Where we first met, Rota added.

"I know." Alexander stared into the fridge. "Kinda hard to forget."

Their current circumstances had been far from voluntary. They'd both woken up inside the Hazel Medical Research Facility with no memory of who they were or how they'd gotten there, both victims of Gronoch, who had taken on the body of the company's CEO and lead researcher to conduct his experiments.

Gronoch had wanted to create an army of Silenced mortals like Alexander who could be easily controlled and serve as conduits for a god's power. He'd had the crazy desire to awaken his father, Salgumel, the God of Dreams and Sleep. Salgumel was said to have gone mad in his dreaming, the deep sleep that all the gods had fallen into when mankind abandoned them, and waking him up would certainly mean the end of the world.

Gronoch and other gods like him wanted the old world where they'd been worshipped and adored, and they were counting on Salgumel rising to make it happen. There would be war, naturally, as not all the gods would be happy about this insane plan, and that's where the conduit program came in.

The idea was to take gods they knew would not support the cause and turn them into mortal slaves to fight on their side in the war that was to come.

It was a plan riddled with multiple issues, countless complications, and a staggering body count. The process was pure agony, and few survived long enough to attempt the actual soul binding. Out of hundreds of Silenced victims, Alexander was the only successful conduit.

Do you ever wonder?

"What?" Alexander directed Rota's tentacles to grab a frozen pizza out of the freezer. He wasn't much on cooking, and he was very tired.

Why us?

"You mean, why did our bond work?"

Yes.

"No, I never think about it." Alexander turned on the oven, using a splash of magic to preheat it instantly. "I know you want there to be some special romantic reason, but I don't think there is one. I think it just… happened."

Rota's thoughts turned sad.

"What?"

I want there to be a reason for all of that suffering.

"Have you seen the world? People suffer every day for no reason." Alexander shoved the pizza in, and he patted his pockets looking for his cigarettes. "We're not special."

You're special to me.

"You're delusional."

You're too young to be this cynical.

"Am I?" Alexander snorted, raising his hands to guide Rota's tentacle over to light his cigarette. "Well, I think you're too old to be this sappy."

Rota laughed.

Alexander grinned, and he leaned back against Rota's invisible body. He could feel him there beside him, firming up so he could get comfortable. This was the limit of the sustained physical contact they could have, and it felt like what Alexander imagined resting on a cloud would be like, cool and weirdly springy.

Maybe I am, Rota mused, *but I can't help it. I want there to be meaning for what happened. Not just to us, but to all those other people. The ones who didn't make it.*

"But there isn't." Alexander took a long drag off his cigarette. "Shit just happens. Gronoch was insane." He took a cautious probe at Rota's side of the bond to see what was wrong. "You know we're not responsible for that, right? It's not our fault."

Oh? It's not? Even though we literally hand-delivered most of them?

"If we didn't do it, Gronoch would have killed me," Alexander said firmly. "We were doing what we had to in order to survive. Then, now, and always, we do what we have to to stay together."

I wish...

Alexander touched Rota's side. "If you want there to be a meaning to all of it to somehow make it all better, I don't think there is one. I'm sorry it happened, but I'm not sorry I did it, and I would do it all over again to keep us safe."

Rota sighed.

"We found each other, right?" Alexander smiled. "In that awful place... you heard me. You came to me."

Yes.

"Now that means something." Alexander kept petting Rota, his fingers moving through the cool silky feeling of what should've been warm skin. "You were there when I was hurt and alone, when I was scared, when I was ready to check right the fuck out. You were the answer to my prayers even after I was too scared to pray because I didn't think anybody was listening. Even if our bond didn't work, I'm thankful for that night."

As am I.

"I know you feel bad because of what we did, because of what I did, but… I did it all because I love you."

And I love you. Rota seemed to smile, though he still felt sad. *Perhaps that's the only thing that matters in the end.*

"It's the only thing that matters to me." Alexander closed his eyes when Rota passed a tentacle over his hand. He tried to fill his side of the bond with the love he felt for Rota in hopes it would comfort him.

Sometimes I wonder which one of us is supposed to be the disenchanted immortal.

"Ha!" Alexander inhaled leisurely and blew out a long puff of smoke. "I happen to like you like this. Rota, God of Sap."

Hmmph. Alexander, Lord of Grump.

"I'm glad you are. Sweet, I mean. Really. Gods know one of us needs to be." Alexander flicked his ashes on the floor and vanished them away with magic. "I don't know why I'm like this…" *And I wonder if I was like this before.*

Grumpy?

"Angry."

However you are is exactly how I want you to be. I didn't mean to upset you. I keep… I can't stop looking back.

"I know." Alexander fidgeted. "You think about it a lot."

Yes. I'm sorry.

"Don't be." Alexander shrugged. "I'm just ready to move on. Gronoch is dead, thanks to Starkiller. The conduit program is over. There's nothing left to think about."

I suppose not.

Rota shifted behind him, and Alexander stood up so he could move away. Rota couldn't go very far, but Alexander could sense he wanted space. He wasn't sure what was bothering Rota so much, but he didn't pry any deeper into their bond.

Alexander left him alone for now, finished smoking, and focused on getting the pizza out of the oven. He ate once it had cooled down, cleaned up the mess, and headed to the bathroom.

He got undressed, ignoring his reflection in the mirror.

There wasn't much to see.

He already knew his once brown hair was white and raggedly shaved around the sides, his eyes were a murky red, and he was covered from head to toe in the binding symbols, circles with a single arrow running through them. Each one had been burned into his skin, and looking at them only reminded him of the pain.

Then there were the ones he couldn't see, the ones *inside* of him. It had taken hundreds of bindings to attach Rota, and Gronoch had run out of room on Alexander's skin so he moved elsewhere including on his bones and even internal organs.

Aside from the reminder of the torture he'd suffered, he didn't like how he looked. He was deathly pale and thin, and he didn't think he was very attractive. He looked tired. He'd seen old pictures of what he looked like before the experiments, and he didn't even recognize himself the first time he saw them.

You're beautiful.

"Get out of my head," Alexander chided affectionately.

Sorry. Can't.

Alexander could feel Rota watching him, and he turned on the water for the tub with his tentacles.

You're the most beautiful thing I've ever seen, and one day I am going to make such love to you....

"Promises, promises." Alexander enjoyed the warmth the words gave him. He could feel that Rota was in a better mood now, and he made a show of bending over to check the water's temperature.

He may not have thought very much of himself, but he knew Rota did.

Oh, you cruel boy.

"Me?"

Yes, you. I'm going to remember this and every other time you've teased me.

Alexander was sure he would. He stepped into the tub and slid down into the water, taunting, "I'll be waiting."

I wanted to take you the day Starkiller let us use his body.

"Right there in front of everyone, huh?" Alexander's heart thumped a little faster, and Rota's desire was strong. It took his breath away, and he knew what was coming.

They had limited options for being intimate, but there was one in particular that was always successful. It was a tease in many aspects, but it was all they had.

Yes. Rota was close now. *I wouldn't have cared.*

"Tell me." Alexander closed his eyes. "Tell me what you would have done."

You want details, I imagine.

Hands sliding down his chest, Alexander nodded. "You know I do."

I would have laid you right out there on the floor, kissing you until neither one of us could breathe. I'd want to taste every inch of you, to memorize the very flavor of you, to worship your entire body.... I would touch everywhere you were hurt and reclaim it as mine.

"Yes." Alexander shifted in the tub, and the heat between his legs grew. His cock was getting hard, but he didn't touch himself yet. He was imagining Rota touching him instead, touching all the binding marks....

A memory resurfaced of being held down, strapped to a metal table, and the burn of the first mark searing into his skin. The pain had been so great that he threw up, begged, pleaded—

Staunchly ignoring it, he said, "Go on. Keep going, please."

I know you'd be hard then. Just as you are now.

Alexander shivered as a ghostly tentacle teased his thigh, and he took himself in hand, stroking slowly. "Yeah... I'd want... I'd want you to...."

Tell me. Rota's voice was silky and low, as if he was whispering right in Alexander's ear.

"I want you to take me fast. I don't want to wait." Alexander stroked faster. His lips parted as his breath picked up, and he could feel the pressure inside of him winding up tight already. He spread his legs and pushed his other hand back behind his balls, pressing his fingers against his hole.

Alexander. Rota was panting. *Yes. I will. I will open you up, with my fingers, my mouth—*

"No. Your dick. Your tentacles, whatever, anything. I need you in me." Alexander groaned, the tips of his fingers pushing in dry. He hissed at the burn, but he didn't stop, jerking himself off and focusing on the head of his dick. "I can't... oh gods..."

Whatever you want. I'll give it to you. I'll give you everything you want. Right there on the floor, I would have taken you—

"Yeah. Please, please, please. Fuck." Alexander kept pushing inside of himself, grunting from the stretch but too desperate to care. The pressure was amazing, and he was getting so close. His face was hot, his heart pounding, and he wanted to come.

All I want is to be inside of you. I want you more than anything. Rota's tentacles glided over Alexander's hips, cool and feathery.

It was such a tease, and Alexander should have asked him to stop. Trying to touch while they did this could be dangerous, but he told himself they wouldn't get too carried away.

It would be fine.

I want to feel you quiver around me, to hear your moans as we make love, to taste the seed you spill as I make you quake—

"Fuck me!" Alexander growled, his eyes flashing open to glare in Rota's direction. "I want you to fuck me! Down on the dirty damn floor, until my back, mmm, until my back is scuffed up and—"

Yes! My love, Alexander. I will. I will fuck you until you're aching and dripping with my seed, I will fuck you until you're weak from screaming in passion—

"Fuck yeah! Give it to me!" Alexander pushed his fingers deeper, holding them there and making himself cry out, his hand a blur on his cock. Rota's tentacles were writhing, hugging his hips and thighs with pressure beyond the usual faint sensation. It should have been concerning, but Alexander was too close to care.

He was right *there*—he could taste it, and his muscles twisted up, readying to melt in climax.

Yes, I will! I will give all I am! I will fuck you until you know nothing but screaming my name! Rota's tentacles tightened down, and the sudden force crushed Alexander's hip.

"Fuck! Rota!" Alexander yelped in pain, grabbing the sides of his tub and fighting back tears.

Alexander! No! I'm so sorry! I—

Alexander held up his hand, unable to speak. *Stop, stop, stop! Don't touch me! Just give me a fuckin' second!*

I love you... I'm so sorry... I didn't mean to....

Sensing Rota's retreat, Alexander summoned him back with a thought of his own: *I need you.* He focused on the bond, guiding Rota's magic through his fingers to heal his hip. It wasn't broken, but there would certainly be a terrible bruise if he didn't take care of it quickly.

Rota's guilt was washing through Alexander in waves, and he was clearly struggling to hold the emotion back.

Any sensual desire forgotten, Alexander tried not to be angry as his cock wilted. It could have been so much worse. He held his hand on his hip until the pain faded, and he slumped down in the water. His heart was still thudding, and his balls were complaining from the abrupt denial.

Do you... do you want to try again? I can leave.

"No. No, you can't." Alexander knew Rota meant that he could distance himself to give him some privacy, but he didn't see the point. The mood was lost, and he was angry at himself for getting so caught up that he didn't tell Rota to back off.

I'm sorry.

"I know." Alexander put his hand back up on the side of the tub, thinking his next words since it was difficult to speak them. *I'm not mad at you. I'm mad at all of this. I want you more than anything, and I'm sick of trying. I'm sick of being hurt—*

I'm here. I love you. Rota hesitantly touched Alexander's fingers, a cool whisper of sensation. *Tomorrow we're going to see Ollie. He will read the book. We'll find the Fountain and reclaim what is rightfully mine.*

"And then we'll fuck?" Alexander attempted a smile.

Yes. Rota smiled. *As many times as you can possibly handle. Even on the floor, if you want.*

"Yeah. Definitely on the floor."

I love you.

"Love you too."

The ache in Alexander's heart lingered long after the frustration of not coming faded, and it was still hurting after he finished his bath and laid down to sleep.

Seven years was a long time to wait. It was a long time to yearn for something so close and yet so out of reach, but now it was right within their grasp. The book was the key to everything, and Alexander dared to hope he would be holding Rota in his arms soon.

He knew sex wasn't everything in a relationship, but being denied it was maddening. It wasn't as if they'd actually chosen to have a celibate romance. Their situation was out of their control, and Alexander longed for a physical connection. Alexander could have taken others to bed, Rota had even given him leave to, but Alexander had refused.

He didn't know if he'd ever been with anyone before he was taken by Gronoch. He couldn't remember, but as far as he was concerned, Rota was going to be his first and last.

Soon, Rota promised. *I will be.*

Alexander drifted off into a restless sleep with those words rattling around in his head. He didn't dream, thankfully, and was able to rest without interruption. When he woke up, he was out of bed and getting dressed before Rota even finished saying good morning.

It was time to go see Ollie.

Alexander grabbed the book and put it in the inner pocket of his trench coat. The pocket was enchanted, a spell of Alexander's own design, and it could have held a small car. He directed Rota to take them over to Ollie's apartment complex, popping up right in front of his door. He could sense powerful protection wards surrounding the frame, and he snorted, reaching out to break them so they could enter.

Knock!

"Why?"

It's the polite thing to do. We need his help. People don't like helping other people if they break into their homes.

"Starkiller helped us."

He is an exception. My point still stands.

"Fine!" Alexander rolled his eyes and banged on the door, thinking, *This is so dumb.*

I know you're impatient—

"I prefer eager."

—but we should try to make a good first impression, all right?

"Whatever. Fine. Good impression. All over it."

The door opened, and Alexander's heart stopped.

Standing on the other side was the most beautiful man he'd ever seen. Alexander said a silent thank-you to all the gods because the man was shirtless, and his body was sculpted perfection. His skin was fair with smatterings of freckles across his face, chest, and shoulders. Alexander didn't even know people looked like this outside of movies and TV.

There was a thick scar over his sternum that had a silver gleam to it, and his eyes were light, maybe hazel or green. His hair was a dark orange, currently arrayed in a haphazard curly mop that indicated he'd recently woken up. His nose was round, his lips full, and when he smiled—still sleepy and a bit crooked?—Alexander blushed.

Attractive, is he?

Oh, for fuck's sake. Get out of my head. Ignoring Rota, Alexander said quickly, "Oleander Logue? I'm—"

Ollie happened to glance behind Alexander, and when he did, instant recognition and terror seized him. He screamed, his eyes rolled back, and he crumpled to the floor in a heap.

"Well, shit."

Oh dear.

"How's that for a first impression?"

K.L. "KAT" HIERS is an embalmer, restorative artist, and queer writer. Licensed in both funeral directing and funeral service, she worked in the death industry for nearly a decade. Her first love was always telling stories, and she has been writing for over twenty years, penning her very first book at just eight years old. Publishers generally do not accept manuscripts in Hello Kitty notebooks, however, but she never gave up.

Following the success of her first novel, *Cold Hard Cash*, she now enjoys writing professionally, focusing on spinning tales of sultry passion, exotic worlds, and emotional journeys. She loves attending horror movie conventions and indulging in cosplay of her favorite characters. She lives in Zebulon, NC, with her husband and their children, some of whom have paws and a few who only pretend to because they think it's cute.

Website: http://www.klhiers.com

FOR **MORE** OF THE **BEST GAY ROMANCE**

CPSIA information can be obtained
at www.ICGtesting.com
Printed in the USA
LVHW081519030522
717853LV00014B/566